An EMBROIDERED Spoon

JAYNE DAVIS

Verbena
Books

Copyediting & proofreading: Sue Davison

Cover design: SpiffingCovers

ACKNOWLEDGEMENTS

Thanks to my critique partners on Scribophile for comments and suggestions, particularly David N, Daphne, Lynden, Kim, JL, Royaline, Violetta and Jim.

Thanks also to Alpha readers Tina, Trudy, Helen, Mary G and Dane, and Beta readers Barbara, Deb, Doris, Fran, Heather-Joy, Leigh, Marcia, Mary R, Melanie, Sue and Wendy.

CHAPTER 1

apel Bodfan, Wales, July 1817

Miss Isolde Farrington peered out of the carriage window, although much of the view was obscured by rain on the glass. It mattered not, she thought with disgust. There would be trees, mist-shrouded and dripping, or soggy hillsides dotted with sheep. If there were a town it would be small, with too many Ls in its name, and not enough vowels.

The post-chaise lurched sideways; Izzy clutched the strap, then let out a breath of relief as another lurch set it into forward motion once more.

"Oh, heaven protect us!" Miss Amberley prayed.

Izzy rolled her eyes. This journey had already taken two days longer than it should, but the only dangers had been the prospect of sliding into a ditch or getting stuck in the mud. Inconvenient, certainly, although unlikely to be life-threatening. But her chaperone saw every ditch as a precipitous ravine, and every muddy road as a quagmire ready to suck the chaise into its depths.

Is that how spinsters end up? Izzy wondered if Miss Amberley had been like that all her life, the worry causing the wrinkles and the grey hair. Thank goodness she was only a temporary chaperone for this journey.

Aunt Eugenia must be nearly as old as Miss Amberley. Papa was forty-five, and Aunt Eugenia was the next oldest sibling. Heaven forfend she was as twittery and fearful as Izzy's companion. This exile in Wales would seem long indeed.

"If only I'd gone to see my sister in June, before all this horrid rain started," Miss Amberley lamented, not for the first time, or even the tenth.

If only you had.

"It was very good of dear Lord Bedley to allow me to go on to Aberystwyth in his post-chaise after I leave you with Miss Farrington. Such a gentleman, your dear papa."

Izzy tried not to listen. Her punishment could have been worse—Papa could have sent Miss Templeton, their governess, with her. But that would have meant Mama having to exert herself to supervise Viv and Lynnie for well over a week. Looking after two daughters should not have been difficult, but Mama preferred to lounge in the parlour with a book, or gossip with her friends. Izzy was happy to be without the governess—even Miss Amberley's twittering was preferable to Miss Templeton's scolds.

"Oh, we must be nearly there." Miss Amberley rubbed the window and peered out. Izzy could see only trees—still dripping—through her own window, and the horses and postboys blocked much of the view ahead. She leaned over to see what her companion was looking at.

They were descending the side of a wide valley. Miraculously, the rain had stopped, and Izzy could make out a river below, flecked with white foam as it flowed through fields and between clusters of buildings. The tree-clad slopes beyond the river rose to bare moorland, still with patches of grey cloud clinging to its top.

"Is that Capel Bodfan?" Izzy asked. It looked more like a village than a town.

"I hope so. Tanner did say we should be there this afternoon."

The buildings resolved themselves into a church and a scattering of dwellings and shops arranged around a street that crossed a bridge over the river.

Why did Aunt Eugenia still live in such an uninviting town? Papa said she'd been left a house by some great aunt on her grandmother's side of the family, but she could have sold it and moved somewhere more civilised.

The post-chaise rattled over cobblestones and pulled to a halt in front of an inn. *Y Ddraig Goch*, the sign said. Izzy supposed it meant 'red dragon', for a painted statue of such a beast adorned the top of the porch. Beside it, lower buildings filled the street, most with shops on the ground floor. The dwellings were narrow, with just one window between each front door.

The footman opened the chaise door, rain dripping from the brim of his hat. "This is Capel Bodfan, Miss Farrington," Tanner announced. "The postboys don't know the town—they will have to ask directions to your aunt's house. Do you wish to wait in the carriage?"

"We will wait in the inn." There was no guarantee her aunt had received Papa's letter, and she might not be at home. It would be good to wait somewhere warm and dry while Tanner called on her aunt. "You may have my trunk taken in."

"Very well, Miss." He let the step down and moved away. Izzy heard him giving orders to someone behind the chaise.

She set her bonnet on her head and tied the ribbons, then fastened her pelisse. Miss Amberley was still fussing about the chaise, collecting her own bonnet, knitting, and reticule. Izzy stepped down without waiting for Tanner's help, grimacing as her foot slid on the slick cobbles.

The air outside was still damp, and cold for July. It might save time if she could ask one of the local people for directions to her aunt's house, but apart from the sodden postboys and a man unstrapping her trunk, the road in front of the inn was deserted. She fished the piece of paper with the address out of her reticule. How on earth did one even *say* the words?

"Tsk, no-one here to meet you, Miss Farrington?" Miss Amberley said. "I hope we do not need to take a room here while someone finds your aunt. My sister was expecting me two days ago."

Yes, I know. You've told me so. Repeatedly.

Izzy sighed, and looked along the street. Was she doomed to spend the next month or more in a tiny house like one of these, in this wet weather?

~

Rhys Williams squinted up at the sky, then back at the track before him. The rain had eased to a fine drizzle, and now was little more than a persistent dampness in the air.

"Only another mile, Seren," he said, leaning forward to pat his horse's neck. "You can have some nice hay and a dry stable."

Seren whickered in reply, and plodded on along the lane. Rhys took off his hat and knocked it against his boot to rid it of raindrops.

Damned weather—last year had been bad enough. The warmth in June had given hope of this year being better, but now the rains had returned. Even so, it was good to be away from home for a while. Away from the office, and from Uncle John's hints about his cousin Sophie's forthcoming seventeenth birthday. But enough was enough —he'd be glad to get indoors. He needed to check if his things had arrived, and perhaps change into cleaner gear before he called on the Lloyds at Plas Coed.

Finally, he reached the outskirts of Capel Bodfan and turned down Bridge Street. A smart chaise stood outside the inn, its sides liberally plastered in mud. A man Rhys remembered as one of Morgan's grooms stood behind it, unfastening a trunk.

A young lady stepped out of the post-chaise, clad in a pelisse of deep blue frogged with gold. A much older woman descended to the cobbles beside her and looked around, an air of faint puzzlement on her face.

Rhys cast another glance at the travellers as he dismounted by the inn door. The young woman turned her head, and Rhys gave a silent whistle of appreciation. Eyes as blue as a Spanish sky, hair the rich colour of chestnuts, and lips like red wine, all set in an oval face. She spoke to the man with the trunk, who just shook his head and walked into the inn. Rhys slung his saddle bag over his shoulder and took hold of the reins.

"Excuse me?"

Her voice carried well. Rhys wondered who she was talking to as he started to lead Seren through the low arch to the stables.

"You with the horse!"

Rhys looked around. The animals from the post-chaise had already been stabled; he was the only person nearby with a horse. He turned to face her.

That expression would curdle milk.

"I'm looking for Miss Farrington, at…" The woman broke off to consult a piece of paper in her hand. "Stryd y Bont," she added, mangling the pronunciation as most English people did. "Do you know where that is?"

Farrington? The only Englishwoman he knew around here was Mrs Lloyd.

His brow creased as a sense of familiarity nudged at his brain; he'd heard the name Farrington before.

Izzy tapped her foot as the yokel puzzled over her words. His mount was a magnificent beast, a black gelding with a white star on its forehead, but the man's serviceable garments indicated he was from the lower orders.

Had he misunderstood her? Or perhaps he had not understood her at all—this place was deep in the heart of Wales.

"Do… you… speak… English?" She made her voice loud and clear to give him the best chance of understanding.

The man nodded, one side of his mouth curling up.

"Where is Stryd y Bont?" Was that the name of a house or a street? Had she even said the words correctly?

He took off his hat, revealing brown hair that curled loosely where it wasn't soaked. His eyes narrowed as he scratched his head.

Was he a farmer? His skin was tanned, as if he spent a lot of time out of doors, and the mud on his steed and on his boots suggested he'd ridden some distance.

"Well?" she prompted.

"By yur, isn't it." He spoke in the sing-song tones of all the natives she had encountered on the journey.

"What...? What does 'by yur' mean?"

He pressed his lips together; the creases at their corners and beside his grey eyes gave the impression of suppressed laughter.

At me?

"This road, Miss. Bridge Street, isn't it."

"I asked you about Stryd..." Izzy shut her mouth with a snap, heat rising to her face as she realised that Stryd y Bont must be the Welsh for Bridge Street.

"Diwrnod da, Miss." He knuckled his forehead and led the horse away.

Izzy's eyes narrowed—were his shoulders shaking? He *was* laughing at her!

"Wait!"

"Miss Farrington, you must not call out like that." Miss Amberley put one hand on Izzy's arm. "It is most unbecoming for one of your station."

"Excuse me, Miss Farrington, Miss Amberley."

"What is it, Tanner?" Izzy took a deep breath. As Papa said, one should not vent one's anger on the servants.

"Will Miss Amberley be staying here, or should I have fresh horses put to?"

"I can't leave you here, Miss Farrington," Miss Amberley said. "Not until I have given you into the care of your aunt."

Izzy sighed. "We will be here for at least an hour, Tanner, possibly more. I'm afraid I don't know yet how long we will be."

"Very good, Miss."

Tanner, too, knuckled his forehead and set off in the same direction as the rider.

"Let us go inside, Miss Farrington, please! We can ask the

innkeeper to make enquiries for us. And we may take some refreshment while we wait."

A sudden sense of guilt rose as Izzy took in the lines of tiredness on her companion's face. The woman couldn't help being irritating.

"You're right. Let us find the landlord." It would be good to sit on something that did not jolt and sway.

A groom came out of the stables to take Seren. Rhys went into the inn by the back door and through to the taproom, something still prodding at his memory.

"Mr Williams, croeso yn ôl." Gwen, rosy-cheeked and plump, greeted him as she pulled him a pint of ale without being asked. "The carrier left your trunk here." She nodded to one corner of the room.

"Thank you." Rhys put his money on the bar. "Gwen, do you recognise the name Farrington?"

The woman nodded. "Yes. That was Mrs Lloyd before she married. Why?"

That was it. The Lloyds were already married when he first met them a couple of years ago, but he must have heard the name when he'd been visiting.

"There's a young woman wanting to find her, but she has an address on Stryd y Bont."

"That'll be right," Gwen said. "Lived three doors down, she did, when she first come here."

Rhys scrubbed his hand through his damp hair. If the young woman was going to stay with the Lloyds, they wouldn't have space for him as well. "Do you have a room here for a few nights? And someone to send a message to Mrs Lloyd?"

"I'll see to it," Gwen promised. "Fancy a bit of mutton pie?"

Izzy laid her pelisse over the back of a chair in the inn's cramped parlour. "A pot of tea, if you please," she said to the innkeeper. "I need to find a Miss Farrington. Do you know her?"

"Someone's already gone with a note, Miss," the man said. "You was expected a couple of days ago, see?"

"Very well. Thank you."

"Miss." The landlord closed the door behind him.

Izzy took off her bonnet and peered in the mirror over the empty fireplace. The curls framing her face had become sadly crushed, and she took a few minutes to wind them around her fingers and tuck in stray strands. The maid at last night's inn had only been able to achieve a simple hairstyle.

"Such a pity your maid could not accompany you," Miss Amberley said. "But the poor girl would have had to ride outside with Tanner in all this rain."

Doing without Mary was part of Papa's idea of punishment.

"Do you think your aunt will be able to find a maid for you here?" Miss Amberley looked out of the window, doubt clear on her face. "It's not a very big town."

"Papa said I would have to share my aunt's maid, and help to look after myself."

"Oh. Oh dear."

What he'd actually said was that managing for herself would give her a taste of what life would be like as an impoverished spinster, but she could not say that to Miss Amberley. It was too close to the woman's own situation.

"Do you think your aunt will come soon?" the chaperone went on, her voice querulous. "Tanner says it will take another four or five hours, at least, for me to get to Aberystwyth, and I would like to get there today."

Izzy made an effort to suppress her impatience—how could she know when her aunt would arrive? "We shouldn't have to wait long." The man with the horse had said the street outside the inn was Stryd y Bont, where Aunt Eugenia lived, so she should be quite easy to find.

"Will you recognise her when she comes?"

"I'm not sure," Izzy said. "I was only nine years old the last time I saw her. We were living at Convale Place then, and she was at Bedley Park with Grandpapa." Izzy had a vague memory of dark hair and laughing eyes, but much could have changed in eleven years.

"Convale Place? Where is that?"

"Hertfordshire. It's one of Papa's lesser estates. I think he didn't want to live in the same house as Grandpapa when he got married. We only moved to Bedley Park when Grandpapa died."

"I do hope she arrives soon." Miss Amberley's face creased in worry again. "I don't want to be on the road when darkness falls."

A serving woman brought a tray with tea and a plate of biscuits. Miss Amberley filled their cups and passed the milk, but the activity didn't stop her chatter for long. By the time Izzy noticed a one-horse gig pull up outside she had started to wonder if the penalty for murder was the same in Wales as in England. This could not be her aunt—why would she come in a gig if she lived on this street?

"Mrs Lloyd is here, Miss," the landlord said as he started to gather the tea things.

"Mrs...?" The query died on Izzy's lips as she gazed at the woman who followed the landlord into the room. It wasn't her pelisse—good quality, if a few years out of fashion—but her face. The shape of her eyes and nose, a slightly wide mouth—there was some similarity to Izzy's own features, but a much stronger resemblance to her father. She had the Farrington chestnut hair as well, although she was shorter than Izzy.

"Aunt Eugenia?"

"Hello, you must be Isolde."

Aunt Eugenia had a friendly smile, Izzy saw with relief. She looked much younger than Papa, too, not to mention slimmer and healthier. Perhaps it was the lack of frown lines.

"Will you introduce me to your companion?"

Izzy remembered her manners. "This is Miss Amberley, who accompanied me here. She is to visit her sister in Aberystwyth, and Papa said the chaise could take her there before going home."

"Miss Amberley." Aunt Eugenia nodded.

To Izzy's surprise, Miss Amberley curtsied. "Can I leave Miss

Farrington with you, then, Miss Farr—, er, Mrs Lloyd? I have some distance yet to go."

"By all means." Aunt Eugenia turned to the landlord, still loitering in the doorway. "Please have the horses put to, Morgan."

"Right you are, Missus."

Aunt Eugenia waited until the landlord had gone before sitting down. "Are you making a long visit to your sister, Miss Amberley?"

"A month, at least. Longer, I hope."

"Excellent. Aberystwyth is very pleasant, is it not? Have you been there before?"

Izzy was consumed with curiosity about her aunt's marriage—a marriage that Papa did not seem to know about—but had to listen to the two older women discussing the merits of Aberystwyth until Morgan returned to say the post-chaise was ready.

"I will leave you in good hands, then, Miss Farrington," Miss Amberley said.

"Have a safe journey," Izzy replied. "Thank you for escorting me."

"Are you ready to accompany me home, Isolde?" Aunt Eugenia lowered her voice to little more than a whisper, even though they were now alone in the room. "It would be best to save our questions for somewhere more private. In a village like this, word will have spread of your visit; there is no need to give them *all* the gossip at once."

Izzy nodded mutely, and followed Aunt Eugenia out of the room. Had her aunt just *winked* at her?

CHAPTER 2

Izzy waved goodbye to Miss Amberley and climbed into the gig to sit next to her aunt. Aunt Eugenia flicked the reins to start the horse moving. "Welcome to Capel Bodfan, Isolde," she said. "Although you are not visiting of your own volition, I think?"

"No." She took a deep breath. "I gather that you did not have much choice about my visit, either. Papa…"

What could—or should—she say about Papa?

"Frederick is still as autocratic as ever, then?" Aunt Eugenia said.

"I… Yes." That sounded promising. And Aunt Eugenia clearly no longer lived in one of the tiny houses near the inn. Perhaps her stay here might not be quite as bad as she'd feared.

"And what sin have you committed?"

"I refused an offer of marriage," Izzy said.

"Ah. Just the one?"

"How do…?" How could she know that?

"You are twenty, are you not? You must have received many offers if you have been out for two or three seasons." Aunt Eugenia inspected Izzy's bonnet, face, and pelisse and gave a nod of approval. "Your looks alone would guarantee that, even without a titled father."

11

She glanced at the sky. "Perhaps now is not the time for this conversation. We will be lucky if we do not get a soaking."

"Do we have far to go, Aunt?"

"A mile, that way." Aunt Eugenia pointed her whip towards a patch of woodland. They had left the houses behind and the stony track climbed gently up the hillside. "Plas Coed is a little way below the edge of the trees," she went on. "That white building. The name means 'Forest House'."

Izzy could just make out a white dot. As the horse plodded on, the walled fields gave way to open grassland grazed by sheep. They passed through a belt of trees, the horse splashing through a stream that flowed across the track, then back into the open. The white dot grew to a long, two-story house under a slate roof, with several sash windows on either side of the porch. Although tiny by comparison with Bedley Park, Plas Coed was still much larger than the houses on Bridge Street that Izzy had thought would be her home for a while.

Fat drops of rain began to fall as the gig drew up. A man came around the end of the house to take the horse.

"Roberts, when you've seen to Castan, please bring Miss Farrington's trunk in."

"Right, ma'am."

As Izzy climbed down, the front door burst open and two little girls ran towards the gig, squealing with excitement.

"Is that her, Mama?"

"Is that Cousin Isolde?"

Cousin Isolde? The girls looked to be seven or eight years old, with chestnut curls and rosy cheeks.

"Back indoors, girls, you'll get wet!" Aunt Eugenia made shooing motions. "You may talk to Cousin Isolde when she has had time to settle in."

The girls stared at Izzy.

"Now! Alis, take Bethan inside."

The taller girl took the other by the hand and they went back into the house.

"I didn't even know you were married," Izzy said. And now she had two new cousins as well.

"A day of surprises then. Come, I'll show you to your room, where you may take off your bonnet and pelisse. Would you like more tea?" Aunt Eugenia chuckled. "You may need some fortification before facing their questions."

The hallway was stone-flagged with a bright rug in the centre, the walls painted a buttery cream. A long-case clock ticked ponderously at the foot of the stairs. Aunt Eugenia led the way up and opened a door at the far end of a landing. "You'll have this room while you're here. Roberts will carry your trunk up. Come downstairs when you're ready."

The room was less than half the size of Izzy's bedroom at home, with a much lower ceiling. The bed, wardrobe, and chest of drawers were made of dark wood, heavy and old-fashioned. It could have felt cramped, but the gaily printed cotton of the curtains and bed hangings, and the pale walls, gave a lighter feeling. The fragrance from a bowl of pot pourri on the chest mingled with a faint smell of beeswax.

Izzy removed her bonnet and pelisse and laid them on the bed. Crossing to the window, she traced the track from Capel Bodfan, half-hidden by the rain. All else faded into grey.

When Izzy came back downstairs, a cheery maid in a mob-cap and apron showed her into a parlour. It felt light and airy, in spite of its small size compared to the rooms she was used to. The walls were papered in pale yellow with subtle stripes, and the curtains were rich gold. There was even a piano in one corner, a pile of music in an untidy stack resting on the stool.

"Come and have some tea," Aunt Eugenia said. She sat at a round table in one corner, the two little girls with her. A pot of tea stood ready, with a plate of sandwiches. The girls each had a glass of milk in front of them.

Izzy's stomach rumbled—it had been a long time since breakfast. "Thank you."

"I think we should let Alis and Bethan talk to you, then Megan can take them back to the schoolroom and we can have a quiet coze."

This was all very different from the reception Izzy had expected. She took a sandwich, but hardly had time to eat it as the girls bombarded her with questions about her gown, where she lived, how many brothers and sisters she had, if she liked needlework and drawing and whether she would tell them stories...

Izzy answered with a smile, entertained by their enthusiasm, until at last Aunt Eugenia intervened. "Time to go back upstairs, girls."

"Oh, Mama—" Alis started, but subsided when Aunt Eugenia gave her a stern look. "Yes, Mama."

Feeling rather limp after the interrogation, Izzy sipped her cup of tea until the door closed behind her little cousins.

"I'm sorry about that, Isolde, but they wouldn't have settled to their lessons again until they'd talked to you." Aunt Eugenia pushed the plate closer. "Have another sandwich. We will eat at six, when Huw and Ioan are both home."

"Huw?"

"My husband. Ioan is our son; he's at the vicarage in the town for his lessons at the moment."

Three new cousins.

"Papa sent me to stay with my aunt, Miss Eugenia Farrington," Izzy said, rather dazed by the way almost all her expectations of this exile had been overturned. "Doesn't he know you are married?"

To her surprise, a flush appeared on her aunt's face.

"No. And that was not well done of me, I think. Huw is a solicitor, you see. A perfectly respectable occupation, but neither Frederick nor my father would have approved of the match, so I didn't tell them beforehand. Nor did I wish the start of our married life to be blighted by a visit from one or the other of them to ring a peal over me. Then it seemed too late. Neither of them came to see me, and only ever sent the briefest of notes. It didn't seem worth the risk of their interference if I told them. They couldn't make me change anything, but the arguments..." Aunt Eugenia shook her head.

"Papa thinks…" Izzy broke off. One of her besetting sins, Papa said, was speaking her mind.

"I have a very good idea of what your papa thinks," Aunt Eugenia said. "He sent a bank draft with the letter announcing your arrival, to cover the extra expenses of having another mouth to feed."

Izzy looked around the parlour—the furniture did not appear as modern as at Bedley Park or the town house, and the fabrics were far less opulent, but there was no hint of poverty either. Mr Lloyd's business affairs were clearly prospering.

"Isolde—"

"Please call me Izzy, Aunt Eugenia." Izzy liked this newly discovered aunt. "I feel I am being reprimanded when people call me Isolde."

Aunt Eugenia smiled. "And you must call me Genie. Being called 'aunt' makes me feel old. Now, tell me what you were expecting. Do speak plainly; I cannot abide people who beat about the bush."

"Um… Papa said that you had been foolish enough to think that you could be independent, and it was a great misfortune that you had been left a house here."

"Let me guess—it is unbecoming, and unwise, in a woman to go against the advice of her male relatives and to live on her own."

Izzy nodded.

"It was a tiny house," Genie said, "but it had the great advantage of not having my brother in it."

Izzy couldn't help giggling. "I'm supposed to learn the value of an appropriate marriage from your, er, reduced circumstances and restricted life."

"Hmm. 'Appropriate' not necessarily meaning a marriage that *you* wish for. What is wrong with the suitor Frederick favours?"

"He knows what I want better than I do."

"Ah. Who is this paragon of wisdom?"

"Lord Ordsall. He's the heir to the Earl of Braxton. Papa says it is a good match as I will be a countess one day."

"Is he old and decrepit or young and handsome?"

Izzy sighed. "He's nice enough looking. I think he's only twenty three, but when he talks to me it feels as though he's much older."

"He's done well, then, to gather so much knowledge of the world and your preferences for only three more years on this earth." Genie made a good attempt at keeping a solemn face, but her lips had started to turn up at the corners.

"Papa said that three seasons to choose a husband are too many, and Vivian came out this year. He says my refusals will harm her chances, and I must be married before Lynnette comes out. But that's several years away."

Genie's eyebrows rose. "How can your unmarried state affect your sisters?"

Izzy shrugged. "He says people will think they are too outspoken, like me, and that men only want obedient wives."

"Are they outspoken?"

Izzy grinned. "I've been doing my best to make them so!"

Genie laughed, but shook her head. "I can see why Frederick wanted to you out of the house for a while."

"Why does he think he can send me here without asking you first?"

"I imagine he thought I would be so grateful for the extra money he sent that I would put up with your rebellious ways."

Izzy smiled at the twinkle in Genie's eyes. That sounded exactly like Papa. She wasn't sure whether to be glad or sorry that Genie hadn't just told Tanner to take her straight home again.

"How is your mama, Izzy? I was fourteen when Frederick married, but I didn't see much of them as they lived in Hertfordshire. You take after her in appearance, I think."

"Yes. Papa says he wishes I took after her in other ways as well. Mama is very…"

"Placid? Obedient?"

Placid—yes, that described Mama. "She doesn't seem to mind that Papa takes decisions for her," Izzy said. And she reliably parroted Papa's strictures on the necessity for obedience and making a good match.

"That's what I remember of her. A shame, really. A wife with a backbone might have made Frederick a little less overbearing."

Izzy giggled. What would Papa say if he could overhear this conversation?

"He means well, I think," Genie went on. "At least, he always told me that his and our father's guidance was for my own good."

It sounded as if Papa hadn't changed much since Genie left home.

"I need to get back to the schoolroom now, Izzy, or the girls will think they've been given a holiday. I'll leave you to unpack. Megan or Ellie can help with your stays and buttons, and your hair if you need it, but I'm afraid you'll have to do most things for yourself. Feel free to borrow any books you would like to read—they're in the room across the hallway."

Izzy looked at the remains of tea as Genie went upstairs. She'd hoped Miss Amberley's comments about not having a maid of her own were only a reflection of her own situation, not the reality.

Papa had said life in Wales would teach her to appreciate what his wealth and station provided for her. She didn't want to have to admit that he might be right.

Rhys leaned on the bar in the taproom at the Red Dragon. The place was almost empty, so he took the opportunity to question Ewan Morgan about the young woman who had arrived that afternoon.

"Mrs Lloyd's niece, she was," the landlord said.

Rhys' brows rose. He'd never heard Mrs Lloyd talk about her side of the family, even though their dinner discussions usually ranged far and wide.

"The older lady, she travelled on to Aberystwyth," Morgan continued. "I heard her say the coach belonged to Lord Bedley."

"Listening at the door, Morgan?" Rhys asked with a grin.

"Can't help it if I have good hearing, now, can I?"

Rhys shook his head. By now the whole town would know that Mrs Lloyd's niece had arrived. He resisted the temptation to ask if Morgan had heard any more. The Lloyds were friends as well as a business connection; he would find out soon enough.

He'd just called at Huw Lloyd's office, but had found only Huw's clerk. He hadn't bothered to make an appointment as he had to visit a couple of farms to the north east tomorrow, and he'd call at Plas Coed on the way to arrange things. For now, he had plenty of time to review his list of things to do on this visit.

"So, Morgan, how's the summer been for everyone here?" It was all part of the background to his trip, and if he had to drink another pint while questioning the landlord, well, one had to suffer for one's work.

Izzy hung her gowns in the wardrobe, wondering if she'd chosen the best ones to bring. Summer in Buckinghamshire had been damp lately, but not too cold. Here in the middle of Wales the land was higher and more rugged, and her muslin gowns might be too thin. If only Papa had allowed her more than one trunk.

Her chemises and stockings went into drawers in the chest, her bonnet on top of it, and her pelisse on a hook behind the door. She laid out her brushes and combs neatly, suddenly feeling quite alone in spite of Genie's friendliness. She would have enjoyed seeing new places if Viv could have accompanied her—even places as wet and grey as this.

It wouldn't be much different if she'd married. She might have been allowed to take her maid with her to her new home, but then she'd also have had to put up with Lord Ordsall dictating what she should think and feel, not to mention his… personal attentions. She wiped her mouth with the back of her hand.

Outside, the rain-shrouded landscape was dim, the sky blanketed in thick clouds. The small garden at the front of the house was very different from the manicured flower borders and parkland at home.

Was there even somewhere she could go for a walk without getting covered in mud, or was she to be confined to the house even when it wasn't raining?

· · ·

The room to which Genie had directed her looked like a combination of a parlour and a study, with several tall cases of books, a cluster of chairs near the fire, and an escritoire against one wall. A newspaper and a book with a length of ribbon sticking out of it lay on a table by the window.

Examining the titles, Izzy first noted books in Latin and Greek. Mr Lloyd must be a man of some culture, but although she recognised a few words, she could not read either language. Other incomprehensible works must be in Welsh. Books in English covered a wide range of topics, from histories, travel accounts, and ancient castles and monuments, to books of household management, recipes, and farming. She was relieved to find the next shelf held a selection of novels. None of these appeared to feature love-struck maidens in deadly peril, although Izzy wasn't sure whether or not she regretted that omission. She'd enjoyed such stories at home, but that might have been because Papa had forbidden the girls to read 'ridiculous novels'. She suspected that without the spice of forbidden fruit, the ones she'd borrowed from Mama's supply might not be as exciting as she'd found them before.

In the end she chose *Waverley*. She remembered starting it in the spring, but she'd lost interest amid the busy round of balls, morning calls, and rides in the park. She would have plenty of time now. Too much, most likely.

They sat down to a family dinner. Huw Lloyd was a tall, thin man, his hair beginning to turn grey at the temples, and he had light eyes and a friendly smile. He welcomed Izzy as if she'd been an invited guest and enquired about her journey, but then confined his conversation to asking his family about their day.

Ioan was a lad of around ten, with his father's gangly frame, and he answered questions about his lessons with serious concentration. He responded politely when Izzy greeted him, but didn't have the same curiosity as his sisters about her sudden appearance in their lives. By the time the children had been sent upstairs for bed, Izzy was failing to stifle yawns.

"Do retire, Izzy, if you wish," Genie said. "Huw will not consider it rude. You will have plenty of time to get to know the family in the next few days."

"Thank you."

She managed to undo her laces and buttons without help, and even remembered to hang her gown instead of leaving it for a maid to deal with. Not that she had a chair to drape it over—the room was too small for that. Brushing her own hair was a novelty, too, and she spent far less time on it than her maid would have done.

Lying in bed as the rain pattered on the window, she considered her situation. Although Aunt Genie was nothing like Miss Amberley, and the house was much larger than the cottage Papa had described, she still felt resentment at her exile. And resentment, too, at the way her life was to be ordered at the whims of men.

CHAPTER 3

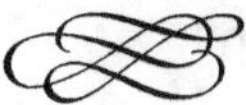

A dazzling beam of sunlight woke Rhys early the next morning. He rolled over and looked at his watch—it was not too early to ask for breakfast, and he should make the most of the unexpected good weather.

An hour later—dressed, shaved, and fed—he turned Seren up the hill towards the woods, along the track that led past Plas Coed and on up to the first couple of farms he was to visit. A few wisps of thin high cloud suggested that the good weather might not last long, but for now it was a pleasure to be on horseback with the sun warm on his face and the air alive with birdsong.

As he drew near to Plas Coed he wondered if it was too early to call on Huw Lloyd to make an appointment, but the front door was ajar so some of the family must be up and about. He left Seren investigating the greenery at the base of the hedge and walked up the path.

"The back door is that way."

It was the impatient beauty from the day before, pointing towards the path that led around the house to the kitchen. She was clad in a white gown with a blue spencer that matched her eyes. Her face didn't have that milk-curdling expression today, merely raised eyebrows at his temerity in coming to the front door.

He couldn't resist. Removing his hat, he tugged his forelock. "Mae'n ddrwg gen i."

"What...?" Her superior expression changed to one of puzzlement, a tiny crease forming between her well-shaped brows.

Rhys turned away before his grin showed—he'd only apologised, but he could have said anything he pleased and she wouldn't know. He headed round the house to the back door—Megan or Mrs Pritchard would tell him if Huw was still here.

Izzy watched the man walk away, convinced that he'd been laughing at her once again. Her indignation rose further as she recalled his lack of reply when she'd asked after Aunt Eugenia yesterday. Had he been deliberately obtuse, or was he a little simple?

Shrugging, she cut a few more blooms and went inside to put the roses into water. The kitchen was full of the appetising smells of coffee and frying bacon; breakfast would be ready soon.

"...coffee before you're on your way?"

That was Uncle Huw's voice, in his study. Who was he talking to?

"Thank you, but no. I'd like to make the most of the sunshine."

The timbre of the voice sounded like the yokel she'd sent to the back door, but without the lilt she'd heard before. Laying the roses on the table beside the empty vase, she went back into the hallway just as her uncle headed for the front door with—yes—the yokel.

"...here for dinner tonight. Ah, Isolde." Uncle Huw nodded a greeting before he turned back to their visitor. "Rhys, this is my wife's niece, Miss Farrington. Isolde, this is my business associate and friend, Mr Williams."

"Pleased to meet you, Miss Farrington." Williams bowed, but the movement did not conceal the laughter in his eyes.

Izzy closed her mouth—had she been gaping? "And you, sir," she managed to say as she dipped the briefest of curtsies, her training taking over while her mind was still trying to deal with what she'd just heard. By the time she came to her senses, Williams had mounted his horse and trotted off up the lane.

"Izzy, are you all right?" Genie stood in the doorway to the dining room as the children trooped in past her.

Izzy managed a smile. "Yes, thank you. I'll just put the roses I picked in water."

Williams' accent—it wasn't quite as truly English as her own, but it was far from the way he'd talked to her yesterday.

He *had* been laughing at her.

And Uncle Huw had introduced her to Williams as though the man were more important than the daughter of a baron. She snapped off the thorns and cut the rose stems to length, her movements jerky.

Once she had arranged the roses in the vase she carried it through to the dining room. She took a deep breath before entering the room —it would not do to let her annoyance show, not if Williams were a family friend. Luckily, all the Lloyds had plenty to say to each other at breakfast, and Izzy only had to pass the butter or jam, and rescue Bethan's cup before the girl knocked it off the table.

After breakfast, Uncle Huw rode into Capel Bodfan with Ioan mounted before him on the horse. Megan had taken the girls upstairs.

"I usually spend the morning with the girls, giving them their lessons," Genie said, closing the front door after a final wave. "You may assist me if you wish; it is entirely your choice."

Izzy recalled the barrage of questions from the day before. "Will I not be a distraction?"

"Perhaps you will. Well, I will see you later. We have something to eat at around one o'clock, then the girls play for a while before more lessons." Genie smiled. "It gives me some peace for a little while."

She went upstairs, leaving Izzy feeling rather unneeded. She hadn't *wanted* to help with the girls' lessons, but the readiness with which Genie had accepted her excuse was rather lowering.

She went into the parlour. Beyond the window the skies were still a clear blue, dotted with puffy white clouds. On such a day at home, she would have walked in the park where there were paths to use if the grass was wet. She might even have gone for a ride. Here, there was only the roughly surfaced road up from the town to walk on, or the garden to stroll around—but she'd made a complete circuit of that this morning in only a few minutes.

With a sigh, she fetched *Waverley* from her room and settled down to read. There was nothing else to do.

Dressed in only a towel, Rhys contemplated the two sets of garments he'd laid out on the bed.

He could put on the clothes he'd worn that day, with a clean shirt. Morgan had sent a maid to collect them earlier, and the woman had managed to get rid of almost all the mud. He'd look perfectly respectable, and the Lloyds wouldn't expect anything more.

Or he could wear his more formal gear. It was still riding dress, but of a finer fabric in lighter colours. He crossed to the window and examined the sky. It remained clear, with only a few streaks of cloud on the western horizon. Plas Coed was about a mile from the town—his best clothes wouldn't smell too strongly of horse if he rode.

He wasn't just dining with the Lloyds—that niece of Genie's would be there, too, with her superior sneer. Those rosy lips had definitely fallen open when Huw introduced him this morning. Would she be as taken aback to see that he could dress like a gentleman as well as speak like one?

It might be entertaining to find out.

He pulled his shirt over his head and reached for his best breeches.

The Lloyds and their guest were at the front of the house when he arrived, seated around a little table set with a bottle of wine and glasses. Miss Farrington, as beautiful as ever, turned her gaze on him as he approached. She examined him from top to toe, her eyes widening slightly as she did so. His lips twitched as he raised an eyebrow. A faint blush rose to her cheeks and she looked away.

"We're enjoying the sunset," Genie said, after they had exchanged greetings.

"And a lovely one it is." Rhys sat down next to Huw. He accepted a glass of wine and sipped it, appreciating its full body and smooth taste. Morgan, at the Red Dragon, brewed a fine ale, but his wine would serve better as vinegar.

"Good day?" Huw asked.

"Useful," Rhys replied. "Lovely day for riding in the hills."

Huw nodded, and the four of them sat in silence as the sun turned the clouds to shades of orange and purple beneath the dusky sky. Rhys was content to relax as the breeze rustled the trees and sheep bleated in the distance. At home, such moments were usually interrupted by his mother or sister with a question, or just with irrelevant chatter.

The sun sank below the distant hill, and Genie stood. "Shall we go indoors? Dinner should be ready by now, and Izzy and I will get cold sitting here in the dusk."

Izzy was relieved to find that she was placed next to Uncle Huw, with Genie opposite. That put Williams diagonally across from her, where it was easy to avoid meeting his gaze. He looked very different from the yokel she'd assumed him to be when she first arrived. His coat was not cut as closely as Lord Ordsall's, and his top boots did not have quite the same mirror-like appearance, but that mattered little. Few men took as much interest in their own appearance as the man her father wished her to marry. Williams would not look out of place in Mama's drawing room.

Megan brought in trays with a ragout of beef, boiled chicken in sauce, and a mutton pie, adding them to the dishes of vegetables already laid out. For a while the only talk was about passing the salt or the sauce.

"How did you enjoy your day, Izzy?" Uncle Huw asked.

"I was… I mean, I spent most of it reading," Izzy said. Good heavens, she'd only just stopped herself saying she'd been bored.

"Do you like Wales, Miss Farrington?" Williams asked.

"Very well," she lied, forcing a smile. It would be rude to give her true opinion in front of Genie and her husband. There was a pause in the conversation, as if everyone was waiting for her to add something more.

"That's good to hear," Genie said. "How did your visits go today, Rhys?" she asked, turning to their guest. "You went to Price's farm, I understand. How are they?"

"Just about managing," Williams replied. "Good crop of lambs, but not quite enough to replace the animals lost in the snow last summer."

"And less wool, I suppose?" Uncle Huw suggested.

Izzy listened in growing boredom as they talked about dead sheep, sickly lambs, floods, and washed out roads and bridges.

"I think most of the damage has been mended now," Williams said. "I didn't need to make any diversions on my way here. Did you have any difficulties on your journey, Miss Farrington?"

"Mud," she said. "We got stuck several times." How would she know if they had taken diversions to avoid damaged bridges? The inns had been small, the food lacking in choice, and the servants had jabbered away in a language she did not understand. By the time she thought up an innocuous comment about pretty villages—there must be some, surely—Uncle Huw had started to discuss the purchase of land for a new mill. Then the talk turned to the price of food, and something about corn laws, whatever they were. Laws about corn? Didn't it just grow?

"Are you going to see Evans while you're here?" Huw asked, addressing his question to Williams. "He must have some of his new-bred lambs for you by now."

Breeding? Mills? What kind of topics were those for a young lady to hear?

Williams answered, but Izzy wasn't listening. If Papa could hear his sister and his daughter being treated to a conversation about trade and animal breeding, he'd probably take her home this instant. That might be a good thing, Izzy thought as she stabbed at a piece of meat pie. She was a guest here, too, and no-one was making an effort to talk to her. She was not excluded from dinner table conversations at home.

"—ride, Izzy?"

There was silence around the table. She looked up to find all eyes on her.

"Ride? Yes, of course I do." She speared another piece of pie, and had put it in her mouth before she realised Genie was waiting for more of an answer, a crease between her brows.

She swallowed her mouthful of food hastily, about to apologise for missing the question, but by then Genie had turned to Williams and asked him how his sister Caris was enjoying her new married life. Genie then passed on what sounded like a year's worth of news about her children. Izzy supposed that she should try to take some interest in that. She might, if anyone bothered to address a remark to her. No-one was interested in *her* or what she might want to talk about.

When the food was finished they retired to the parlour, but Williams declined the offer of port or tea.

"I have an early start tomorrow," he explained. "Good night, Miss Farrington." He bowed briefly in her direction, and Genie and Huw accompanied him into the hall to bid him farewell.

Rhys let Seren amble down the track back to Capel Bodfan, his belly full and his mind content. The dinner table conversation had ranged far and wide, from farming to market prices, from family to politics. It had been the kind of conversation he only got at home when Uncle John came to dinner.

Seren splashed through the stream that crossed the path, barely visible in the moonlight filtering through a sheet of high cloud. Rain again tomorrow, Rhys predicted. All the more reason to enjoy the peace of this night.

His uncle's chest pains at Christmas had changed things. Following strict instructions from his physician, Uncle John had handed over all the day to day business to his nephew. Now he only discussed major decisions with Rhys, such as the new mill they were planning. Talk at home was almost exclusively about fashion, local gossip, or Caris' interesting condition.

At least there were no sour faces at home, he reflected as they passed between the first houses. His cousin Sophie favoured the same tedious topics of conversation as his mother and sisters, but unlike Miss Farrington she didn't scowl at the dinner table. If Uncle John had his way, they'd marry soon.

Rhys sighed, some of his good mood evaporating. A union made to secure the future of Granger & Williams wasn't his ideal, but he had to marry at some time. Sophie was pretty, and genial. They'd rub along well enough, he supposed, trying to suppress the thought that he'd be bored to distraction with her chatter.

"Will you come into the dining room with me, Izzy?" Genie spoke as the Lloyds returned to the parlour.

Izzy stood up. She didn't know her aunt well, but only a fool could interpret that tone and expression as anything other than a direct order.

"Do you realise how impolite you were?" Genie asked, as Izzy followed her across the hall. "You took little part in the conversation, and your expression made plain you wished you were elsewhere."

Izzy felt heat flushing her cheeks. "I was bored," she muttered. "I didn't understand what you were all talking about."

"You could have asked one of us to explain. We would have happily done so."

Izzy shook her head. She couldn't say to Genie that lack of understanding wasn't the only problem. She wasn't *interested* in dead sheep and the way corn grew.

"Rhys Williams is a friend, and a guest in this house," Genie went on. "An *invited* guest. I'm afraid your behaviour appeared childish as well as rude."

"Childish?" She was twenty years old, in her third season. "He was making fun of me."

"Who was?"

"Will— *Mister* Williams. He pretended he..." Izzy's voice tailed off as Genie raised her brows.

"Did you give him cause to make fun of you? If he did, that is."

"It's not my fault I'm here," Izzy retorted, her resentment at the whole situation boiling over. "And I'm not used to associating with... with tradesmen."

"I see. If you do not wish to associate with Huw, you may have your meals in your room."

"What do you mean?" Even as Izzy said the words, she understood. "It's not the same, Mr Lloyd is—"

"Huw works for a living," Genie stated. "Would your father sit to dinner with him?"

Would he? Probably not. "No."

"Then perhaps you should consider whether you wish to remain, Izzy. You are welcome to stay here if you *wish* to—and that would mean treating our guests as you would treat guests in your father's home. But remember that I am not obliged to have you here, so if you wish to go home I can make the arrangements. You should be able to leave within a couple of days. Think on it."

In her room, Izzy set her candle on the chest and looked at her reflection in the mirror. Her pursed lips showed her resentment.

She closed her eyes and took a deep breath. That was a scowl, not just a sour face, and the way her bottom lip stuck out did indeed resemble a child in a sulk.

Such behaviour was ridiculous, particularly as she would be of age in a few months. She'd sat through far more tedious dinners at home —why had she behaved so badly this evening?

Did I give him cause?

Shame washed through her as she recalled their first encounter. She'd thought him simple, but he might only have been considering her question. After that, all he'd done was to act the part she'd assigned him and taken a little amusement at her expense.

Had *he* been childish? Perhaps, a little, but nothing to her own subsequent behaviour.

Mechanically, she undressed, hung her gown on its hook, and brushed her hair, thinking about Genie's final comment.

Did she want Genie to send her home?

CHAPTER 4

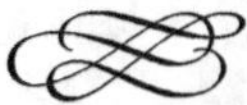

*I*zzy did her best to appear cheerful at breakfast the next morning, although she said little. After yesterday's sun the weather had reverted to damp greyness, but in spite of the dreary view from the window she didn't want to leave this place. Not yet.

When Huw and Ioan had set off for Capel Bodfan, Genie turned to Izzy. "Have you come to a decision?"

Izzy nodded. "I'm sorry. I will not be so childish again if you allow me to stay."

Genie sat down, her expression serious, and gestured for Izzy to do the same. "Do you *wish* to stay?"

"I think so, yes."

"Why? It's better than the alternative, I suppose."

"I don't know whether it's better, not yet." Izzy wondered if absolute honesty really was the best approach, but she'd committed herself now. "I was bored yesterday, but that is usually true at home as well." And she didn't want to be packed off home like a child sent to its bedroom in disgrace.

Genie settled back in her chair, her expression relaxing into its normal friendliness. "What do you usually do in the summer?"

"Walk or ride in the park with Viv. Help Lynnie with her piano and harp practice. Dine with neighbouring families. Embroider."

"What do you *want* to do?"

"Anything that's not tiresome." Izzy's words came out without thought. That wasn't a helpful answer, but it was true. "I… I don't know."

Genie waited.

"I mean, I've always known I will marry and have children, and run a household."

"And do as your husband tells you."

"Yes. I mean, not wanting that is what led to my being here."

"Did *none* of your suitors make you feel you would enjoy being married to him?"

"And obeying him?" Izzy added, and shook her head. "No. For different reasons, but… no."

To her surprise, Genie smiled. "I found that, too. I was twenty-five when Aunt Elena left me her house and a small annuity. I'd refused several offers, quite probably for reasons similar to yours."

Izzy gazed at her aunt. It had been arrogant to assume that she had not received any offers. Although she must be around forty, Genie's hair was still the same rich chestnut colour as her own, and the few lines beside her eyes could be due to laughter as much as age. She would have attracted as many suitors as Izzy when she was younger.

"Is that why you didn't just send me straight back?" Izzy asked. She couldn't say out loud what she'd been thinking.

"Partly," Genie admitted. "The life here *is* a little restricted, as you will find out if you stay, so new company is welcome."

"*If* I stay?" The pang of disappointment confirmed her wish to remain, for a while at least.

"You may change your mind, or your father might. Izzy, what do you think will happen when Miss Amberley finally returns home from Aberystwyth? She seemed the nervous type to me, anxious to oblige her benefactors."

"She'll probably call on Mama to reassure her of my safe arrival here. She might have already written a letter to that effect."

"And is she a woman of few words?" Genie's eyes twinkled.

Izzy almost snorted with laughter. "You must have noticed she is not, even in the short time… Oh—she will tell Mama that you are married."

Genie nodded, her face becoming more serious. "And your mama, naturally, will tell your papa…"

"…who is likely to fetch me home," Izzy finished. "A woman who married without the consent of her male relatives is an unsuitable influence."

"Not to mention one living in considerably more comfort than Frederick supposes," Genie added. "Well, make the most of your time here while you can, my dear."

"Thank you."

"There may be some books you would not be able to read at home," Genie went on. "I see you've borrowed *Waverley*."

Izzy grimaced. "I put that aside in the spring, so I thought I'd try again. But I'm up to Chapter Fifteen and all he's done is visit his uncle."

Genie laughed. "If you don't feel like persisting, you might find something to interest you that isn't a novel. And when you've had enough of books, you're welcome to help me teach the girls. You could even bother Mrs Pritchard to show you how to bake, if you wish. You might learn some skills you would never learn at home."

"Baking?"

"I know fine ladies do not do their own cooking, Izzy, but there's no harm in knowing how, is there? I find it quite enjoyable." Genie smiled. "Although that is partly because I know I may also choose to have Mrs Pritchard do it instead."

Izzy decided to accompany Genie upstairs to the schoolroom, and spent a surprisingly enjoyable hour listening to Alis read and talking with her about the stories. It reminded her of her own nursery days. When it was time for the girls to practise their numbers, Genie left Izzy in charge, saying she needed to talk to Mrs Pritchard.

At one o'clock Megan brought plates of sandwiches into the dining room. The girls sat at one end of the table, talking to each other while they ate.

Genie looked out of the window. "The weather might be clearing up a little," she said. "I have a few errands in town, and owe Mrs Jenkins a visit—Alis and Bethan play with her girls sometimes. You are welcome to come if you wish, although it will be a bit of a squash in the gig."

Izzy looked at the grey view outside. It didn't look any more appealing than it had that morning, but she had to assume Genie knew more about the weather here than she did. And an excursion *would* be a change of scenery.

"Thank you, I will." Izzy glanced at the girls. They were still deep in a conversation. "Genie...?"

"Yes?"

"How did you know Mr Lloyd was the right man for you? After all the others, I mean."

"Sometimes you just know, Izzy." A smile spread across her face and she stood up and left the room. When she returned she placed an oddly-carved piece of wood on the table beside Izzy.

"I think I knew for certain when he gave me this," she said.

Izzy looked at it doubtfully. The kind of gifts she was used to receiving included flowers, fans or gloves, sometimes even a book. Not a wooden... spoon?

It had a bowl at one end, like a proper spoon, but the handle was too long and wide, carved into a sequence of shapes. Izzy could make out a heart, a padlock, and a book, joined with curved lines. Picking it up, she could see it had been carved out of a single piece of wood.

"It's a Welsh tradition," Genie explained. "A young man gives his love a spoon like this, that he's carved himself. It demonstrates that he can provide for the family using his hands."

Izzy examined the spoon more closely. The surface was smooth, polished, but the objects in the handle were not entirely symmetrical, and there were a few scores and gouges where it appeared that a tool had slipped.

"It's just as well he was a solicitor," Genie added.

Izzy met her aunt's eyes, laughing with her. "Brave of him to show you his attempt?" she hazarded.

"It was the time he must have spent, as well," Genie said.

Looking at the fond smile, Izzy thought there was more to it than that. But instead of prying, she asked Genie what other lessons she did with her daughters.

❦

In Huw Lloyd's office, Rhys leaned back in his chair, the documents spread before him forgotten. "Rhodri Evans is going to lose his farm?"

Huw nodded. "So I believe. Stannard, the landowner, means to enclose much of the land in the valley, and part way up the hillside. What he hopes to grow there, I've no idea, but word has it he's in financial straits."

Damn. The breeding project was going well, but Rhodri was the only farmer he'd met with both the intelligence and the interest to work with it.

"Will Stannard evict him?"

"He may be able to keep the house," Huw said, "and the upland grazing, but if he loses the lower lands he won't be able to pay the rent."

"Does Stannard know that?"

"Rhys, this is all hearsay at the moment. It may not be true. Stannard will have to go through the petition process, which takes time."

And would cost money. It would take some time, too, for enclosed land to show a profit, even without the disadvantages of this rough countryside and thin soil. He gazed at the plans on Huw's desk. Which was more important, the mill or the new wool?

"Huw, can you find out if Stannard would be amenable to selling his rights in the land?"

"You'd pay for that?"

"I don't know—I need to think about it." He would if he could persuade Uncle John to agree.

"Certainly. I'll write to Patterson, in Llangenydd, see what he can find out."

"Thank you." Rhys took a deep breath, and leaned over the plans. "Now, this site for the mill near Llanidloes…"

Two hours later, Rhys stretched and closed his notebook. Nothing was concluded, and he still had a lot to consider. He could make no decisions on the mill yet in any case, after the news about Stannard and Rhodri's farm.

"Now there's only the payments for wool and cloth to deal with," he said. "I'll give you a list of what I'm expecting when I've finished the visits."

"No-one else visits all the suppliers," Huw said. "And certainly not in person, nor do they feel responsible for them."

Rhys shrugged. It wasn't the first time Huw had made that point. "It gets me away from Shrewsbury for a while. I'm managing almost all of the business now." Uncle John's hints about Sophie were becoming irritating, too—he'd have to make up his mind soon.

"Will you go to see Rhodri?"

"Tomorrow, probably, or the next day. I might give my backside a rest this afternoon."

"Hah! Well, invite yourself to dinner any time you like." Huw's lips twisted in a grimace. "My wife's niece may improve her manners."

It might be better if she didn't, Rhys thought. She'd be stunning if she smiled, and the last thing he needed now was to take a fancy to someone he could not have.

Rhys went back to the Red Dragon for a pint and a bite to eat, wondering what to do with the half day holiday he'd just awarded himself.

Although it was over three years since he'd sold out, his time in the Peninsula had spoiled him for office work. Riding to the various farms was exercise of a sort, but he felt the need of more. A walk, perhaps, as the grey drizzle of the morning had eased. He remembered Huw telling him last year about the ruined chapel in the woods above Plas Coed. It was time he visited the place that had given its name to the town.

He changed into his riding gear and old boots. He was starting up Bridge Street when he met Genie Lloyd and Miss Farrington, the two little Lloyd girls trailing behind them. Miss Farrington didn't look sulky today, as far as he could tell from the brief glimpse he got of her face before she looked down and gave him a splendid view of the top of her bonnet.

"Rhys," Genie said. "You've finished with my husband, I take it?"

"Indeed. I was setting out for a walk. Morgan gave me directions to the old chapel."

"Ah, yes. It's quite easy to find—Huw likes to visit it."

"It's somewhere to aim for," he said, puzzled at the way Genie's lips began to curve.

"Excellent." She turned to her niece. "Izzy, I will be some time with Mrs Jenkins, and she does run on, rather. Why don't you go home and read instead? Rhys will set you on the right road. Then you'll have had some fresh air, but won't be bored by Mrs Jenkins' chatter."

What?

Miss Farrington stared at Genie, her jaw dropping a little. Her gaze slid towards him for a moment, and she pursed her lips. "Genie, I don't think Mr Williams—"

"It would be my pleasure," Rhys found himself saying. What was a gentleman to say, after all?

"But Genie, it..." Miss Farrington glanced his way again, then said something to Genie too quietly for him to hear.

"Nonsense," Genie said. "This is Wales, not Hyde Park. I hope you are not implying that Rhys would—?"

"No." Miss Farrington shook her head.

Ah, it would be improper for a young lady to walk unaccompanied.

"Good." Genie smiled. "It's only a mile. I'll see you later. Thank you, Rhys."

She swept past him before he could speak. Rhys' surprise was overtaken by amusement at the look of horror on Miss Farrington's face.

"If it is too far for you, Miss Farrington, I can borrow a vehicle from the Red Dragon, or use Mrs Lloyd's gig to drive you back."

"I can walk that far." Her brows drew together in a scowl, but she smoothed her features before she spoke again. "But thank you for your consideration."

The words sounded as if she'd had to force them out. Rhys' lips twitched. He couldn't help wondering if she'd had a scold about her manners.

"The lane is rather muddy," he pointed out.

"I know. We drove down it to get here."

"Of course you did. My apologies for assuming you hadn't noticed."

She cast a sharp glance at him, as if unsure whether he was baiting her or really apologising. In truth, he wasn't entirely sure himself.

"It is also very rough underfoot." He glanced down—she wore a pair of half-boots, leather by the look of them, but not very sturdy.

"I assure you, sir, I am perfectly capable of walking a mile." She looked away, and her chest rose as she took a deep breath. "Shall we go?" She turned as she spoke, and set off up the street at a brisk pace.

Well, that saved him having to decide whether or not to offer his arm. He chuckled. It also saved her from having to be polite and taking it. Her rear view was rather attractive, as well.

Izzy had to slow down as they passed the last cottages in the town. The road here was indeed rough, with mud-filled ruts where wheels had left tracks. Stones the size of her fist filled the centre. Some were embedded in the ground, while others rolled beneath her feet when she stepped on them. It looked a lot worse now than it had when seen from the gig.

"You'd be more comfortable in—"

She spun around to face him. "*Thank* you, Mr Williams, but I have had *quite* enough of *men* telling me what I would like and what to think." Biting her lip, she looked away. Her promise to Genie hadn't lasted long.

"Do men often tell you what to do?"

The calm question drew her eyes back to his face. He was smiling at her again, but not with the suppressed amusement she'd seen before.

"All the time," she said, resuming their journey. He came up to walk beside her this time, even though that meant he had to walk in one of the muddy ruts. He didn't offer his arm, but he was close enough to steady her if she slipped.

"Every man knows better than me, it seems," she went on, trying to keep the bitterness from her voice. Although in this case, he did—he'd been right about the road. If he'd been going to suggest she would be more comfortable in the gig, he was right about that too, although she wasn't about to admit it.

She could do this. There were places this rough at Bedley Park, and she would *not* show herself up by turning her ankle.

"Are you enjoying your visit?"

As he spoke, one of her feet slid sideways into a puddle and water seeped coldly through her boot. A quick glance at his face showed only polite enquiry.

Or was that a curl to one side of his mouth?

"Of course. What could be more pleasant than a stroll in such surroundings?" A wave of her arm took in the low clouds, the mud, and the trees beside the lane still wet from the morning's rain.

"It is refreshing, certainly. I've slept outside in worse. Better than all that sunshine we had in June."

He *was* baiting her. She clenched her teeth, keeping her head pointing forwards so the brim of her bonnet hid her face from his view. She had promised Genie she would be polite.

"If you dislike it so much here, why did you come?" His tone was still one of polite enquiry.

She didn't answer—it was none of his business.

Another stumble; this time his hand took her elbow, steadying her.

Annoyed at her own clumsiness more than his help, she jerked her arm away.

"Peidiwch â'i sôn amdano." His words were a mutter, one she was not meant to hear.

About to remind him it was rude to speak in a language she did not understand, she thought better of it. He *had* stopped her falling.

"I was sent here." She forced the words out through stiff lips, still trying to control her temper.

"As a punishment?" She heard a chuckle. "It appears to be working —if whoever sent you thought you'd hate it here, it appears they *did* know what you'd like. Or wouldn't like."

She walked on. The fact that he was right did nothing, nothing at all, to improve her mood.

The track curved ahead, into a narrow belt of trees. The sound of running water blended with the squelch of their footsteps. She stopped at the sight of a stream flowing across the road.

Of course. The ford.

It was far too wide to jump. The swirling water was brown and opaque, but it was clearly deeper than her boots.

Ah, stepping stones at the side of the track. They were close enough together for her stride, and looked fairly flat on top.

"Miss Farrington, you do not need—"

"*Thank you*, Mr Williams. When I *wish* to be told what I should think or what I want, I will let you know."

Left foot there, reach out with her right foot…

Rhys hurried over the stream to lend her his hand if she needed it, but her foot slipped before he could reach her. He heard a whimper above the babbling of the stream, then a shriek as she hit the water.

He shivered in sympathy, memories of wading chest deep through ice-cold rivers in Spain coming back to him. At least she wasn't far from the house—she needn't stay wet for long.

She ignored the hand he held out to her, scrambling to her feet and standing calf-deep in the stream, staring at his feet.

"I didn't see you use the stepping stones. Why are your boots dry?" Her glare turned to his face.

He pointed at the footbridge a few yards into the trees, awaiting her reaction with interest. Her body stiffened as her gaze followed his pointing finger, then she looked down. Her pelisse was soaked up to the waist and clung to her legs. The soggy mess of her bonnet floated nearby, stuck between two protruding stones.

Her lips compressed, she splashed over to the bonnet and picked it up, then held one hand out as if needing a pull. He obeyed the implied request.

At the last minute, some quick change of expression in her face made him brace his feet, just as she gave a sudden, hard jerk on his arm. Instead of pulling him in after her, as she'd clearly intended, she stumbled forwards, landing with her chest against his and nearly knocking him over backwards.

He held onto her hand until she was steady on her feet and then took a hasty step away. He'd known women who would give him a slap for less—camp followers, admittedly, but who knew what this one would do?

"I *did* try to tell you," he said.

She looked down at her gown again for almost a minute, her chest rising and falling as she took deep breaths. Her gaze moved to the bridge and then, to his astonishment, she started to laugh. It wasn't a girlish giggle, but a real, heartfelt laugh, her eyes dancing and shoulders shaking.

Oh hell, she's lovely.

"Come, you should get home and out of those wet clothes," he said, dragging his eyes away. He took her arm, and this time she let him, leaning on him as they made their way on up the track.

CHAPTER 5

*I*zzy's laughter bubbled up as they walked on to Plas Coed. She would have laughed at Viv or Lynnie for falling in a stream after refusing to listen to advice, and for some reason the ridiculous situation was just as funny when she was the victim. No sooner had she calmed down than she'd catch his eye and go off into giggles again. It wasn't only her dishevelled state, but his answering laughter and her memory of his earlier pretence.

When they reached the gate she took several deep breaths and pulled on his arm to stop him. "Mr Williams, I must offer my sincerest apologies for my discourteous behaviour, both when we first met and since then."

"Are—?" His mouth snapped shut on his words.

"Yes, thank you, I *am* feeling quite well."

His mouth opened but, rather than speaking, his lips curved in a smile. It reached his eyes, now alight with friendly humour. She felt he was laughing with her, not at her. A novel experience, and one that she found she liked.

"That *was* what you were about to say, was it not?"

"I'm afraid so, Miss Farrington. I, too, must apologise. It was impolite of me to speak in a way I knew you would not understand." There was no trace of amusement in his face now; he sounded as sincere as she had been.

"What did you say before I fell in the stream?" If it had been something derogatory, would he tell her?

"Miss Farrington, at the risk of causing further offence, do you not think it wise to change into dry garments?"

He was right. The weather was cool for July, and her skirts clung to her legs in clammy folds. She pushed the gate open and headed for the front door, but stopped and turned when she heard no footsteps behind her.

Mr Williams was still waiting in the lane. As she looked, he closed the gate, tipped his hat, and began to move away.

"Wait!"

Oh dear, how imperious!

"I… I mean, thank you for escorting me home, Mr Williams. Will you not come in for some refreshment?" She still wanted to know what those Welsh words had meant.

He hesitated, and for a long moment she thought he was about to decline. Then he pushed open the gate and, with a glance at his boots, set off down the side of the house towards the back door.

Why? She'd apologised for her rudeness; surely he knew that included sending him to the back door yesterday? She set off towards the front door, but glanced down at her pelisse and boots; she would make a terrible mess on the rug in the hall. She wouldn't have thought twice about such a thing at home, but she couldn't imagine Genie being pleased if she caused extra work for Megan or Ellie, particularly as her sodden state was entirely her own fault.

With a sigh, she followed Mr Williams round to the back of the house.

"Oh, Miss Farrington!" Mrs Pritchard looked up from her chopping board as Izzy entered the kitchen, Mr Williams a pace behind her. "Are you hurt, Miss?"

"Only my dignity, Mrs Pritchard. Please send up a bath—" She stopped as she took in the activity in the kitchen. Megan sat at the table, a knife in one hand, a potato in the other, and a bowl of peelings in front of her. Ellie stood at the range, absently stirring a pot even though her eyes were fixed on Izzy.

Izzy cleared her throat. "If you could spare someone, a jug of hot water in my room, please."

"Boots in the scullery, Mrs Pritchard?" Mr Williams asked.

"If you please, sir. Megan, show Mr Williams where to leave them. The potatoes can wait. Ellie, you put some water on to heat."

Izzy looked at where she'd walked in. A trail of prints led from the door to the slowly spreading puddle around her feet. She started to unbutton her wet pelisse.

"Megan'll take that for you, Miss," Mrs Pritchard said, picking up her knife again. "Leave your boots here, too, if you like." She inspected the blue pelisse. "I doubt that'll ever be the same again. Shame, it's a lovely colour."

Izzy doubted it too. Still, there was no-one here who minded what she looked like. She unlaced her boots and squeezed what water she could out of the bottom of her gown before heading for her room. Her stockings left damp marks on the hall tiles, so when she got to the stairs she did the best she could to walk on the wood beside the carpet.

She paused in horror as she caught a glimpse of her appearance in the bedroom mirror. There was nothing wrong with the top of her gown, which had been protected by the pelisse. But there were muddy streaks on her face and her hair had come undone; half of it straggled in a lopsided bun while the rest tumbled down her back.

What must he have thought of her? Laughing like an idiot and looking a total hoyden, not to mention her stupidity in refusing to listen when he tried to tell her about the footbridge. No wonder he'd laughed.

No time for that now, she told herself sternly, undoing tapes and laces until she stood in nothing more than her chemise. That, too, was wet where she had sat in the stream, but the mud in the water hadn't penetrated through her other layers. Her gown was a different matter. Would the muddy marks wash out? She had no idea; at home, she would have given it to her maid to keep, to do with as she would.

She could ask Genie about that later. For now, she'd asked Mr Williams in for refreshment, and she should not leave him kicking his heels in the parlour for too long. A knock on the door heralded Ellie with a jug of water. Izzy washed quickly, a brisk rub with the towel afterwards helping to reduce the chill in her legs, then pulled on a clean chemise and laced her stays over it. She tidied her hair as she tried to decide between the primrose and cream gowns, wincing as the comb encountered tangles.

Her gown should not matter, and the primrose one was closer. She pulled it on, then her fingers stilled as she wound her hair into a knot.

Why did he accept the invitation?

Nothing she'd said or done could have endeared her to him. She pulled a shawl around her shoulders, and gave her hair a final check in the mirror.

He was probably only making sure she wasn't hurt, or likely to take a chill.

Rhys sat back on his heels, watching to check that the parlour fire had caught. The room wasn't particularly cold, but Miss Farrington had spent at least a quarter of an hour in wet clothes, and the water from the hills was chilly, even in summer.

Mrs Pritchard had agreed that making sure Miss was warm was a sensible idea, but Rhys had overruled her when she told Megan to see to it. Megan would have enough to do trying to clean Miss Farrington's clothes, and he was partly to blame for that.

He shook his head. He couldn't have *made* her use the footbridge, but he should have finished telling her it was there.

"You shouldn't be doing that, Mr Williams."

He straightened at her voice. "The maids are busy, and I'm perfectly capable of lighting a fire, Miss Farrington." He tried not to sound defensive, but wasn't sure if he'd succeeded.

A charming blush appeared on her cheeks. "I know. I'm sorry."

"Miss Farrington, do you think we could start again? There was fault on both sides."

"Perhaps, but I think I was far more…" She shook her head. "Thank you, Mr Williams."

Her smile this time took his breath away.

Remember her scowl, her sharp tongue.

"I'll let Mrs Pritchard know you're ready for your tea," he said, making his escape.

Izzy relaxed into the chair and pulled the shawl a little tighter around her shoulders. The fire was not yet blazing, but the little warmth it gave off was welcome nonetheless. What warmed her, too, was his offer of a new beginning. In truth, she had been far more at fault than he, and it was kind of him not to mention that.

Had it been improper to invite him in, unchaperoned? Probably, but Genie trusted him, and Mrs Pritchard and the maids were within call. She suspected that Mama would be more horrified at her talking to one of the 'lower orders', but it was difficult to think of Mr Williams that way when he was such a friend of Genie and Huw.

He soon returned bearing a tray with tea, a plate of biscuits, and a tankard of ale. He set it on a table next to Izzy's chair before taking a seat himself.

"You are not hurt, Miss Farrington?" he asked. "There must have been some sharp stones on the bottom of that stream."

She shook her head, flexing her wrist as she spoke and feeling twinges of pain. "I may have landed too hard on my hand; it feels a little sore. It will wear off soon enough, I dare say. I've had worse falling off a horse." She had a sore bottom and a bruise on one thigh, too, but she wasn't about to discuss those parts of her anatomy.

"You are not too chilled?"

"A little, but I will soon warm up."

He wasn't going to fuss over her, was he, as if she were made of glass? That was almost as annoying as being told what she would or wouldn't like.

But no; he sat back in his chair, ale in hand. "I don't suppose today's experience has improved your opinion of Wales."

"About as much as it has improved your opinion of my intelligence, Mr Williams."

He gave a crack of laughter. "I refuse to comment on that."

"What was it you said just before I fell in the stream?"

He frowned, as if trying to remember. "Oh, only 'you're welcome' or something similar. It was sarcasm, I'm afraid."

She felt heat rise to her face, wishing she hadn't asked. He'd taken her arm to stop her falling, and she'd jerked it away again without a word of thanks. "You were quite justified."

"It's past; we're making a new start." His lips curved, the creases beside his eyes adding to the warmth of his smile, and Izzy felt a fluttering in the pit of her stomach.

What could they talk about? He would finish his ale soon; she didn't want his visit to finish so quickly.

"Last night, Mr Williams, you mentioned snow in the summer. Did it really snow here?"

"In May, yes. You must have experienced bad weather, too?"

"Yes. One does not notice so much in Town, of course, but when we moved to Bedley Park there were so many days when it was too wet to go riding." She stopped, remembering the comment had been part of a discussion involving lost sheep and destroyed bridges. "That is a trivial consequence, I'm sure, compared to most."

"Where is Bedley Park?" he asked.

"It is in Buckinghamshire, not far from Aylesbury."

"You must find this countryside very different."

Izzy nodded. "Bedley isn't far from the Chiltern Hills, but they are not like the hills here. I've never seen such wild countryside."

"You haven't seen it at its best," he said. "On a fine day, there's nothing to beat being out on the hills, with skylarks singing and nothing but mountains as far as you can see." He glanced at the window, a rueful smile on his face. "It does look grim when the cloud is down, but even then I find the landscape has a certain majesty. It makes me feel small, powerless even."

"That is good?" She'd felt powerless, often enough, but it was not something she'd expected to hear a man say.

"I... it does seem an odd thing to say, I'm sure," he admitted, putting his mug of ale down.

He wasn't about to leave, was he?

"I felt small after Genie... er... reprimanded me yesterday," Izzy said. "But you don't mean that, do you?"

He gazed at her without speaking.

"Please, Mr Williams, I *am* interested."

Letting out a breath, he shook his head. "Small compared to the world, Miss Farrington. Compared to the universe. We all try to do our best, but often fail despite our efforts. Sometimes it is comforting to feel that a tiny creature such as myself cannot make much difference overall." He shrugged, his face reddening slightly. "Although that is not an excuse not to try." He stood as he spoke. "Thank you for the refreshment, Miss Farrington. I really must not impose on you any longer."

It was on the tip of her tongue to ask him not to go, but she seemed to have put him off with her questions. She stood without speaking—he *had* stayed as long as was proper for a social call.

"Thank you for your understanding, Mr Williams."

"Stay by the fire, Miss Farrington. I can see myself out." He gave a bow and padded out, silent in his stockinged feet. She heard Mrs Pritchard talking to one of the maids, the sounds cut off as he closed the kitchen door behind him.

She walked to the window, following him with her eyes as he appeared round the side of the house and let himself out of the gate. She was surprised to see that he turned up the lane, not down towards the town, and she recalled him mentioning a chapel.

Not much more than an hour ago, she would have wished him at Jericho. Now, she was sorry not to be able to continue their conversation.

'We all try our best,' he'd said. She wasn't sure that was true, not of the many men she knew. What best was he trying to do? It wasn't true of her either, although what she could do besides obey Papa she wasn't sure.

Shaking her head, she went back to her seat. She should be thinking how to explain her wet and dirty clothes to Genie.

Rhys turned into the narrow path that led from the track to the chapel ruins, the world darkening as the trees closed above him. His boots squelched as he walked, the path covered in sodden grass and moss.

It had taken a real effort to stand and take his leave, nearly as much as it had taken not to stare at her. Her vivid blue eyes had attracted him when they first met, but her manner and scowl had made his appreciation impersonal, as if admiring a statue. Dinner last night had only served to reinforce his impression of a spoilt beauty, and one he didn't care to be around.

He swore as he stumbled over a tree root, becoming aware of the moisture in the air, the feel of fine droplets against his face. The damned drizzle was about to start again.

The chapel was his target, and not far now, but he needn't linger very long once he got there. He concentrated on keeping his footing, walking as fast as he could. Finally he came to the rectangle of low stone walls, all that was left of a place of worship said to be over a thousand years old. He stepped over tumbled stones into the centre.

Rhys examined the base of the walls in search of an inscription Huw had mentioned, but the drizzle was turning to rain and he decided to come back to look for it in more pleasant weather. He turned back down the path, contemplating the happenings of the last hour.

Who would have thought Miss Farrington could laugh at herself?

He paused on the footbridge by the ford, gazing at the water as it burbled below. The new Miss Farrington was more attractive than the woman he'd first encountered. She was someone he could come to like. Very much indeed.

That was not good. His uncle wanted him to secure the business by marrying Sophie. And in any case, barons' daughters did not associate with men in trade.

Genie married out of her class, a tiny voice said, but a solicitor was a profession, not a business. In the eyes of the upper classes, buying wool and selling cloth was definitely a step below solicitors and doctors.

Forget her—he'd be on his way in a few days.

By the time Genie returned, Izzy had decided that honesty was the best policy. She helped her aunt get the girls settled in the nursery with biscuits and glasses of milk, leaving Megan with some mending in a corner to keep an eye on them.

Izzy told her story once she and Genie were settled in the parlour.

"You fell in the stream?" Genie's eyes danced with amusement. "Really?"

"Yes, I'm afraid so."

"Then you laughed?"

"Like a fool, yes, but I did apologise as well."

Genie nodded. "I'm pleased about that. Rhys has been doing business with Huw for three years. He has become a good friend in that time."

Izzy wanted to ask more about Mr Williams—where he came from, and what his business was. But Genie had a speculative look in her eye, and Izzy was wary about betraying too much interest.

"Did he accept your apology?" Genie asked.

"Yes. I *am* sorry I was rude, Genie. It was not well done of me." She recalled the muddy pelisse and gown. "I made a lot of extra work for Megan, cleaning my clothes. Is there anything I can do to—?"

"Best leave that to Megan." Genie tilted her head to one side. "But if you truly wish to help, you can do some of the mending in her place. The girls…" She shook her head. "I don't know how they do it, but they are forever tearing their aprons and making holes in their stockings."

Not the most interesting of tasks, Izzy thought, but better than learning to wash clothes.

"If you really want to be helpful, do it in the nursery. You can listen to the girls read at the same time."

"Tyrant," Izzy muttered as she stood up, trying to keep a straight face.

Genie laughed.

That evening, Izzy finally had time alone to consider the events of the day properly. There wasn't much to do here, but was it really much different from home? The sewing she'd done today was useful, unlike the embroidery that Mama insisted on. She'd enjoyed reading with the girls, too.

Megan had done wonders with the blue pelisse and the gown she'd worn beneath it, and Izzy had hopes that both would be presentable again once they were dry. It had taken Megan half the afternoon, though. Izzy recalled with a grimace the number of times she'd come home with hems and stockings muddy from riding, and wondered what the servants at home really thought of her. Megan hadn't seemed to mind, and had even been proud of what she'd achieved. Mama wouldn't approve of her chatting to the servants at home, but she seemed to be doing a lot of things that Mama would not approve of.

She turned her thoughts to Mr Williams. Rhys—she tried the name out in her mind. What a difference it made when someone laughed with her, not at her, and what a difference a smile and a laugh made to a face. He was really rather attractive.

CHAPTER 6

Izzy looked with longing at the blue skies beyond the dining room window. At home, she would have had plenty of choice for things to do out of doors. Here, she would be limited to wandering around the garden.

"Are you visiting the farms with Rhys today?" Genie asked her husband as she passed the toast.

Huw nodded. "I can afford a day or two out of the office. I want to take a look at Rhodri Evans' farm." Izzy listened as Huw talked about enclosure acts and grazing rights, not understanding most of what he said. She would have to ask Genie about it later.

Or perhaps…

"Could I come with you, Uncle Huw?" she asked. "I would like to see more of the countryside on such a lovely day. It is so different from the places I'm used to." That was true, but she might also find out a bit more about Mr Williams.

Huw regarded her closely, brows raised.

Izzy dropped her eyes. "I will be polite, Uncle. I apologised to Mr Williams for my rudeness—it will not happen again."

"Very well. We were going to ride, but if you'd like to come I'll take the gig. We can squeeze Ioan in as far as the vicarage."

A strange feeling settled in Izzy's stomach. Anticipation? She wasn't sure.

"I've an old pelisse you can borrow," Genie said. "Yours is probably still wet, and too fine, besides."

Too fine for what?

"You had better take one of my bonnets as well," Genie added. "One that won't disintegrate if it rains. A stouter pair of boots, too, although they might be a little large on you."

Izzy glanced down at the cream muslin of her gown, its hem edged with lacy vandyked points. If mud were to be involved, and she was certain it would be, it might be wiser to wear a darker colour. She had a forest green walking dress.

"Thank you, Genie, Uncle Huw. I'll go and change." She didn't want to keep them waiting. Especially as Huw also seemed to have forgiven her for being rude to his friend.

Rhys waited for Huw outside the inn, with Seren saddled and bread and cheese wrapped in a napkin in his pocket. He'd normally have been well on his way by this time, but Huw had met him on the track yesterday and suggested accompanying him. That meant he had to wait until Ioan had been delivered to the vicar for his day's lessons.

Rhys spotted the gig coming down the northern side of the valley. It appeared to have two adults in it, both clad in drab colours. Was Huw giving Genie a ride into town?

It was only as the gig approached along Bridge Street that he realised the shape next to Huw was too slim, and a little too tall, to be Genie. What business did Miss Farrington have in town?

Huw brought the gig to a stop next to Rhys. "Thought we'd let Izzy see a bit more of the place," he said. "The gig will get to everywhere we're going today, won't it?"

"I think so," Rhys had to admit. "We're heading for Aled Thomas' place first; you should have no trouble getting up there."

Damn. He'd tried to consider last night what he was going to do about Sophie, but Miss Farrington's smiling face had repeatedly intruded into his thoughts. He didn't need to be distracted by her while conducting his business today. Or to remember what he'd said about feeling small in the face of the universe—what had possessed him to tell her his private thoughts like that?

He nudged Seren into a walk and set off down the valley. All this countryside would be new to Miss Farrington. The road was too narrow for him to ride beside the gig, so Huw would have to answer any questions. He wasn't sure whether he was glad or sorry for that.

Izzy gazed around as the gig bowled along the main road, jolting over ruts and stones. The countryside in the valley bottom was similar to home, the hedgerows brightened by campion and purple spires of foxgloves. But the backdrop of wooded hillsides and the white foam of the river tumbling between rocky banks made everything feel different.

"That flows into Cardigan Bay," Huw said, pointing with his whip. "But not far to the east of here the rivers flow the other way, into the Severn Estuary."

Izzy nodded. She had no notion of the geography of the area, but she didn't want to be rude again. "Where are we going today?"

"Down the valley a little way, then up there." This time the whip pointed up and to the left, where the fields rose to a band of trees with rough moorland visible above.

"It looks very high," Izzy said.

Huw laughed. "A bit higher than your hills, eh? They're far from the highest in Wales."

They were lot steeper than the Chilterns. Izzy shivered—these hills were impressive enough—not only steep, but rocky, too, their tops bare of trees. How high were other mountains in this country?

"Why are we going there?" she asked, her eyes on the man riding in front of them. Mr Williams was clad once more in the rustic style that had led her to make that first, disastrous misjudgement.

"Buying wool, or yarn," Huw replied.

Izzy had worked out that much from what she remembered of the dinner table conversation. "What happens to it?"

"The farmers'll send it down to the valley, and I'll arrange a carrier to take it all to Williams' family firm. They will dye it, and weave it into cloth. You'll have to ask him if you wish to know more."

Mama, and Papa, would definitely *not* approve of her associating with such a man.

"Is it a big company, Uncle?"

Huw glanced at her, and shook his head. "That depends on how you judge such things. Big enough, but it's not for me to give financial details."

Izzy sighed. "Tell me about the farms, then," she said. Even she could see that making a living here must be harder than in Buckinghamshire.

Huw talked about crops in the valleys and sheep on the mountains; of how the bad weather in the previous year had caused starvation, with wheat rotting in the fields; about lambing time and shearing time, spinning and weaving.

Izzy listened with half an ear, watching Rhys Williams as he rode ahead. He had a good seat on a horse, at ease, as if he was used to riding long distances.

"…not changed much for hundreds of years, or even longer," Huw was saying. "The oldest building near us is the chapel in the woods that Rhys walked to yesterday. We call it a chapel, but it may just have been where a hermit lived. Dafydd ap Owen, you know, in his work on early Christianity in Wales, speculates that…"

Huw's words tailed off and he cleared his throat.

"I'm sorry, Uncle Huw, I was—"

"No, no, my dear. I was about to apologise for boring you."

Izzy felt her cheeks warming. She'd been rude again.

"Don't worry, Izzy. Genie never lets me prose on about such things to guests. Now, it's a little bumpier up here, see? You might need to hold on."

Huw guided the gig up through the trees and onto the grassy slopes above, where the view opened out. Across the valley, the hill was backed by higher ground with sharp shadows in the creases where streams ran. As they rounded a curve in the track, a low stone house came into view. A chimney at one end sent a thin spiral of smoke into the blue sky, and a higher roof behind could be a barn.

Mr Williams urged his mount into a trot, getting far enough ahead to lean over and open the gate before the gig reached it. A girl ran out to hold the gate, and a couple of rangy dogs loped out of the barn beyond the house. Izzy heard him say something in Welsh to the girl as he dismounted. She nodded, and dashed back inside.

Mr Williams dropped the reins and offered his hand to help Izzy down from the gig. "Thomas and his family have little English," he explained. "I'm afraid you won't understand what is said. Our visit should not take long, though."

"Don't worry, Rhys," Huw said. "I came along to see Rhodri's sheep. I'll make sure Izzy doesn't get bored here."

Izzy looked away, embarrassed at Huw's assumption that she would take little interest in the visit. She couldn't blame him, though, after her behaviour when Mr Williams came to dinner.

"Croeso!" A short but broad man approached from the barn, calling a greeting.

"I'll leave you to make the introductions, Huw," Mr Williams said. "Excuse me, Miss Farrington." He walked off towards the barn with Mr Thomas.

Izzy straightened her skirts as the farmer's wife approached, talking with Huw in the lilting tones of the local language. Gazing beyond them to the house, she noticed a spinning wheel by the open door. The lintel was low, the house squat with small windows. Some of the cottages near Bedley Park looked similar, she realised, but this one was more solid, its walls thicker. On the slopes below, stunted trees grew with sloped tops, nothing like the lush woodland at home.

Huw followed her gaze. "The wind does that. Always windier up here than down in the valley." He held out one arm, his elbow crooked. "Come, Mrs Thomas has offered refreshments."

Izzy paused inside the door. Sunlight streamed in through two windows, but the bright patches of light served only to make the rest of the room seem darker.

A table occupied half the floor, with low benches down each side and a chair at either end. Pots and pans stood on shelves beside a fireplace, with two more wooden chairs set before it. A dresser held plates, bowls, and mugs.

Mrs Thomas reappeared from a doorway at the far side of the room, holding a tray with jugs and a plate spread with what looked like biscuits. She set them on the table, and gestured for Izzy to take one of the chairs. Fetching mugs and plates, she poured milk for Izzy and ale for Huw.

"Diolch," Huw said as he sat down on one end of the bench nearest to Izzy.

"Does that mean thank you?" Izzy asked.

Huw nodded.

"Diolch," Izzy said hesitantly, and was rewarded with a beaming smile and a flood of incomprehensible words from Mrs Thomas. The girl who had opened the gate came in. She stared at Izzy's pelisse and murmured something to her mother.

Huw laughed, and the two of them exchanged more words before Huw turned to Izzy. "Anwen says your coat is very smart." The little girl giggled, and looked away. Huw gestured to the plate. "Picau ar y maen. Genie calls them Welsh cakes. Mrs Thomas made them for Rhys' visit, so we had best leave a couple for him."

Izzy took one—it looked and tasted like a scone, but not quite. "It's very good."

"Da iawn," Huw translated for her.

He made a few remarks to Mrs Thomas, who answered briefly, casting uncertain glances in Izzy's direction. It felt awkward not to know what they were saying, but it would be impolite to talk to Huw in a language that Mrs Thomas did not understand. All Izzy's practice in drawing room talk was useless here, in another country where, she realised, she was the interloper. But perhaps there was a way to communicate.

"Huw," she said, "could Mrs Thomas show me how the spinning wheel works?"

Rhys finished his inspection of the wool to be delivered to the warehouse in Capel Bodfan ready for the carrier. It had taken a little longer than he expected, Aled wanting reassurance that Rhys would still buy his wool in spite of the quantity being far less than previous years.

"It's the same elsewhere," Rhys said. "I'll not be losing an honest supplier like you for something you couldn't help."

Aled nodded his thanks. "Come in for a mug of ale before you go."

Hoping Miss Farrington wasn't too bored by now, Rhys followed Aled to the front of the house. He halted in surprise as he rounded the corner of the building. Miss Farrington sat on a bench by the door, her feet on the treadles of Mrs Thomas' spinning wheel and a look of fierce concentration on her face. She'd discarded her bonnet, and the sun made copper gleams in her hair. Mrs Thomas was beside her keeping a close eye on the spinning, her hands ready to guide the younger woman's.

Huw, leaning against the wall nearby, looked up at Rhys' approach, one brow raised and an amused smile on his face. It *was* an unexpected sight. Rhys wondered whether or not to interrupt, but the decision was made for him as Aled continued into the house and Miss Farrington let the wheel slow to a stop.

"I'm afraid I've probably spoiled this batch of yarn," she said, managing to both pout and smile at the same time.

"No matter," Rhys said. Why was the ability of a woman—*this* woman—to laugh at herself so endearing? "I'm sure Mrs Thomas can fix it," he added, grateful for Aled's return with two mugs of ale. His son Dai followed him out, notebook and thermometer in hand.

"Excuse me, Miss Farrington." Rhys moved to a bench at the other side of the door, nodding to Dai to sit beside him. Taking the book, he flicked through the pages, noting that the columns of neat figures and notes changed part way through to much wobblier writing.

"My da helped at first," Dai said in Welsh, pointing to the earlier ones. "Then I did it all."

"Good work, Dai." Rhys took an empty notebook from his pocket and handed it over, together with the coins he'd promised.

"I think I should have half of that, Dai," Aled said, laughing at his son's sudden frown. "Rhys, he should do it without payment—it's helped improve his writing no end, and his English."

"There's nothing like the prospect of payment for encouragement," Rhys countered, and ruffled Dai's hair.

Izzy accepted the length of spun wool Mrs Thomas handed her. It was rather lumpy, and thicker than the rest of the yarn on the bobbin, but it was her own work. Catching Uncle Huw's eye, she smiled her thanks to Mrs Thomas and wound the yarn around her fingers before stowing it safely in a pocket of the pelisse. She knew where wool came from, of course, but she'd never wondered what happened to it between the sheep and something like her pelisse. Trying the spinning wheel had been a way of avoiding awkward silences, but it had quickly turned into a challenge.

Mr Williams was talking to the Thomas boy by the cottage door, and Izzy saw him hand over some coins. Curious, she glanced at her uncle, but he would probably just refer her to Mr Williams again.

Her gaze slid to the mare harnessed to the gig. The docile beast was attempting to crop the bits of grass within reach. She wondered if Uncle Huw enjoyed driving such a horse, or if he might prefer riding Mr Williams' mount. Then Mr Williams would have to drive the gig.

"Uncle Huw?"

Rhys handed his empty mug to Dai. "If you'll excuse us, Aled, we've other farms to visit, and we're later than I'd hoped to be. My thanks for the ale."

Huw and Miss Farrington were waiting for him by the gig. "Magnificent beast you've got there," Huw said, as Rhys gathered Seren's reins.

Rhys patted the animal's neck. "He serves me well."

"I'd love to ride Seren a little way, if you don't mind driving the gig up to Rhodri's farm. Both our horses are easy for Genie to manage, but they make for a tedious ride."

Put like that, what could Rhys say? "Help yourself."

"Thank you. Perhaps you can answer some of Izzy's questions on the way." Huw took Seren's reins with a smile and swung himself up into the saddle.

Rhys sighed—so much for not getting distracted. Or not getting too attracted, come to that. He might as well see if he really did enjoy her company, as it seemed that fate was throwing them together.

"Miss Farrington?" He held one hand out, and she leaned on it as she stepped up into the gig. Aled opened the gate for them, and Rhys flicked the reins to get Huw's mare moving.

Sitting beside her, he wouldn't be beguiled by her pretty face. Maybe, just maybe, he could get her out of his mind.

CHAPTER 7

*I*zzy didn't speak until they were through the gate and bumping down the track behind Huw and Seren. Mr Williams hadn't seemed pleased at Huw's request, but the impression was fleeting. It *was* forward of her to suggest it to Uncle Huw, but he had liked the idea.

She wondered if Mr Williams would start the conversation, or if it was up to her. She'd had years of practice talking about meaningless topics such as the weather and the latest fashions. That wasn't what she wanted now—she wanted to talk to the man who'd laughed with her yesterday, and spoken of this wild country with affection. The man who had briefly shared his inner thoughts.

"Have you lived here all your life, Mr Williams?" A standard opening gambit, to be sure, but something she found she really was interested to know.

To her surprise, he laughed. "I don't live here at all, Miss Farrington. My home is, and always has been, just outside Shrewsbury."

"Oh." She'd made assumptions again. "You seem to speak Welsh well."

"My father was Welsh, but set up his business in England. Shrews-

61

bury is close to the Welsh border, and I learned both languages as a boy."

That answered her question. What next? She couldn't talk about the weather—they'd done that yesterday.

Rhys broke the silence. "Huw said you had questions?"

Izzy felt heat rise to her face. Now she had the opportunity to ask, it felt too inquisitive. Mr Williams had not invited her along on this trip, and it was really nothing to do with her.

"Miss Farrington?"

"I… I asked Uncle Huw about your business," she said. "He told me you bought and sold wool, and I should ask you if I wanted to know more. But it seems…" Not rude, exactly. Prying?

"It's no secret," he said, casting a quick glance towards her before returning his attention to the road. "I buy wool, and some yarn and cloth. I'm off to Llangenydd tomorrow for cloth."

"Then you sell it again?"

"Yes." He negotiated a bend in the track before turning his head to face her. "You are really interested?"

"Yes. I mean, I think so." Good grief—she sounded a complete shatterbrain. She was aware of his body next to hers in a way she had never been with Lord Ordsall, or any other man—and most of them had taken her driving in the Park on at least a few occasions. Was that addling her brain?

What had she been talking about? Interest, that was it.

"Young ladies do not need to trouble their heads about matters of business," she said. "According to Papa, and almost every other man I've met."

"Which makes you the more interested."

She could only see the side of his face, but that was surely a smile. "I do not do things *only* to be contrary," she protested.

He chuckled. "I meant no offence, Miss Farrington. I was teasing, a little."

Izzy took a deep breath. "I know. I'm not used to being teased." Not by personable men, that was—her sisters were a different matter. Strangely, she found she liked it.

She saw a flock of sheep being herded by dogs on the slopes below the road, and the foaming river beyond. "Things are strange to me here," she said, with a glance at his face. "I know that seems obvious, but I find myself interested in the differences. This countryside seems more… hostile. Harder."

"Life can be just as hard in England for the poor," he commented.

She flushed again. Neither his words nor his tone had been critical, but she felt she'd been too selfish to take an interest in anything beyond her own future.

"I know, really, but I'd never thought about it before."

"It's particularly bad now," he said. "With last year's weather and crop failures. Not so bad for the hill farmers, perhaps, apart from losing some animals in the snow. There's not quite so much wool for me this year."

"Is that why you gave the Thomas' son money?"

"I… yes." To her surprise, he looked embarrassed.

"I could have given them some, if I'd known."

He shook his head. "No, Miss Farrington. These people do not readily accept charity. I pay young Dai for doing this."

He pulled a notebook out of a pocket and handed it to her. Flicking through the pages, she saw it was filled with columns: dates, temperatures, and notes on the weather.

"You study this?"

"No, but I'm sure it would be useful for meteorological studies. I know someone who might be interested, although I haven't spoken to him about it yet."

Izzy remembered the times she'd watched the staff making up baskets for the poor on her father's estate. She'd always assumed the recipients must be happy to receive them, and had never thought they might have their own pride.

"That is an excellent idea," she said, handing the book back. And he was both generous and considerate to have thought of it.

His face reddened again, his gaze fixed ahead. She had better change the subject. "What happens to the wool and cloth that you buy?"

"The cloth I buy is processed further and sold abroad, mostly. The wool with short fibres is carded, then—" He shook his head. "My apologies, Miss Farrington, I'm sure you don't wish to know that much detail."

"You get it spun," Izzy suggested.

"Yes, in a factory. I sell it to weavers, then buy the cloth back later."

Rhys watched as Miss Farrington digested his information, a crease forming between her brows. Was she really interested or, in spite of her words, only asking because she'd been told it was an unsuitable subject?

She ran a hand down her pelisse. "And the cloth makes things like this?"

The pelisse she wore was not as fine as the blue one that had been in the stream. It was one of Genie's, he guessed, but still made of more costly fabric than the stuff his uncle concentrated on. "Not the fabric I sell. That is mostly used for more… more workmanlike clothing."

"Like this?" She touched his sleeve briefly.

"Er, no. Most of it is sold to plantation owners in the West Indies, to clothe the slaves." Not by his choice.

"Oh? I thought the slave trade had been abolished," she said. "I'm sure I heard Papa saying something about it."

"Before he told you it was not women's business?" He took his eyes from the road for a moment; his comment drew a smile, but she met his eyes squarely, waiting for an answer.

"I'm afraid it was only the trade that was abolished, Miss Farrington. It is still legal to own slaves. In the Indies, at least. Unfortunately there are many more battles to win before slavery is completely abolished."

She appeared to be contemplating his words as he turned the gig onto the road by the river, then she turned to face him. "Is it not supporting slavery to supply cloth to the owners?"

It was, and although the slave owners could easily get cloth elsewhere if he refused to sell it to them, that wasn't the point. He took his eyes from the road again to say so, wanting to counter any criticism there might have been in her words, but she wasn't waiting for an answer. Instead, she was fingering the length of wool she'd spun.

"Do you employ many people?" she finally asked.

"Not at present, no. Not compared to the number of weavers and farmers I deal with."

"But you are helping them to make a living." She nodded her head. "It seems like employing them."

"In a way, I suppose, it is." He flicked the reins, trying to encourage the mare into a trot. The going was faster here on the smoother surface.

"So if you stopped selling cloth to slave owners, these people would lose your business?" She waved a hand that took in the whole valley.

"Yes. I only started to work in the business in '14. Until then my uncle had been running it, with my father while he was still alive. Uncle John sees nothing wrong in selling to the plantations. It will take time to change his views, and to find new markets."

She still had that little crease on her forehead, but he was fairly sure now that she was puzzling things out, not showing boredom.

"That's how business works," he added. "I depend on these people, and they depend on me."

"And Papa's tenants depend on him," she said.

He chuckled. "He depends on them, too, don't forget."

Her brows rose—that idea seemed new to her. Where did she think the family money came from? Her family did have money, he was sure; the fine pelisse she'd been wearing yesterday could not have been cheap.

"I never thought about it before."

She'd said that earlier. What did young ladies like Miss Farrington think about?

"I was taught the use of the globes," she said, as if she'd heard his question. "I know where different countries are, and can list some of the things we buy from them, but that's all. We don't learn anything about *how* things are made, or how other people live. We learn French only so we can converse."

"And drawing and painting, I suppose?" Mama had ensured his sisters received instruction in those subjects, as well as more useful ones.

She nodded, pouting her lips for a moment. "Embroidery, too. The harp—"

"A fine Welsh instrument!" He was glad the conversation had taken a lighter turn.

"So it is." She looked at him, her eyes dancing and that glorious smile on her face. "That may be the one Welsh thing I can do that you cannot!"

"You have the right of it there, Miss Farrington."

"Call me Izzy, please. The other sounds too formal." She laughed. "Especially when you've seen me sitting in a stream."

He hesitated. Using her first name seemed too intimate. Dangerously so, for his peace of mind. But he was unlikely to see her again once he returned to Shrewsbury. Ignoring the sudden heaviness inside, he managed a smile. "Very well, Miss Izzy."

"Now you sound like a servant," she scolded, shaking her head. "Are you buying wool at the next farm?"

A safer subject, less personal. "Yes, but not only that. The farm's up there." He pointed to the hillside ahead. "Rhodri Evans has a bigger farm than Aled Thomas. He breeds sheep as well as raising them for wool."

Half an hour later Rhys was leaning on the wall around one of Rhodri's pens while the farmer explained sheep breeding to Miss Farrington. Life was good: the sun warmed his shoulders, skylarks sang above him, and he was spending time in the company of a beautiful woman.

His sisters' eyes always glazed over quickly when he mentioned breeding sheep to obtain better wool; Izzy seemed to be genuinely interested. He wasn't sure whether to be sorry or glad for Rhodri's excellent English. On the one hand, Rhodri was getting her undivided attention, but on the positive side, Rhys could gaze at her without her noticing. She nodded as Rhodri's talk covered such things as fleece weight, staple length, rams and mules, Exmoor Horns and Lincoln Longwools. Those were not subjects a gently brought up young woman normally discussed, he suspected. Huw, leaning on the wall next to him, seemed to have no objection, and was listening intently himself. Rhys wondered how Sophie would react if he brought her here—but his cousin had grown up with his sisters, and he doubted she'd be any more interested than they were.

Rhodri whistled to his dogs, and they trotted down to the far side of the pen, rounding up the sheep there and herding them up to their master. The farmer grabbed one of them and held it between his legs.

"One of the cross-bred lambs from last year," he said, jerking his head to summon Rhys and Huw over as well. "Most survived the wet and the snow. I left a few unshorn for you to see."

Rhys stuck his hand in the animal's fleece, feeling the length of its wool, soft and oily on his fingers. "You've some wool for me to take back, as well?"

"Some, yes. More next year."

"Excellent." Better quality wool from hardy sheep was only the beginning of his plans. It didn't seem as if the appalling weather had set him back too much.

"Is the longer wool easier to spin?" Izzy asked, rubbing her fingers together after feeling the animal's fleece.

"Yes; it can produce finer, more even yarn." Rhodri nodded towards Izzy's pelisse. "That coat's made of fine yarn, Miss, but most likely from lowland sheep that wouldn't survive winters in these hills."

"Thank you for explaining, Mr Evans," Izzy said. "I'm afraid I have taken up too much of your time."

"No, indeed," Huw put in before Rhodri could speak. "I wanted to see for myself how the breeding was coming along. But we do have other matters to discuss."

"Come inside," Rhodri offered. "Bronwen has some bara brith for you."

. . .

Izzy followed the stocky figure of Rhodri Evans as he limped towards the farmhouse, gazing about her with interest. Mr Williams—Rhys— had said it was a larger farm than Aled's. The farmhouse and barns were bigger, but she guessed that he had also meant the amount of land. A flowerbed in the shelter of the building held a colourful mix of sweet peas, phlox, and marigolds.

Indoors, Mr Evans showed them along a dim corridor into a bright and airy parlour. The furniture looked very old-fashioned to Izzy's eyes, but was solid and sturdy, and polished to a soft gleam. A cheery young woman hurried in with a tray, setting it on a low table near the fireplace. There were mugs of ale for the men, a pot of tea for Izzy, and slabs of rich fruit cake. This must be the bara brith that Mr Evans had mentioned.

Bronwen Evans was plumper than her husband, her black hair tucked neatly beneath a white cap. She handed round the ale and cake, and asked Izzy in heavily accented English how she liked her tea.

"A little milk, please," Izzy said, and Mrs Evans poured it for her.

Huw took a packet from his satchel, unfolding it to reveal what looked like a plan.

"Best take it into the other room," Mr Evans suggested. "Spread it out on the dining table."

"We shouldn't be too long, Izzy," Huw said as the three men rose to their feet.

"Won't you stay and talk to me?" Izzy asked, as Mrs Evans stood as well. Belatedly, she wondered if the woman had enough English for conversation, but Izzy felt she had to try. "This looks a very comfortable house," she started, hoping she wasn't making some faux pas.

Mrs Evans beamed. "It is. Lucky, we are, to have it. It belonged to Rhodri's uncle, but he had no sons. He's old now, lives in Llangenydd in a little house. He gave the farm to Rhodri to look after when he was discharged and we got married."

Discharged?

"Lucky, too, that Captain Williams is in the wool business. Got us off to a good start, it did, when we got married."

Captain?

"Mr Evans was in the army?" Izzy asked, although he wasn't the one she wanted to know about.

"Oh yes. Fought in Spain and France in Captain Williams' company. Captain Williams sold out after Toulouse, and Rhodri got leave, but he was sent to Belgium when Boney escaped. Served under Captain Pelham there. A good officer, he was, too. Friend of Captain Williams, Rhodri says. Rhodri got his leg broken and a bad sword slash at Quatre Bras, but he was lucky, really."

"You haven't been married long, then?"

"Two years this summer," Mrs Evans said, laying one hand on her stomach. "Second one on the way. The babi's sleeping, thank the lord."

Izzy wondered if it would be polite to ask more, but she needn't have worried. Once she'd started, Mrs Evans needed no further encouragement.

"Joined up when he was seventeen, Rhodri did. Old Mr Thomas was talking of leaving the farm to one of his other nephews, but he turned out bad. Drink, you know. I was only fifteen at the time, but I reckoned Rhodri was worth waiting for. Taught himself to read, he did, while he was in Spain. Got to be a sergeant in the end." She nodded in satisfaction. "I got a good man there, I reckon, and a good living if Captain Williams wants him to carry on with this sheep breeding." Mrs Evans smiled. "I reckon you've got a good man there, too."

Feeling the heat rise to her cheeks, Izzy opened her mouth to protest that she'd come with her uncle, and that Rhys—Mr Williams— was not a suitor. But she was strangely reluctant to deny outright what Mrs Evans had assumed. "What is it like here in the winter?" she asked instead. "The country is much flatter where I live."

"Cold. Not used to living this high, I wasn't, but the house is solid..."

Izzy let out a breath of relief as the woman chattered on about snow, rain, and gales, but also of warm summers that might come again if this strange weather ever stopped.

"We've finished, Izzy," Huw said from the doorway. "Time to head home, I think."

Izzy stood. "Thank you for the tea and cake, Mrs Evans."

Outside, Rhys was helping Huw to check the harness on the horse, but his own mount still cropped grass in a nearby field. She suppressed a pang of disappointment as she realised that Rhys would not be travelling back with them.

"I'll bid farewell, Miss Farrington," he said, handing her into the carriage. "I've more business with Rhodri, and more still at farms beyond here."

"Thank you, Mr Williams. I enjoyed our talk." Very much. She wanted to shake his hand, or have him make that offer, but Huw had picked up the reins.

"Come to dinner when you get back, Rhys," Huw said, flicking the reins to get the horse moving.

Rhys remained by the gate as the gig drew away down the track, a warm glow starting inside as he saw Izzy turn to look back at him.

"Good lass you've got there, Captain," Rhodri stated. "Sharp as a tack. Now, come and see this land Stannard wants. You can ride on to Hafod Rhos from there."

"She's not mine, Rhodri," Rhys said, regret stabbing him as he spoke. "Her father's a lord, and lords don't let their womenfolk associate with trade."

He had to keep reminding himself of that.

CHAPTER 8

"Well, Izzy, did you enjoy your outing?" Genie asked as they sat down to dinner that evening.

"Very much, thank you. The countryside *is* lovely when the sun shines."

"Interested in Rhodri's sheep, she was," Huw said, taking a mouthful of the mutton stew.

"Really, Izzy?" Genie asked.

Izzy toyed with the peas on her plate, admitting to herself that she'd listened to Rhodri Evans at first because Rhys was involved. But Mr Evans' enthusiasm, and his wife's, had caught her own interest. She was certain she hadn't understood everything, but she could always ask R... Uncle Huw.

Taking a deep breath, she met her aunt's enquiring gaze. "I am coming to realise how little I know about the world," she said. That was also true. "The only things we ever talk about at home are fashions or social engagements. It's all so... *trivial*. There must—" She broke off as she registered the amusement on Genie's face. "Oh. Of course—you thought the same."

"Indeed. But I was lucky enough to escape. It's not an easy life, though, Izzy, if you've been used to living somewhere like Bedley Park with numerous servants."

Izzy nodded. She already knew that Genie did some of the household tasks that fell to maids and the housekeeper at home. But it wasn't as if she was planning on giving up her old life.

Not *planning*, exactly. Perhaps wondering what it would be like.

"Would you like to ride about the countryside a little, Izzy?" Genie asked. "It's been quite a while since I've ridden over the tops. I could borrow another horse and side saddle."

"Yes, please, I'd enjoy that."

"Good." Genie smiled. "Did you bring a riding habit with you?"

"No, Papa said…" Izzy closed her mouth. It would not be polite to repeat Papa's assumptions.

"Frederick said I could not afford a horse?"

Thankful to see that Genie didn't appear to be offended, Izzy nodded.

"You'll have to spend some time adjusting an old one of mine, then. I'll look one out after dinner and you can start on it this evening, if you wish."

"Thank you."

A ride with Genie would be interesting, but a ride with Mr Williams would be better.

Izzy continued working on Genie's spare riding habit the next morning. It was made of moss-green kerseymere with paler green trim up the front, and the jacket was loose on her. Tucks in the back would take care of that, she hoped, as she finished unpicking two of the seams. It wouldn't be a stylish fit, but it would be good enough for riding around the countryside.

"That colour suits you," Genie said, as Izzy tried the partially dismantled jacket on. "Hold still, now, while I pin the seams up."

Izzy gazed out of the window as Genie tugged and pinned. Clouds scudded across the sky, white puffs against blue, sending patches of sunlight racing over the fields and woods. If she were at home now, she would not be doing anything much different—practising the piano instead of sewing, or looking out at the park instead of this wilder country.

"There, that should do." Genie moved to look at the fit of the jacket from the front. "What amuses you?"

"The idea that Papa thought coming here was a punishment," Izzy said.

"You thought so at first," Genie commented, setting the pincushion on the table. "Remember, he didn't think I had anything more than a one-bedroomed cottage."

"And you have to be rich to be happy?" Poverty produced unhappiness, but she wasn't sure if the converse was true.

"And pay due deference to the edicts of your male relatives," Genie said, "who always know what is best. Now, if you don't make the stitching too fine, it'll be easier for me to let the seams out again afterwards."

"Thank you."

While Izzy sewed, she thought about the two farms she'd visited the day before. The tenants that Mama took baskets to had never seemed like real people to her. None of them had offered Mama food or drink, as Mrs Thomas and Mrs Evans had done. Nor would Lady Bedley have accepted. Izzy could imagine her horrified expression, and protests about the dirt, and the risk of disease. In fact, on the occasions when Izzy and Viv had accompanied her, Mama had merely sat in the barouche, sending a footman in with the basket, and nodding her head regally when one of the grateful recipients emerged from their dwelling to curtsey their thanks.

Izzy snipped off the final thread on the jacket and turned her attention to the skirts, wondering what those people had *really* been thinking. Had Mama just been seen as Lady Bountiful rubbing their noses in the differences in their wealth?

But Mrs Thomas had happily shown her how to spin, and Bronwen Evans had been friendly. They were people with hopes and fears as real as Izzy's own. Recalling Genie's comment about the excessive fineness of her blue pelisse, Izzy wondered how much their friendliness had been encouraged by the fact that she had worn her aunt's old one. She smoothed her hand across the fabric she was working on. The habit, like the pelisse, had sparse ornamentation and a practical dark colour.

Izzy's best pelisse—safely back at Bedley Park—was cream with white lacy trim, worn with white kid half-boots. She imagined herself picking her way across the muddy farmyards in that ensemble while trying to stop her fringed parasol blowing away in the breeze. Anyone watching would have laughed. Then she wondered how long it would have taken her maid to clean her garments afterwards. Even one's choice of clothing had consequences for others.

You'll be turning into a revolutionary next, she told herself as she tidied her sewing away and joined Genie and the girls for luncheon. After they had eaten, she tried on the whole outfit before the girls resumed their lessons. As she'd expected, the skirts were a few inches too short. At home, Mama would have had a fit and sent it back to the modiste. However, there was nothing Izzy could do about the lack of length, and who would notice in any case?

"You look lovely," Alis said as Izzy twirled in front of them.

"I'm sure he'll think you look fine in that," Genie added, her expression one of bland innocence.

"Who will?" Izzy asked, feeling her face redden.

"Why, Huw, of course!"

Izzy wrote to her sisters that evening, wishing she could see their faces when she revealed that Aunt Eugenia wasn't the poverty-stricken spinster Papa had made her out to be. But as she started to describe her young cousins, she paused, pen held in mid-air.

Would Papa read the letter? Even if he didn't open it before giving it to Viv and Lynnie, he would ask them what was in it, hoping to be reassured she was having a suitably miserable time. And she preferred him not to know that Genie was married. Miss Amberley might have written with this news, but there was nothing she could do about that.

She screwed up the paper, smiling at the challenge before her. How to avoid writing untruths, while giving the impression her father would want to hear?

The weather, perhaps—it didn't rain this much at home. The length of the journey would be a suitable complaint, too, although it wouldn't be nice to mention Miss Amberley's worries and fidgets. Helping Aunt Eugenia with her sewing and mending. The muddy track down to the town—but not the part about falling in the stream.

She signed the finished letter with mixed feelings. It *was* deceiving whoever read it, but it was up to Genie, not her, to decide when Papa found out that his sister was now married.

Feeling at a loose end once the letter was completed, she went to look for something to read. *Waverley* still wasn't holding her attention, and she scanned the shelves for something more interesting. She had selected a book recounting travels in Italy when her eye was caught by the word 'chemistry' on the spine of a book. Chemistry was a science and therefore deemed unsuitable for women, so she'd never been taught anything about it. She added *Conversations in Chemistry* to the travel book and took them to her room to read in bed.

"Not long now." Rhys patted Seren's neck as the church tower in Capel Bodfan came into view. He felt as if he'd been gone longer than three days. The sun had finally emerged from dark clouds, and the slanting rays turned drops of water on the trees into glittering points of light. The beginnings of a red sunset boded well for the next day.

The clock on the tower showed nearly five—too late to discuss business with Huw today, but perhaps not too late to accept that dinner invitation if the Lloyds were going to eat after the children were abed. The landlord could send someone to Genie with a note while he was changing.

Dismounting outside the inn, he handed Seren to an ostler and headed to the taproom. He ordered hot water and took an ale up to his room.

He wrote a quick note while he waited for the water, and gave it to Gwen when she arrived with the jug. He stripped off his coat, waistcoat, and shirt, tested the sharpness of the razor and soaped his face.

It had been a productive time, he reflected, scraping off a few days' worth of stubble. He'd done all he'd set out to do; Huw would pay the farmers when they delivered their wool and cloth to Morgan's barn behind the inn, then Jones the carter would take it to Shrewsbury. There would be more profit than last year, but not much.

After wiping his face with a towel, he laid out his more formal—and cleaner—clothing. He'd confer with Huw in the morning about the wool, and that matter with Stannard and Rhodri's farm, then it was time to return home.

He didn't want to, he realised, as he pulled a clean shirt over his head. He'd allowed a few days' contingency in his plans, so he didn't have to go back yet. It wasn't a wish to see more of Genie and Huw, good friends though they were. No—he had to admit that he wanted to stay to see more of Miss Farrington.

Izzy.

Images of her face had disturbed his dreams these last few nights. One moment of shared laughter after she fell in the stream, and a few hours the following day of nothing more than intelligent conversation—that shouldn't have him thinking about her at random times while he was supposed to be concentrating on business. It was ridiculous—he'd scoffed at friends who'd said they'd fallen in love at first sight.

Not that he was in love.

No. This fascination would wear off. And it wasn't at first sight, either. He'd admired her beauty at their first meeting, when she was looking down her nose at him, asking directions, but it wasn't until that fateful walk up from the town that he'd *liked* her.

She seemed to like him, too, as far as he could tell. He'd had more experience with willing camp followers than courting respectable young women. But her apparent interest in him and his business surely couldn't last.

He shook his head, trying to banish such thoughts, and reached for a neckcloth. "Come," he called as someone knocked on the door.

"Note for you, sir." The groom held out a folded paper.

In spite of his resolution, his heart accelerated as he read that Genie would expect him at seven.

CHAPTER 9

"Never mind, Bethan," Izzy said, as the girl hit more off-key notes and stuck her bottom lip out. "Try again."

Tongue poking from one corner of her mouth in concentration, Bethan worked through the tune once more, managing all the right notes this time and something that resembled the correct rhythm.

"Well done. Alis, you try now."

Izzy walked over to the parlour window as Alis fussed with the height of the piano stool. A man appeared from behind the house heading for the gate. She didn't recognise him—a groom from the inn with a message, perhaps? Alis was finishing her warm-up scales when Genie came into the room.

"Uncle Huw will be late?" Izzy guessed.

"No, he's coming up the track with Ioan. We have a guest for dinner."

Rhys?

"That's nice." Izzy tried for nonchalance, but wasn't sure she'd succeeded. "Anyone I know?"

"The vicar," Genie said. "We won't need to speak at all once he and Huw start talking about ancient ruins. It should be a most educational evening."

Despite her best efforts, Izzy's lips drooped.

"I thought so," Genie said, an unmistakable note of triumph in her voice.

"What?" Izzy's eye met her aunt's. "I mean, I beg your pardon?"

"You're disappointed in our guest."

"No, indeed. As you said, it should be most educational."

"I lied," Genie laughed. "Rhys should be here at seven."

Izzy couldn't help smiling, and braced herself for whatever Genie might say next.

"He'll probably be returning home soon," Genie went on. "His trips here usually only last a couple of weeks."

"Oh."

Silly—of course he wouldn't stay here for long. He had a life of his own—one that did not involve her. And why should it? She'd only met him a week ago, and they had almost nothing in common. She forced her lips into a smile. "It will be pleasant to talk with him again."

"Very pleasant," Genie agreed. "I need to have another word with Mrs Pritchard. I'll send Megan up to help you with your hair."

Izzy mechanically set Alis' music on the piano rack as Genie left the room. Why would Genie say that? Izzy hadn't needed Megan's help on other evenings.

Of course, Genie knew she liked Rhys.

Liked. That was all.

She had to force her mind to focus on helping Alis instead of thinking about which gown she should wear.

Izzy dithered over her gowns, finally picking the cream coloured one with the silvery grey overskirt, for no better reason than its colour reminded her of Rhys' eyes. It was a walking dress, not an evening gown, but Rhys...no-one would mind.

At home, she'd have ribbons, silk flowers, and jewelled pins to decorate her hair, but she'd not been allowed to bring those. She remembered there were white roses blooming in the garden, so she hurried outside to pick some buds before changing.

"That dress looks lovely on you, Miss," Megan said, when she arrived to help Izzy with her hair. "I can't do much fancy, see, but Mrs Lloyd sometimes has me help with her hair when she goes to a ball."

"A ball?" Here?

"It won't be like you're used to, Miss." Megan twisted Izzy's hair into a knot. "They go all the way to Aberystwyth sometimes, or to Llanidloes, and stay a day or two. Take the children, they do, and me to help with them."

Megan managed a more elaborate style than Izzy could on her own, and teased a few curls down to frame her face. "Makes a nice change, it does, from Capel Bodfan. Where d'you want them roses, Miss? All together here?"

"Yes, please." When Megan finished, Izzy turned her head from side to side to admire the maid's handiwork in the looking glass. "That's lovely, thank you Megan."

"You're welcome, Miss."

Mama would exclaim over the colour in her face, from that day out in the gig, but probably no-one else would notice. Her stomach felt hollow, but not from hunger. She hadn't felt so nervous since her first ball, over two years ago now.

The chimes of the clock in the hall sounded.

Seven o'clock. She should go downstairs.

Rhys handed his hat to Megan as Genie emerged from the parlour, one hand held out in greeting.

"Welcome, Rhys."

"Genie. Thank you for having me at such—"

His eyes caught a movement, a swirl of shimmering cream and grey, as Izzy descended the stairs. Her hair was done up in some fancy style, white rosebuds in it highlighting her clear complexion. It was her smile, though, that stopped his words—tentative, almost shy.

"You look lovely this evening, Miss Farrington," he said, hoping his tongue-tied pause hadn't been too noticeable.

"Thank you." A delicate blush spread over her cheeks. "Do call me Izzy, please."

"Some wine, Rhys?" Genie was gazing at him with her lips pursed in what looked like suppressed amusement.

"Er, yes, please. After you, Miss… Izzy."

In the parlour, Genie poured them glasses of white wine, and Rhys took a seat opposite Izzy.

"Huw will be here in a few minutes," Genie said. "Did you have a successful few days, Rhys?"

Rhys took a sip from his glass, trying to turn his mind back to business. "Yes, thank you."

"You've been to Hafod Uchaf, I think? How is Mrs Price doing with the new baby?"

Rhys answered her questions as well as he could, trying to keep his attention on her, not on her niece.

"Give the poor man a chance, Genie dear," Huw said, as he entered the room. "I think you should write a list of questions for him, next time." He winked at Rhys as he poured himself a glass of wine.

Megan appeared in the doorway before he could sit down. "If you please, Sir, the dinner's ready."

"Shall we go through?"

"Your business here is finished, then?" Genie asked, having already extracted further details about Rhys' travels over the last few days.

"I need a couple of hours with Huw tomorrow," Rhys said. "If that's convenient, Huw?"

"By all means," Huw said, taking another helping of mashed parsnip.

"So you'll be off home after that?" Genie added.

"Trying to get rid of me?" Rhys caught a sudden turn of Izzy's head from the corner of his eye.

"Not at all," Genie said. "As you well know."

He did—he counted the Lloyds as good friends.

"If you have time, I wondered if you would escort Izzy and me on a ride," Genie went on. "Huw hasn't the time, and it looks as if we might have good weather tomorrow."

Rhys cast a glance at Izzy. She met his eyes briefly, a shy smile appearing.

He shouldn't. He really shouldn't. She was already on his mind too much as it was, and he could claim urgent business back in Shrewsbury.

He opened his mouth to decline. "I'd be delighted to."

Damn it, his mouth seemed to be operating independently of his brain. But a wider smile from Izzy banished his concern, for the moment at least. "I may be back here again in a month or so," he added. But would she still be here?

"The mill?" Huw asked.

"Yes, if your enquiries about the land purchase are successful."

"Where will it be?" Genie asked.

"Near Llanidloes." Rhys remembered Izzy's sulks the previous time they had all sat here. Educated as she had been, she would have under-stood little of their conversation. "That's about fifteen miles from here," he added, looking at her. "The town lies on the Afon Hafren—"

"That's the River Severn, to you and me, Izzy," Genie put in.

"When in Wales…" Huw said.

"When one has English-speaking guests…" Genie retorted, her smile removing the reprimand from her words.

"Is the mill to be for spinning, Mr… Rhys?" Izzy asked.

"Spinning and weaving, hopefully. It will be a year or more before it is built and running, though. I hope the building of it will…" His voice tailed off. She wouldn't be interested in all his reasons.

"Will that put people like Mrs Thomas out of business?"

Rhys glanced at Genie, uncertain if this was a suitable subject.

"Women are quite capable of understanding such things, Rhys," Genie said.

Rhys felt a flush rise on his face. "I didn't mean that, but—"

"It's not a subject my father would allow to be discussed, at the table or elsewhere," Izzy interrupted. She smiled, her eyes crinkling in amusement. "Do, pray, continue."

Rhys laughed. "Very well, since you ask. I will do my best to keep buying spun yarn from the cottagers, but if I do not also reduce my costs by using machinery, my company is like to go out of business. Other manufacturers are mechanising, so I must, too."

Izzy nodded. She didn't know anything about business, but that made sense. "Will some of the people get work…?" She broke off and shook her head. That was silly. "No, they would have to leave their homes to work in your factory."

"It's a problem I am still working on," Rhys admitted. "Once the mill is running, profits would be greater if I bought no spun yarn from the farms, but I don't like to do that."

"You have no obligation to those people," Genie said. "At least, that is what my brother would say, if he were in a similar situation."

That sounded exactly like something Papa would say.

"Enclosed all the nearby land, has he?" Huw asked.

Izzy had no idea—that was yet another topic she would have to ask Genie about later.

"Undoubtedly," Genie said. "If my father hadn't already done so. Can't have the lower orders getting in the way of profit, you know."

Izzy pressed her lips together and looked down at her plate. She'd heard her father say that several times, and had thought nothing of it. "Genie, did you think like Papa when you came to live here?"

Genie shook her head. "Not really, but I'd never given it much thought. It didn't take long for me to realise how… how isolated I was from most people. The rich really have no idea how the rest of the population live, and care little as long as their own income is maintained."

Genie's words hadn't been aimed at her; Izzy knew that. Nevertheless they were true. She slid a glance at Rhys. What did *he* think of her, really?

She wasn't to find out this evening, as Huw turned the conversation to the recent debate in parliament on continuing the suspension of the Habeas Corpus Act. Izzy, bewildered by the discussion, grasped only that it had something to do with the attack on the Prince Regent at the beginning of the year. Rather than demonstrate her ignorance now, she did her best to follow the discussion until the topic changed again. She would ask Genie or Huw about it later—and about many of the other things their discussions had touched on.

"Where do you wish to ride tomorrow?" Rhys asked Genie.

His gaze met Izzy's, a smile curving his lips. Had he noticed her lack of contribution and changed the subject on purpose?

"You could visit the cromlech up on Bryn Moel, perhaps," Huw was saying. "I'm sure Izzy would be interested, and I don't think you've seen it, Rhys?"

"I'll give them the short version of the history," Genie said, with a laugh. But Huw had got started on his pet subject, and the rest of dinner was taken up with tales of times past, although it was clear from Genie's expression that she had heard most of them before. Izzy was fascinated by stories of mythical beasts, wizards, and gods. They reminded her of some of the folk tales the nursemaids had told when she was a child, before Mama found out and decreed that such stories of common folk were not suitable for the children of a baron.

Rhys finished the evening by relating Owain Glyndŵr's struggles against the English hundreds of years before, and how the bad weather in the hills had sometimes helped the Welsh army. It was strange to Izzy to think of herself as one of the interlopers, daughter of a country that the Welsh had fought to expel from their lands. He spoke well, and Izzy enjoyed the sound of his deep voice and the faint lilt in his speech as much as the stories themselves.

It was dark when Rhys finally took his leave, promising to return late the following morning for their excursion. Izzy watched him ride away in the moonlight, standing in the doorway with Genie.

"That was one of the best dinner parties I've ever attended," she murmured to her aunt.

Enough light spilled from the hall to reveal Genie's quizzical expression.

"The conversation," Izzy clarified. "I've never been included in such discussion of laws and parliament before, even if I didn't understand a lot of it. Nor have I heard so many stories told."

Genie chuckled. "Huw has plenty more of them, I assure you. Rhys, too. Be careful what you ask them."

It wasn't just being included in the conversation, Izzy thought as she brushed out her hair ready for bed. It was being included in a way that made her feel an equal participant. She knew she was not—the more she listened to them talk, the more she realised how little she knew. That wasn't her fault—well, not entirely. She hadn't paid much attention to their governess, but Miss Templeton had a knack for making even interesting subjects dull, and not much had seemed relevant to real life. She would make a point of asking Genie and Huw to explain things to her.

Of course, a pair of smiling grey eyes had nothing to do with her enjoyment of the evening. And the warm feeling inside her was not because she would see him again tomorrow.

CHAPTER 10

The promise of the previous evening's red sunset held, and Rhys rode up to Plas Coed under a blue sky. His business with Huw was complete, and he had the rest of the day to enjoy himself. His anticipation was fuelled by the glorious weather, but he had to admit to himself that the main cause of it was the prospect of spending the afternoon with Izzy.

He dismounted outside the gate, leaving Seren cropping the hedge. Izzy, garbed in green, was as beautiful as ever, the slight tan she'd acquired enhancing, rather than marring her complexion. She gave him a tentative smile as Genie called a greeting and they mounted their horses.

"We're going that way." Genie pointed her whip up the hillside. "We'll start slowly, to give Izzy a chance to become accustomed to Castan."

Rhys recognised Izzy's mount as the chestnut the Lloyds normally used to pull the gig—a docile beast, he recalled.

They followed the track up the hill, Genie in the lead, and passed the path to the chapel. The world opened out around them as they ascended. Rhys said nothing as they rode, not wanting to distract Izzy.

She seemed to have little trouble, her seat relaxed, her body moving easily with her mount.

They reached the top of a rounded hill, an outlier to the higher land ahead. The moorland was covered in rough grass, broken by isolated outcrops of rock and patches of bracken. A skylark rose, trilling its song to the heavens.

"How do you like the view, Izzy?" Genie asked.

Rhys nudged Seren to move sideways so he could see Izzy's face. She gazed at the scenery, her lips parted slightly, and then smiled.

"It's… impressive," she said, appearing to consider her words. "Not pretty, but it goes on so far."

"And mountains beyond," Genie said, pointing to shadows on the far horizon. "Our way lies along this ridge." She set off westwards. Rhys guided Seren behind her, riding next to Izzy.

Very aware of Rhys' presence beside her, Izzy looked around at the scenery again before turning to him. Even riding up onto the Chilterns at home had never given her such views, or made her feel on top of the world as she did now.

"I can understand why you like this place," she said. "I feel… free."

He smiled, a grin as wide as her own must be. "Any mountain top will do that for you."

"As long as the sun is shining? You must ride a long way for business—do you enjoy it?"

"It's better than sitting in an office, although I might give you a different answer if I've spent the day with rain trickling down my back."

"Like the day you arrived here," she said, and then looked away. No need to remind him of her rudeness.

"At least now I'm guaranteed a warm bed at the end of the day, and dry clothes."

No bed? He hadn't grown up in poverty…?

No. He'd been in the army—he must be referring to his time in Spain. Until now the fighting on the continent had been bare statements of battles won or lost, something she'd taken little interest in on the few occasions Papa mentioned it at the dinner table. How much else of life had she never bothered to concern herself with?

"Izzy?"

"I'm sorry, I was thinking."

"Oh dear." He shook his head, the action belied by his smile. "Your father would not approve."

He'd said it for her, and she couldn't help laughing.

"We're getting behind," she pointed out, and urged her horse into a canter. That was all it could do, she thought, admiring the way Rhys' mount moved effortlessly across the rough ground. She rode better horses at home, but she wouldn't change this moment for the finest of steeds.

The ridge must have been a mile long, or more, but Genie led them off it before they reached the end, descending the slope into a shallow valley where sheep grazed. The sun was warm on Izzy's back here, sheltered as they were from the breeze. They paused to let the horses have a quick drink from a stream before they rode on. Izzy said little, enjoying the day and the little bubble of happiness inside her. It seemed like years since she'd felt this way.

The cromlech, when they finally reached it, turned out to be a large, flat stone balanced on the tips of three upright ones. Smaller stones stuck out of the earth around it, or lay on their sides in the grass. They dismounted, leaving the horses loose. Izzy walked up to the structure and found she could stand beneath the top stone if she bent her knees a little.

"What is it?"

"An old tomb," Genie replied. "Sometimes called a dolmen. Huw says the capstone was once buried under a mound of earth, but that's been worn away over the years."

Izzy listened with half her attention, standing with a hand on the lichen-covered surface of one of the vertical stones. They were rough, irregular, not shaped as building stones were. On such a sunny day, it was difficult to imagine this structure buried in permanent darkness, a body laid beneath it.

"...difficult to tell, but over four thousand years old, so it's not surprising..."

So long ago. Such a different life, yet they had lifted these great stones here on this hillside, then gone to the trouble of covering them.

Rhys hadn't visited this cromlech before, but he'd heard Huw's theories about them. Rather than listen to Genie, he watched Izzy. Her gaze was unfocused as she stood by the structure, one hand pressed against a stone as if communicating with it. What was she thinking?

"How did they live, those people?" she asked, as Genie finished her explanation.

"They were farmers, I think. As far as anyone knows, at least. You'll have to ask Huw... if you have a couple of hours to spare."

Rhys laughed. "Ignore her," he said. "Huw won't bore you, not if you are truly interested."

"Shall we see what Mrs Pritchard packed for us?" Genie said. "Rhys, if you would fetch the bags from my horse?"

The bags contained small pies wrapped in napkins, bread, cheese, apples, and bottles of lemonade. He laid the food out on a fallen stone.

"Not the kind of picnic you are used to, I expect," Genie said to her niece. Rhys could detect neither censure nor apology in her tone.

"No, not at all," Izzy said, taking a pie and lowering herself to sit on a rock. A few wisps of hair had come loose and blew about her face. "No picnic basket, no strawberries and cream, no footmen." Her mouth curved into a smile as she spoke, and she waved a hand at the scenery around her. "I prefer this."

She bit into the pie. Rhys missed Genie's next comment, gazing instead at Izzy's lips, wondering what it would be like to kiss them.

"Rhys, do pay attention!" Genie's smile had something knowing about it. "Izzy asked what your horse is called."

Rhys took an apple and found himself another flattish rock to sit on. "Seren," he said. "It means star."

"After his face." Izzy nodded. "I had a pony with white on her legs when I was younger. I called her Socks." She looked at Seren's white feet.

"I could never give him such an undignified name," Rhys protested.

Izzy laughed. His sisters would have giggled, but her laughter was lower pitched. Endearing rather than irritating.

It's because she's not *your sister, you fool.*

"Are there any more burial mounds near here?" he asked Genie, trying to distract himself.

"One or two," she said. "But nothing as impressive as this. Now eat up. We'll go back a different way. Unless you're too tired, Izzy?"

"Not at all," Izzy said, taking another pie. Rhys got up and went to examine the cromlech himself. There was something about watching her lick pastry crumbs off her fingers that was testing his self-control.

To his dismay, or delight, she followed him, leaning against one of the uprights and looking up at him.

"Are *you* ever curious about the lives of the people who built these things?" she asked.

He clasped his hands behind his back to stop himself reaching out to tuck those stray wisps behind her ears.

"Not really," he admitted. Was that disappointment that crossed her face? "But I have lain outside at night looking up at the stars. Each one is a sun like our own, they say, but millions of miles away. I've always wondered if any of those have planets, with beings on them."

"Looking up and wondering about us?"

He'd lost himself in his thoughts, gazing up into infinity on those warm nights under Spanish skies. He could as easily lose himself in her eyes, imagining what it would be like to kiss her, to hold her close. To wake up beside her. To talk over their plans.

"Time to go!" Genie called from somewhere behind the stones, and they both started.

Rhys took a deep breath. "After you," he said, following Izzy to the horses, and making a stirrup of his hands to help her mount. She settled on the horse without fuss, smiling her thanks. He looked into her face, breathing the faint scent of roses that hung about her.

"Ready?" Genie asked.

No.

"Ready," he admitted with reluctance, and mounted Seren.

Genie took them back by a different route. Izzy hardly noticed their surroundings for the first mile, reliving that moment by the cromlech. Rhys' grey eyes had gazed into her own, something in his expression making her unable to look away; only Genie's summons had broken the spell. Then when he'd helped her onto the horse, his closeness had produced that same strange feeling within her. Nervous, but in a new, exciting way.

Now, while they rode on across sunlit moorland and through woods in dappled shade, her joy in the day was more from the presence of the man beside her than the beauty of their surroundings.

Genie finally reined in above an expanse of trees. Izzy thought she recognised Capel Bodfan in the valley below.

"Do you want to see the old chapel, Izzy? It's what the town was named after."

"Yes, please." Anything to extend this day.

"I need to go back to see to the girls," Genie went on. "They've been in Megan's charge long enough. Rhys, that path will take you to the chapel from here, although you'll need to lead the horses. I think you've heard enough about it from Huw to be an adequate guide."

Rhys laughed. "To be fair, I *did* ask him."

"I'm going to ride along the top of the woods to meet the track down to Plas Coed. Don't be too long."

"Thank you, Genie," Rhys said, dismounting. "For everything."

Genie smiled at Rhys, although there was something odd about it to Izzy's eyes. A warning?

Then Rhys was waiting to help her down, and she slid off the horse. The touch of his hands on her waist was brief, but it warmed her and she felt its absence when he stepped back. He took the reins of her horse in one hand and offered his other arm. "Seren will follow," he said.

She laid a hand on his arm, conscious of the man inside the

clothing as she never had been before. Glad of his steadying presence on the rough grass, she had to release him once they were in the trees. The path was narrow and muddy, but she was used to that now.

"Be careful of tree roots," Rhys said from behind her. "They're very slippery when they're wet."

"I will, thank you." She knew that—they had plenty of woodland in Bedley Park—but she was grateful for the warning.

She heard a short laugh.

"I *can* listen to advice, Rhys." She glanced behind, and he returned her smile. "Although it does depend on the way it is given, and by whom."

She paid attention to where she put her feet until they reached a set of tumbledown walls, her breath coming faster than it should for such an easy walk. The chapel was only about twenty paces long, mostly filled with brambles and nettles.

"How long ago was this abandoned, do you know?" Izzy asked, regarding a small tree growing in one corner. "Uncle Huw started talking about it in the gig when we went to Mr Thomas' farm, but then he remembered Genie's orders not to bore people to death." She chuckled.

"Centuries ago," Rhys said. He was sure Genie hadn't suggested this visit to talk about ancient history. He took a step closer to her. "Izzy?"

"Yes?" She must have heard something in his voice, for the smile vanished.

"I return home tomorrow."

"Yes, of course." She bit her lip, glancing away briefly. "Will you be coming back?"

A little of the hollow feeling inside him dissipated. If she didn't want to see him again, she wouldn't have asked that question. "I will have more business here this year, but not for several weeks. A couple of months, even."

"Oh."

He hadn't meant to say the next words, but they came out anyway. "I… I find myself wishing to kiss you before I leave. May I?"

The widened eyes, the sudden step backwards, acted like a bucket of cold water on him. He moved back himself—clearly she did not share his feelings. It was time to escort her back to Plas Coed before he said anything else.

"My apologies, Miss Farrington. I did not mean to offend you."

"No!" Izzy reached out a hand, touching his sleeve. "I'm not offended." It was a compliment if a man wanted to kiss you, wasn't it? Even if, like Lord Ordsall, he didn't wait for her agreement before pressing his lips wetly against hers, his tongue trying to push her lips apart.

But this was Rhys. He had asked, but was also prepared to take no for an answer. She liked him far more than she'd cared for any of her other suitors, and no-one else had ever given her that warm feeling inside when he was close.

"If you wish to." She closed her eyes and tilted her face up, her lips pursed a little.

Nothing happened.

She opened her eyes.

"That's how Alis and Bethan put their faces up for Huw to kiss," Rhys said, his eyes narrowed. "Izzy, I don't mean to be rude, but how is it you've reached your age without being kissed?"

"I *have* been," Izzy said. "Once." She felt a blush rising to her face. It was too embarrassing to discuss how distasteful she'd found it.

"You didn't enjoy it?"

She shook her head, her face getting even hotter. Was it some failing in her?

"At the risk of sounding arrogant, perhaps they weren't doing it properly."

Her eyes flew to his. "Properly? What is…? I mean…" She took a deep breath. "I'm sorry, I'm babbling. I… I didn't know there was a right and a wrong way. How…?"

No, she could not stand here and ask him to explain. He looked amused—was he laughing at her? Not laughter, no. Amusement, perhaps, but something else, too. Something in his eyes that almost stopped her breath.

"I can demonstrate. But only if you wish it."

"Are you good at—?" One hand flew to her mouth, aware of how improper that question was. Mama would have a fit if she'd heard.

"I've had no complaints," he said. "But few men would admit it if they had."

His words sounded half-joking, but he wasn't laughing as he put one hand out towards her, hesitating with it close to her face.

She stepped forward, moving her head so her cheek rested on his palm. "Show me," she whispered.

He leaned closer. His thumb stroked her cheek gently as he came closer still, then his lips were brushing hers. Lightly, so lightly it almost tickled.

Izzy took a deep breath, her mouth opening slightly, and his lips moved along hers again, stroking gently. A tingling feeling spread through her. Wanting more, she took one more step towards him, one hand going up to his shoulder, then to curl around his neck, her fingers tangling in his hair.

With a strangled moan, he deepened the kiss. A vague thought that this felt nothing like Ordsall's kiss flitted through Izzy's mind before she stopped noticing anything other than the feel of his mouth on hers, the warmth heating her body, and the pressure of his hard chest against her.

Rhys finally made himself pull away, his hands almost shaking as he stepped back. That had felt so good, better than any other he recalled. He couldn't regret kissing her, although he knew he'd pay for it later. The kiss had only made him want more, more of what he could not have.

Izzy seemed as affected as he'd been, her face delightfully rosy as her breathing slowly returned to normal.

"I..." She put one hand to her lips. "I think... I think the other one *must* have been doing it wrong."

He laughed—he couldn't help it. "I'm pleased to hear that you approve."

That brought a smile, but then her face sobered. "I... I'd like to do it again..."

So would he.

"...but Genie will be expecting us."

She was right—Genie would be coming back after them if they stayed too much longer. Much as he wanted to, he wouldn't break Genie's trust in him. Or Izzy's.

"Come then." He followed her out of the ruin, ready to steady her if she slipped on the slippery stones, almost regretting that she didn't need his help.

Seren and Castan were where they'd left them, idly cropping grass. Rhys took Castan's reins, as before, and they picked their way through the trees. Too soon, they reached the main track, but he made no move to mount. It seemed hardly worth it for the short distance to Plas Coed, and walking allowed him to be closer to Izzy for longer. She took his offered arm, and they walked in silence.

Genie was waiting by the gate as they approached. "Would you like to come in for refreshment, Rhys?"

He did, and he didn't. Caution finally won.

"Thank you, Genie, but no."

He ignored a sudden movement from Izzy beside him. Disappointment, he hoped, although he knew he shouldn't. Being with Izzy was one thing. Having Genie with them, observing, was something else. He wouldn't be able to hide his feelings from her. He needed time, away from temptation, to make sure this wasn't just a temporary infatuation.

He had to hope it was temporary—what future was there for an attachment between a man in business and a baron's daughter?

"I will take my leave of you both now," he said, handing the chestnut's reins to Genie. "My thanks for your hospitality, Genie."

"A pleasure, as always, Rhys. You will call when you are in the area again."

"Of course."

Genie rubbed the mare's nose. "I'll take her round to the stable." She led the horse through the gate, and out of sight behind the house.

"Go safely, Rhys." Izzy's soft smile took his breath away.

Should he ask for a final kiss?

No, he dared not. Instead he took her hand. "I hope to see you again, Izzy."

"I hope so, too."

He lifted her hand and kissed the back of it, then resolutely mounted Seren. He twisted round to look behind him before the bend in the track took him out of sight.

She was still standing by the gate.

He tipped his hat. She waved her hand in reply, but his view of her was soon blocked by the trees alongside the track. Closing his eyes for a moment, he let Seren make his own way down the track.

If this was only an infatuation it would wear off, surely, once he was back in familiar surroundings, back to his normal routines.

And back to Uncle John hinting about marrying Sophie.

Against all the arguments of the logical part of his brain, he fell to wondering how he could convince his uncle that returning to Capel Bodfan very soon was necessary.

CHAPTER 11

Izzy stood by the gate for several minutes after Rhys had gone from sight. She'd never said goodbye to someone with so much regret, or so much hope that their parting would be short. She cupped the back of her right hand with her left, cradling the place he'd pressed his lips in farewell. The sensation of their bodies close, their lips touching—that was new as well. New, and intriguing. Exciting.

Genie was drinking tea in the parlour, a spare cup ready for Izzy. "You like him?" she asked as Izzy sat down.

"Very much." But Genie must know that—she had surely suggested the diversion to the chapel to let them say their goodbyes in private.

Genie tilted her head to one side. "Did he say anything?"

Izzy didn't pretend misunderstanding. "Only that he wants to see me again."

"And you him." It was a statement, not a question. "How much?"

Izzy blushed, and looked away.

"I'm not prying, Izzy. Well, I suppose I am, in a way. I'm merely wondering if I need to ask if you've thought things through."

"What do you mean?"

"You've had several offers of marriage. More than your mama or Frederick know about, I suspect."

Izzy nodded. "Most of them had the courtesy to find out my feelings before they approached Papa."

"And you probably managed to put off a few more before they got to that stage." Genie's lips twitched.

"I'm afraid so. They were not all men my parents would have approved of, though. They say I should be marrying someone with a title."

"Not even a second son?"

Izzy shrugged. "Papa hasn't explained his requirements. I suspect a younger son of a duke or marquess might have been acceptable. I would still become Lady Isolde then." She shook her head. "As if that were important!"

"And if Rhys had asked you this afternoon?"

Izzy's face heated, but she met her aunt's eye and took a deep breath. She'd known this question was coming. "It is too soon to be sure, Genie. But I would have been tempted to say yes."

"Knowing Frederick would not approve?"

Izzy nodded.

"Life would be very different, Izzy. You would miss the balls and all the other social events you attend in London. Oh, there will be assemblies and so on in Shrewsbury, but smaller than the ones you have been used to, and with different kinds of people."

That might not be all bad, Izzy thought. She had only a few close friends amongst the people she saw in London.

"Some of your friends may not wish to associate with people in trade," Genie went on.

"I would find out who my *real* friends are, then. Genie, do you see your friends that you had before you left home?"

"Not very often, but we write."

"Well, then." Izzy's chin went up as she spoke. "And you haven't tried to stop us spending time together, have you? *You* must approve?"

"I think he'd make a good husband, yes, but you need to consider the consequences of marrying into a different way of life." She sighed.

"Izzy, there's one thing I would ask—if you tell your father, or he gets wind of it, please do not base any decision about Rhys on doing the opposite of what your father wants."

Izzy gave a wry smile. "You know me too well. But you're right, as usual."

Genie leaned forward and patted her hand. "Good. In any case, you might find your feelings diminish if you don't see him for a few weeks."

His might, too. Izzy felt a heavy knot of disappointment in her stomach.

"Now, how about reading to the girls, Izzy? That should take your mind off things for a little while."

Rhys handed Seren to his groom and followed the path around to the front door. Although he was looking forward to a hot bath and dinner, his normal pleasure in arriving home was absent. The world seemed to have shifted around him, as if he'd left something important behind when he'd ridden away from Capel Bodfan two days ago.

"Welcome home, sir." Dobson stepped aside to allow Rhys to enter. "Mrs Williams and Miss Williams are in the parlour."

Taking a deep breath, Rhys crossed the threshold. "Thank you, Dobson. Order a bath for me, will you?"

He pushed open the parlour door. "Hello Mama, Gwynne."

Both women stood to greet him, Mama laying down her embroidery and Gwynne a magazine. Rhys gave first his mother, then his sister, a quick kiss on the cheek.

"Did you have a good trip, dear?" Mama asked. "You must tell me all about the business things tomorrow. How were the Lloyds?"

"Very well." He wasn't ready to mention Izzy—he needed to work out what he was going to do first. He'd had to force himself to stop wondering how a kiss with Sophie would compare to that kiss with Izzy. He suspected he knew the answer.

"I'm glad you came back today, Rhys," Gwynne said. "There's an assembly in Shrewsbury tomorrow—you can escort us. We're taking Sophie as well."

He wished he'd stayed an extra day in Wales.

"It will be my pleasure," he lied, suppressing the thought that he would have looked forward to it if Izzy were to be there.

"That's good, thank you! And Uncle John is holding a big dinner, with dancing, for Sophie's birthday next month. Did you get very wet, Rhys? It's been horrible weather here."

"There was some good weather," he said, and changed the subject by asking them how they'd spent their time while he'd been away. He made that topic last until Dobson came to say his bath was ready.

Rhys settled into the hot water with a sigh. Tomorrow would start with telling Mama about his trip, then doing the same with his manager at the mill. He was never sure why Mama wanted to know the details, for she took no part in any business decisions. But since he'd sold his commission and started to run the business, she'd wanted to be kept informed. He could only think that it was a habit she'd got into while his father was still alive, and she clung to it in his memory.

Izzy would question him, he was sure, and make suggestions. Probably quite sensible ones, if she was interested enough to learn about the business. She might even have accompanied him on the trip.

Stop it!

He sat up and soaped himself, trying to dismiss a vision of chestnut hair and blue eyes.

The next evening, Rhys danced the first set with Gwynne, then retreated to a position at the side of the assembly room. The air was thick with the smells of candle wax, sweat, and mingled perfumes. If it was up to him he'd leave now, but he had his mother, sister, and cousin to look after.

Gwynne and Sophie danced their way down the current set, smiling and giggling at their partners and looking remarkably similar. Both had soft brown hair dressed high at the back with ringlets framing their faces, and were garbed in pale gowns with knots of ribbon at sleeves and hems.

The set ended, and Sophie's partner brought her over. Bates, he recalled, a junior partner in a solicitor's business.

"Here you are, Williams. Miss Granger says you are her next partner."

Rhys nodded in thanks. Duty called.

The next set was already forming, and they took their places for another country dance. As Rhys grasped Sophie's hand and released it, swung her round and stepped back, a vision of doing this with Izzy intruded. There'd be some frisson as they came into contact, more than just fun in her eyes as they met.

Dancing with Sophie felt no different from dancing with Gwynne.

"...tomorrow evening?" Sophie gave him a small frown as they came together again. "Rhys?"

"I beg your pardon; my attention had wandered."

"Papa would like you to come to dinner tomorrow evening."

"Thank you, I'll be there." What else could he say? If he declined, Uncle John would want to know why when they met tomorrow morning.

"Did your business in Wales go well?"

"Yes, thank you." He looked into her eyes, detecting only polite interest. "The sheep that Evans is breeding..."

They moved apart—two steps back, two steps forward.

"...are coming along nicely. Hardy animals, with good fleece..."

Back, turn, forward.

"...high staple strength. Lovely pink wool, too. With blue spots."

Sophie's rather glazed expression did not change, and Rhys wondered if she even realised he'd stopped speaking. It was unfair to judge her when he'd spoken knowing she wouldn't understand the details. But her father's wealth had come from this very business, and he wondered why she took so little interest. Gwynne, the same age as Sophie, had managed to make some relevant comments this morning.

"Tell me about your birthday dinner," he said. "Who is coming?" He did his best to concentrate as she chattered for the rest of the set, and was glad when it ended. He had promised one more dance with Gwynne, but then he could retire to the card room until Mama decided to return home.

~

John Granger's study was stuffy, the windows kept closed on his physician's advice. Rhys straightened his pile of papers, glad that he could soon escape into fresh air.

"So that's it, Uncle John. There's a little more wool to be had than last year, but not up to previous amounts. Next year should be better."

Uncle John nodded as he reviewed the notes he'd made. Rhys regarded his bent head with concern. He hadn't been in Wales for long, but his uncle seemed to have aged noticeably in that time, his face thinner, the bags beneath his eyes more prominent.

Finally, Uncle John looked up. "I was a bit wary, handing all the day to day matters over to you this spring," he admitted. "But Sophie persuaded me that I had to listen to the physicians." He tapped his notes. "You're doing well, in difficult circumstances. I'm not sure about this breeding business though."

He held one hand up as Rhys opened his mouth to protest.

"No, I'm not about to suggest you stop. I just want you to be sure about your plan to secure farming land when the money should be put towards the new mill instead."

Rhys sighed and leaned back in his chair. "We can do both, Uncle. And there's little point rushing ahead with the mill when we barely have enough wool to keep the one in Shrewsbury going. It won't cause much of a delay to our plans."

"Very well. But Rhys, I also want to secure the future. You know Sophie turns seventeen next month."

Rhys nodded, making an effort not to grimace. He'd known this discussion was coming.

"This has been a family business since the beginning—your father and I only met because our wives were sisters. When Williams died..."

When his father had fallen ill, Rhys had been with Wellington in

France. The letter had taken over a month to reach him, and by the time he returned home his father had been dead for weeks. Mama hadn't wanted him to go into the army in the first place, and with Boney's abdication there had seemed no reason not to sell out and take over his father's side of the business. He'd felt bad, not being with his regiment at Waterloo, but he had responsibilities here, too. One of his brothers could have managed the business if he'd been killed, he supposed, but Owen was already settled in his parish near Monmouth and Alun was making good progress in his law career in Chester.

"You'd get on well together, Rhys. You've known her all her life."

"And she's like a sister to me." He'd felt that way even before he met Izzy. "Anyway, you've years in you yet, Uncle, if you do as the doctors bid you." He wasn't sure that was true, but what else could he say?

Uncle John leaned forward. "I'd like things to be settled. You've got most of your father's shares, and Sophie will get mine. But her shares will belong to her husband when she marries, and who knows what he might do with the business." He shook his head. "No, Rhys, better to keep it in the family."

Uncle John did have a point, but Rhys didn't want to marry for money. And didn't Sophie deserve to have a choice, too? From what he'd seen at the assembly last evening, she'd treated him no differently from any of the other men she'd danced with. His refusal could be no betrayal of her expectations or feelings.

"I'll give it some thought," he promised, admitting to himself that the thought would mostly be about how to change his uncle's mind.

"Thank you. Well, Sophie says you accepted my invitation to dinner. I'll see you all this evening."

"I look forward to it."

So many white lies.

CHAPTER 12

*I*zzy sat near the parlour window, making the most of the grey afternoon light to see her needlework. Alis and Bethan were on the window seat itself, frowning in concentration as they embroidered flowers around the edges of handkerchiefs. Izzy was working pink and yellow roses onto the necklines of the girls' new summer dresses.

Her hand paused as she gazed at the raindrops on the window, wondering yet again what Rhys was doing. She wasn't sure how long it would have taken him to ride to Shrewsbury—surely only one night on the road. He should have reached home days ago, then, although he'd have got very wet if all of Wales was suffering this rain. He'd probably just laugh, and say that no-one came to harm from a soaking in such mild weather.

Alis leaned over to inspect Izzy's work. "Can you do another pink one?"

"If you wish. Here?"

Alis nodded, her curls bobbing.

Izzy selected a different length of silk, and started on a new set of petals. For once, she was enjoying her embroidery; it must be because she had a purpose for it. At least, a purpose that seemed more useful than working yet another fire screen or purse. For, naturally, embellishing one's clothing was a task for the modiste, not a young lady.

Smiling, Izzy formed the petals, adding a paler pink to give them shape, and then the green leaves that Alis demanded.

"Mine too?" Bethan asked, coming to watch.

"I'm sure Izzy will do a splendid job on both," Genie said from the doorway. "Time for your tea, girls. Megan is waiting for you upstairs."

Izzy glanced at the clock—it seemed a little early. Genie shook her head before Izzy could speak, and waited until the girls had left.

"Huw's just sent a lad up," she said as she closed the door. "I think your father has arrived."

"Papa? Here?" Izzy turned her head—the rain had stopped, but mist still blurred the distant landscape. She could see nothing out of the ordinary.

"He'll be here soon. The lad said there's a coach with a crest on the door at the Red Dragon, and someone asking for Mrs Lloyd."

"Oh. Oh, dear. Miss Amberley must have written to him."

"I think so, yes."

"Will he come up here, do you think? Or summon me to the town?"

Genie sat in the chair facing Izzy's. "I suspect he'll come. He won't want anyone in the inn to overhear. Does he still shout when he's angry?"

Izzy nodded. "I'm afraid so."

"He'll have come for you, but I cannot imagine Frederick missing the chance to berate me for marrying without our father's permission."

"You were of age!"

"Ah, but my father was head of the family at the time. A dutiful daughter would have been guided by him. And now Frederick considers himself in that position."

Izzy let out a breath. That *did* sound like Papa.

Genie's eyes were on the track. "This may be him now."

Her father's familiar travelling chaise drew up by the gate. A heavy feeling settled in Izzy's stomach as she watched a dripping footman let the step down. Her life was about to be ordered for her again by her father, with no reference to her own wishes, and that meant that she would not see Rhys when he came here again.

"Izzy, if you need to, you may make your home with us," Genie said. "I hope it will not be necessary, but bear that in mind. I'll not see you forced into a marriage you don't want."

Izzy's jaw dropped. "You think I will need—?"

"Frederick always insisted that his way was the correct one, my dear. I doubt he's mellowed with age. Now that his punishment seems to have failed spectacularly, he may…" Genie sighed. "Well, I don't know what he'll do."

"Thank you, Genie. I hope I don't need to accept." It was good of Genie, very good, but she would have to consider carefully before taking her up on the offer. She'd come to enjoy the countryside and the Lloyds' way of life over the last fortnight—that might change if she had to live here permanently, but it would probably still be better than what Papa had in mind. If only Miss Amberley had not told him about Genie's marriage so quickly, she could have had more time here. More time with Rhys.

They watched as her father approached the house, a footman beside him holding an umbrella. The coach moved off to turn in the space further along the track.

"At least Papa doesn't know about Rhys," Izzy said, as her father drew close enough for her to make out the thin line of his mouth and the crease between his brows.

The knocker sounded. Izzy stood, but Genie put a hand out to restrain her. "Let Megan open it, Izzy. Whatever he may have wanted, you are not here as a servant."

They heard the sound of Megan's footsteps, then the door opening.

"Where is she?" Although it was not a shout, her father's voice carried clearly through the door.

"Mrs Lloyd is in—"

Heavy footsteps drowned Megan's words, and Izzy's father pushed open the door and walked in. Larger than Huw, and broader of shoulder, his presence seemed to fill the room. His face was set, but Izzy could not make out his expression. He was angry, yes, but not nearly as much as she'd expected, and there was something else mixed in.

His gaze swept over the room as he deposited his hat on a side table and ran his hands through his hair. His brows drew together when he spotted the two women by the window.

"Isolde, go and pack your things. I'm taking you home."

"Papa—"

"Now, Isolde."

Izzy knew better than to disobey that tone.

"Very well, Papa." She stood and carefully put all her embroidery threads into her sewing bag. "Excuse me, Aunt Eugenia."

The sound of her father's footsteps followed her as she walked towards the door. She wondered if he was going to reprimand her now, but he only closed the door behind her.

That was strange—he was prone to slamming doors when he was really angry.

"Ooh, Miss, is something wrong?" Megan, still standing in the hall, regarded her with wide eyes. At the end of the corridor, Mrs Pritchard stood in the open kitchen door, Ellie visible behind her.

"It is my father, come to take me home." She might as well tell them; they would find out soon enough.

"What, right now, Miss?"

"I'm afraid so. I need to pack."

"I'll help you, Miss, shall I?"

Izzy nodded, and Megan followed her up the stairs. Izzy changed into her green walking dress; it was more practical for travelling than the muslin morning gown. She laid out the blue pelisse and her bonnet. Packing the rest of her clothing didn't take long, her hands moving mechanically as she folded garments into the trunk. She felt as if she were in a dream, or a nightmare. Only ten minutes ago she'd been helping Alis and Bethan, and now she was being taken home. Away from her new friends, and from the chance of seeing Rhys again.

Izzy put the books she'd borrowed from Genie into the trunk and closed the lid. Genie wouldn't mind, she was sure. She took a deep breath. Thinking about Rhys would have to wait—she had Papa to face first.

"I'll go and get Roberts to fetch it down, Miss," Megan said, hurrying off.

Izzy checked her reticule for coins as she went downstairs, finding that she had some left from her journey here. She could hear her father's voice through the parlour door—loud, but fortunately not shouting.

The rest of the staff were gathered at the end of the hall nearest the kitchen door. Trying to listen, Izzy guessed, without being so close they'd be caught when someone opened the door.

She gave the coins to Mrs Pritchard, asking her to share the money out. "For all the cleaning of my muddy clothes," she said quietly.

"Why, thank you, Miss," Mrs Pritchard said. "Sorry I am that you're going so sudden."

Izzy grimaced—the cook wasn't nearly as sorry as she was. She paused outside the parlour door, listening. Papa's words were not easy to make out—something about keeping secrets.

Putting her shoulders back and chin up, she knocked on the parlour door and pushed it open. Her father spun round to face her, interrupted in his pacing. Genie, behind him, shrugged, aiming a wry smile at Izzy.

"I'm ready, Papa," Izzy said.

Her father drew a deep breath. "Very well. Go and wait in the coach."

"Thank you for having me to stay, Aunt Eugenia."

"It was a pleasure to—"

"Go to the coach, Isolde. Now."

"Yes, Papa." He hadn't raised his voice, but now was not the time to argue.

"I am disappointed in you, Eugenia," her father said as Izzy stepped into the hall, leaving the door ajar. "Deceiving the people who care for you, who are responsible for your well-being, is a wretched example for—"

"Yes, I know," came Genie's calm interruption. "You have just told me so, several times."

Izzy shook her head. Papa resorted to repetition when he had no other arguments.

"Are you sure you won't wait until my husband returns?" Genie went on. "I'm sure you'd enjoy meeting him."

"You… you… Pah!"

Izzy hurried to the front door as heavy footsteps sounded in the parlour and Mrs Pritchard and the maids disappeared into the kitchen. Papa's footman waited outside the door, sheltering under the umbrella. It was the same man who'd accompanied her and Miss Amberley.

"Tanner," Izzy said. "You must hardly have reached Bedley before coming back again?"

"Was only back a day or two, Miss." Tanner squinted at the sky. "At least it's not too cold." He held the umbrella over Izzy's head.

"You'd better wait for Papa. He'll be out in a minute." Anything to avoid making his mood worse.

"Right, Miss."

Clasping her bonnet to her head, Izzy made a dash for the coach. She pulled open the door and scrambled in without bothering with the step. It was very unladylike, but it got her out of the rain quickly. She would miss this place, she thought, looking back. Genie, too. But she would miss Rhys the most, and the chance to get to know him better.

It was less than a minute before her father joined her. Tanner closed the door and the coach started jolting down the track. Papa was silent until they reached Capel Bodfan; Izzy sat with hands clasped in her lap, eyes downcast.

"I am very disappointed in my sister," he said, once the coach was on a better road. "Marrying such a man. And so lacking in family feeling that she did not inform me of it."

"Yes, Papa." Best not to argue with him now, not when they would be in the carriage together for several days.

"Such an error of judgement, marrying someone of Lloyd's class.

Look at this place." He gazed out of the window. "This is the life she has chosen? I hope you see what refusing to marry well does for you, Isolde."

Izzy nodded. She had learned that lesson, but not in the way Papa thought.

"How did you enjoy managing without a maid?"

"It was not easy." But not particularly difficult, either.

"Hmpf. Well, I suppose I cannot blame you for Eugenia's deceit."

That was something, she supposed. She understood why Genie hadn't told him.

Her father leaned back against the squabs. "Damned poor roads here. Godforsaken country."

"Yes, Papa." That was rather unfair. Buckinghamshire wasn't attractive in rain, either.

He fell silent. Thankful for the temporary peace, Izzy gazed out of the window. He'd return to her own failings soon enough.

Rhys sat in his office long after the sounds of machinery had died away and the workers had gone home. He'd dealt with all the orders and correspondence that had piled up while he'd been away, and there was no reason to stay here instead of returning home.

No reason apart from Mama and Gwynne discussing young Doctor Feltham to the exclusion of almost everything else. He knew the man slightly, but it seemed that Feltham had been promoted from an acquaintance to a suitor while Rhys had been in Wales. Why that required endless debate about the physician's tastes, income, and prospects, he had no idea. He didn't remember the same fuss with Caris, but he'd been in Spain when her long courtship started.

It would be only a step from there to Mama wondering how the house would feel with Gwynne gone and Rhys at the mill during the day, and whether it was time that Rhys found a wife. And what a lovely young woman Sophie was turning into.

Rhys eyed the decanter of Madeira on the table near the window, kept for visiting customers or suppliers. Drunken parties had whiled away long winter evenings in Spain, but that wasn't the answer here. Part of the problem, he had to admit, was that the continual chatter about marriage prospects didn't let him forget his own dilemma.

Writing lists often helped him to think through a problem. He wasn't going to put his thoughts about marriage on paper, but if he did…

Item One: I can't get Izzy Farrington out of my mind.
Item Two: Sophie feels like a sister.
Item Three: Even if she didn't, it would not be fair to marry her while thinking about someone else.
Solution: Stop thinking about Miss Farrington.

That wasn't much help. It was a week since he'd last seen her, and his wish to be with her again was growing stronger, not fading.

The business…? Rhys shook his head. It didn't matter. He was not going to marry just to suit the family business. He would just have to explain the situation to his uncle, and politely decline. Uncle John could not force him, after all, nor would he want to.

No, his problem was Izzy. Or his feelings for Izzy, to be precise, and whether she returned them. That kiss showed she did feel something for him, but was it enough? Enough to marry him in spite of the differences in their situations?

He had to see her again. He'd have to be honest with Uncle John, but as far as Mama and Gwynne were concerned, he'd suffer fewer prying questions if he said he had to go back to Wales to see about the new mill. No need to mention Izzy to them yet.

The interview with Uncle John would be the hardest. He pulled out his watch. Uncle John ate early these days; if he called on the way home, he would probably catch his uncle having his evening glass of port.

"I've been thinking about Sophie," Rhys started, once the manservant had brought in a decanter and glasses. He poured port for them both, and handed a glass to Uncle John.

"Good, I'm glad you've..." Uncle John's words tailed off as he looked at Rhys' face. "You've come to say no, haven't you?"

"Yes, I have." No point in beating about the bush.

His uncle's shoulders slumped a little, and he shook his head. "I can't say I'm surprised."

"I've nothing against Sophie, please do not think that. But..." He had to be honest. "I met someone in Wales, staying with the Lloyds. I can't get her out of my head." He took a deep breath. "Your marriage was a love match, was it not, Uncle? And my parents' too. Do you not wish that for Sophie as well?"

Uncle John rubbed his temple. "I hoped you would come to feel affection for each other, at least. If this young woman does not return your affection, what then?"

Rhys tried to put that possibility out of his mind. "Do you really want me to marry Sophie while wishing for another woman?"

"No." His uncle sighed. "But my reasons for wanting the match still remain."

"There are other ways to make sure the company is managed properly, whoever Sophie marries. You could leave your shares in a trust, for example. Or I could buy some of yours—now, if you wish. I don't need many more to have a controlling interest. My brothers will follow my judgement in any disagreement."

"That could work." Uncle John nodded. "I will think about how best to arrange matters."

Rhys sat back in his chair, surprised he'd managed to persuade his uncle so easily. But Uncle John's brow was creased as he sipped his port, and Rhys suspected he hadn't won yet.

"Rhys, I haven't told Sophie this, but my chest pains are getting worse."

Rhys stared into his glass for a moment, collecting his thoughts. It was a shock, even though he had suspected his uncle's health was deteriorating. "I'm sorry to hear that, Uncle."

Uncle John waved a hand. "It will help if I don't have to worry about Sophie. If the two of you were wed, I'd go knowing I need not fear for her future. She will need someone to look after her financial interests, as well as making sure no-one marries her just for her inheritance."

"Mama will take her under her wing," Rhys said.

"I'm sure she will. But Rhys, if you will not marry her, will you agree to be appointed her guardian when I die?"

"Yes, I will, happily." Better her guardian than her husband.

CHAPTER 13

*B*y the second day of the journey, as the Welsh hills gave way to the more rolling countryside of Herefordshire, Izzy had found herself thinking longingly of Miss Amberley. Even her endless twittering would have been preferable to her father's silence. He had immersed himself in a newspaper or book the entire time, only speaking to inform Izzy when dinner would be served or what time they would set off again. Now, rattling out of Oxford after another couple of days, she was beginning to wonder, with growing resentment, if he would speak to her at all.

She had done nothing wrong. Well, nothing that he was aware of. He didn't know about Rhys, and it was hardly her fault that Genie had got married without telling him. He must still be angry with her for refusing Lord Ordsall's offer.

Izzy leaned her head back on the squabs as they left the buildings of the city behind and the coach picked up speed on the turnpike. The father she remembered from her childhood had been a laughing man, happy to spend time teaching her and Viv to ride, proud of their progress when he asked them to read to him or when he admired their watercolours. He'd done the same with Lynnie.

She missed the way he used to be. When had he begun to change?

114

Sometime towards the end of her first season, she thought, casting her mind back. Probably about the time that Lord Crompton made her an offer and she turned him down. He wasn't the first she'd refused but he was the highest ranking suitor she'd had until Lord Ordsall came along this year. Papa, and Mama, had begun to talk more about the importance of being married, and wanting her to be wed before Viv came out. If her refusal to accept titled suitors was the reason for Papa's current ways, it did not bode well for her chances of being allowed to see Rhys again.

The coach finally passed through Aylesbury—not far to go. The continuing silence had given her too much time to think. To wonder what Rhys was doing now, if he would return to Capel Bodfan to find her gone, and what he would do when he found out.

Probably nothing, she'd concluded despondently. What could he do? He could not introduce himself to Papa—quite apart from the fact that Papa would not receive him, a visit from an unknown man would give the impression of more... more serious intentions than they had discussed. A wish to see her again and kiss was just that, nothing more.

Rather than moping because she might not see Rhys again, she should take Genie's advice and think about what she would do if it turned out that he *did* want to marry her. And if she wanted to marry him, of course.

And what she could do when her father did not give his permission.

As Izzy began to recognise the countryside only a few miles from home, her father finally turned to look at her.

"We will remove to London the day after tomorrow," he said.

"So soon?"

"Ordsall is in Town. It is to be hoped your initial refusal has not put him off, and he will make another proposal. You have seen what your life would be like if you remain unwed."

Izzy grimaced. She should have expected this. "Papa, what will you do if I decline his offer again?" She had to find some way of avoiding that match.

Her father's eyes narrowed. "Have you learned nothing from your sojourn in Wales?"

Yes, but not what you hoped. "Will you send me back to Aunt Eugenia?"

"Certainly not! She is not a good example."

That was a pity. "You will buy a cottage for me somewhere out of the way?"

Her father's mouth opened and then snapped closed again. "No. Good grief, Isolde, that would be even more unsuitable!"

She waited.

"Izzy, I'm trying to arrange a good marriage for you. Ordsall is pleasant enough to look upon, is he not?"

Izzy had to nod.

"He has sufficient status and wealth, and has no vices that I can discover."

Apart from a kiss like a wet fish. And not asking before slobbering on me.

Her father pinched the bridge of his nose and took a deep breath. "Izzy, every woman needs a husband to look after her and guide her."

Izzy bit her lips against a retort. She disagreed with that statement even more now than she had before.

"Your mama struggled to supervise both you and Vivian this season past. She cannot do it again next year."

"I'd be out of sight and out of mind if you sent me back—"

"No! How many times must I say this? You need to be married. If you do not wed, you will become a burden on the rest of your family."

Izzy bit her lips, unaccustomed tears pricking her eyes. The Papa she remembered from earlier times would never have called her a burden.

He sighed. "Izzy, you are not a burden *now*. A damned nuisance at times, but not a burden. But if you are still unwed when Vivian and Lynnette are married, you will end up as a companion to your mama. Is that what you want, rather than having your own establishment?

And when I'm gone and your cousin James inherits the title, you will be a dependant in his household."

That sounded gloomy indeed. "If you gave me an income instead of my dowry, I could—"

"No, Izzy, it's out of the question. Young ladies do not set up their own establishments. It's just not done, you know that."

Unfortunately, she did. She would be regarded as peculiar, probably ignored by many of her acquaintance, and looked upon as an object of pity.

"I'm not against marriage, Papa."

His brows rose.

"But I would prefer to marry someone I like, at least." Someone with a sense of humour, an imagination, with laughing grey eyes and—

"I do not see what is wrong with Ordsall," her father said.

Izzy sighed at the impossibility of persuading him.

"I would like your promise that you will accept Ordsall if he renews his addresses," he went on. "And if he does not, you will curb your tongue when you are with any other suitable young men. I am sure your lack of respect for them will have put off several potential suitors."

Izzy turned her gaze out of the window, feeling as if a hand squeezed her heart. Whatever possibilities there might be with Rhys would be instantly negated by her betrothal to someone else. Lord Ordsall's wet lips came back to her mind—if kissing him was so unpleasant, what would marital relations be like? She had only the vaguest idea of what would happen, but surely if a man could not even kiss well, the rest would not be enjoyable.

"Izzy? For heaven's sake, girl, have some consideration for your mama and sisters."

The feeling in her chest eased as she recalled the words of the promise her father required. *If he renews his addresses.* But she could try to prevent that.

"May I have more time to get to know him before deciding?"

"You've had weeks, Izzy."

"I've only met him at balls and parties. One cannot get a very good idea of a man's character in such public places." Her stomach knotted as she waited for his reply.

His eyes narrowed. "You will promise not to be rude to him?"

Izzy let out a breath of relief. "Yes, Papa."

"That's my good girl. Your mama will be relieved."

She hadn't promised to accept the man, but her father would expect it if Lord Ordsall did renew his addresses. She would have to make sure he did *not* do so.

"Oh, Rhys, I've just remembered," Mama said, pouring the tea and handing Rhys a cup. "A letter came for you while you were at the mill. Dobson put it in your study. Now, what do you think about repainting this room? I noticed when Doctor Feltham was here this morning that it looks sadly shabby."

Rhys glanced around at the familiar furnishings and walls, wishing he'd stayed at his office for longer. "We could repaint above the fireplace, I suppose," he suggested, noting traces of soot around the mirror and below the cornice.

"Oh, I was thinking of doing all the walls, dear. In a nice primrose, or pink, perhaps."

About to take a slice of cake, Rhys changed his mind. He couldn't face a discussion of colours and fabrics. "Talk it over with Gwynne, Mama. But now is not a good time to spend money on such things." As she should have realised when he'd told her about his trip to Wales. "If you will excuse me, I will take my tea into the study." The letter must be personal: a business letter would have gone to the mill.

It *was* personal. Genie wrote that Lord Bedley had arrived at Plas Coed only a few days after Rhys had left, and had taken Miss Farrington away immediately.

Damn. He screwed up the letter, a hollow feeling in his stomach.

No use going back to Wales. He knew he should try to forget her, no matter how impossible that seemed.

No. Izzy had said she wanted to see him again. He should not let her go without trying to see her at least once more. He flattened the paper out—Genie had written more, even crossing her lines for the last sentence. The reason Izzy had been sent to Wales was because she refused to accept an offer from one of her suitors.

He'd never asked Izzy what particular sin she had committed that resulted in her banishment. Ironic, really, that both of them were being pressured into marriage. No doubt the intended suitor was one of the men who told her what to think.

Turning to the letter again, he focused on the rest of Genie's message. She was concerned that Izzy might be forced into a marriage she did not want, as Lord Bedley had mentioned moving the family to London as soon as possible.

That was all. Genie didn't suggest he do anything, but why else would she tell him the reason Izzy had been sent to her?

He would have to go to London instead of Wales, to find out what *Izzy* wanted. It would be more difficult to see her there than in Wales, but he'd manage somehow. He'd have to spend a couple of days at the mill to make sure everything went smoothly in his absence, but in the meantime, who did he know in London who might help?

Half an hour later he had letters ready to be sent to the Lloyds and to Algy Pelham.

"Welcome back, Izzy." Her mother set her novel on a side table, and patted the sofa beside her in invitation. "I've asked Parker to get tea sent in. Did you have a good journey?"

"It was all right," Izzy said. Her pleasure at being out of the coach was tempered by the discussion she knew was about to come.

"How did you enjoy your visit to Eugenia? Is she well? You must be glad to be back."

"Very well, Mama. She sends her best wishes." Or she would have done, Izzy was sure, if Papa hadn't rushed her away. The familiar furnishings of Mama's parlour felt formal—unfriendly, even—compared to the lived-in feel of the Lloyds' house. There was more than one reason she was not pleased to be home.

"That's good. We didn't know each other well before she went to live in Wales. She had some odd ideas, and she seemed a very… determined person. Quite fatiguing."

Izzy chuckled. "She is indeed. She is married now, did Papa tell you?"

"He said so before he left to fetch you." She shook her head gently. "Such a shame to marry so low, no concern for the family reputation. Still, it cannot be undone, I suppose. Does she have any children?"

"Yes, three of them." Izzy described the children, and the lessons she'd given to Alis and Bethan. "They are a lovely family, and very happy."

"I'm pleased she married, even if he is not of our class," her mother said. "I would never have made such a match, but a woman does need to marry someone."

"Yes, Mama." Izzy had listened to the reasons why no woman should live alone too many times; there was no point in arguing. "Mama, may I write to Aunt Eugenia to let her know I have arrived safely? The weather has been so bad she might be worried."

"Why, yes, dear, that would be polite. Your father had a word with me while you were changing your dress, Izzy. I'm very pleased you agreed to accept Lord Ordsall."

"I didn't!" Izzy protested, horrified. Papa had twisted her words. "He agreed I could get to know him better."

"Indeed, yes, with a view to encouraging him to renew his offer. I'm sure he will do so—you have some of my looks." Her mother patted her hair complacently—it still showed no signs of greying. "You have good breeding, too, and a respectable dowry. Who would not renew their addresses once your father tells him you are amenable?"

Izzy closed her eyes and took a deep breath. She hadn't thought her father intended to be so direct in approaching Lord Ordsall.

"I don't know why you are protesting so much, dear," Mama continued. "An earl's heir is a very good match for you, and your parents know best."

Not in this case, Izzy thought.

"Your Papa was chosen for me, you know, and that has worked out nicely. I have a higher title than my mother's, and I have many titled friends."

As if that mattered!

"Your Papa doesn't bother me often. Lord Ordsall would be discreet in his affairs, I'm sure."

Izzy's eyes flew open at this comment. "I… I will think on it, Mama."

"Make sure Mary packs all your best gowns for London, Izzy."

"Yes, Mama. If you will excuse me?"

Her mother waved a casual hand. "Yes, dear, you must be weary indeed from all the travelling."

Piano notes filled the hallway. The scales and warming up exercises indicated that Viv and Lynnie were starting a music lesson. Miss Templeton would not release them until their half-hour was finished, no matter what the excuse.

Izzy went first to the schoolroom and wrote a short note to Genie, folding it and sealing it with a wafer. Then she went to her bedroom, where Mary was tutting over the state of her gowns, some still with muddy hems from the last few days at Plas Coed.

"You can finish the unpacking later, Mary. Please put this on the hall tray on your way down." Izzy handed her the letter. Papa would frank it for her.

The door closed behind the maid, and Izzy sank into a chair, some of her mother's words still running through her mind.

He doesn't bother me often.

Normally, Izzy would have interpreted such a statement as meaning that her father made few demands on his wife's time, allowing her to choose what entertainments to attend with Izzy and Viv. But coupled with the remark about Lord Ordsall being discreet in his affairs, she wondered if Mama had been referring to marital relations.

If she were married to Lord Ordsall, she would doubtless be grateful if he didn't bother her often. But she'd seen the affection between Genie and Huw, obvious in the way they talked to each other, and in little physical touches she'd never seen between her parents.

She put one hand to her lips. Rhys' kiss had demonstrated that there *were* great pleasures to be had from the physical side of marriage. More than she knew about thus far. They were pleasures she wanted for herself, and that she would not get from Lord Ordsall. Not to mention his lack of imagination, sense of humour, or any recognition that some women had minds of their own.

"Izzy!" The door burst open and Lynnie ran in, dark curls bobbing and a beaming smile on her face. "Miss Templeton wouldn't let us come and see you sooner. How was Wales? Papa was furious when he got the letter saying Aunt Eugenia was married. What's she like? What's her husband like? Papa says she married beneath—"

"Lynnie, calm down." Viv had followed her sister into the room. "Let poor Izzy answer." Viv crossed the room and gave Izzy a quick hug. "It's good to have you back."

"It's good to see you two, as well." Good to be with people who weren't going to lecture her.

"What's Aunt Eugenia like?" Lynnie asked again.

"In looks, it is obvious she is Papa's sister, but she is—"

There was a knock on the door, and Mary entered. "If you please, Miss Izzy, Lord Bedley wants to see you in his study." Lynnie stuck her lip out at the interruption.

"Thank you, Mary." Papa must have read her letter.

"You'd best go right away, Izzy," Viv said. "He's been in a bad mood ever since he got that letter from Miss Amberley. You can tell us the rest later."

Izzy knocked on the study door, waiting to hear her father's summons before she entered. He sat at his desk, an open ledger in front of him and his face set in stern lines. "Sit down, Isolde." He picked up a folded paper. "This letter to Eugenia—it says 'Give my thanks to Castan for a lovely day out.' Who is Castan?"

"Castan is Aunt Eugenia's horse, Papa. Genie took me on a ride in the hills, and let me ride Castan." Izzy folded her hands in her lap and maintained what she hoped was an innocently enquiring expression.

Her father glared at her. "You want her to thank a *horse?*"

"It was a figure of speech, Papa. Shall I rewrite it to thank Aunt Eugenia directly for the day out?"

"That's not what I… Gah!"

Izzy managed not to smile. Papa suspected she was up to something, but couldn't work out what.

"Will you send the letter?"

"Yes, yes." He refolded the letter and scribbled his frank on one corner, then resealed it. "I will give it to Parker with my other correspondence."

"Thank you, Papa."

"Izzy, I will be looking out for Lord Ordsall at my club as soon as we arrive in Town. Remember your promise to me."

"I will be polite, Papa." She waited, but he did not add any further conditions. "May I go?"

He waved a hand, returning to his perusal of the ledger.

Izzy left. Her suspicion that her father would read any letters she sent had been confirmed, so she would have to think of a different way to send a message to Genie. The only friends she had who could be relied upon not to gossip had left Town early, so she couldn't ask them to forward a letter. Slipping out to post a letter herself would be difficult, not to mention improper, and it wasn't fair to expect the staff to risk their positions by helping her.

She also had to work out how to dissuade Lord Ordsall from renewing his suit. If she had to break her word to Papa and be downright rude to the man, she would do so, but she should try to keep her promise first.

But now she had to answer Lynnie's questions.

Izzy finally escaped to her bedroom long after dinner, feeling drained. Conversation at table had been undemanding, but she was already tired from describing her time in Wales to Viv and Lynnie. It wasn't the talking, but the need to avoid mentioning Rhys. Any reference to her interest in a man, particularly a man in trade, would inevitably get to her parents. Not that Viv and Lynnie told tales, but they would talk about it and the servants or Mama would overhear. She'd mentioned touring the countryside, but had bent the truth by saying that Huw and Genie had been showing her some of the old ruins and standing stones.

She turned her thoughts to Lord Ordsall again while Mary brushed her hair out that evening. Politics would be a good start. She was still largely ignorant of such matters, but talking with Genie and Huw had provided enough information to at least start a discussion. Ordsall wouldn't like a mere female questioning the laws of the land. No, he would think she should stick to lady-like occupations. Not that there was anything wrong with flower arranging or embroidery, she enjoyed both at times, but she was no longer happy to be limited to such pastimes.

Embroidery.

She could send a piece of embroidery to Genie as her message.

Waiting until Mary had left the room, she found her sketchbook and worked out a design. It would have to be a bookmark, she decided —not too big, so it wouldn't take long to complete nor be too bulky to send. The basic shape was quick to sketch, and she pricked the design onto a scrap of fabric from her bag. She would find some stiffer backing material later.

Dark and light brown threads, and some yellow, with black for outlining. That would do nicely. Once it was embroidered, all she had to do was persuade her father that ornate spoons were a traditional Welsh symbol of hospitality, and thus suitable as a thank-you gift for Genie.

Izzy wasn't yet sure if she should send it, but if she did decide to she wanted it to be ready.

CHAPTER 14

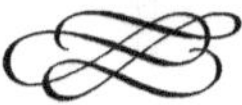

"*L*ord Ordsall, my lady."

Silence fell amongst the morning callers gathered in the front parlour as all eyes turned to the door. Izzy swallowed hard as her mother stood to greet her latest guest. They had not yet been in Town two full days and here he was already, impeccably dressed as always. His hair was carefully brushed into a fashionable crop, his cravat neatly tied, and his jacket close-fitting but not tight— not for him any of the excesses of fashion. That was a point in his favour, Izzy had to admit. One of very few.

She couldn't help comparing him to Rhys. They were of similar age, she guessed, and an impartial observer might judge Ordsall better looking. But Ordsall's smile lacked the friendliness that made Rhys so attractive, and there was no humour in his eyes. Izzy also sensed that Ordsall's admiration for her went no deeper than her looks.

"Pray be seated, my lord," Mama said, indicating a chair close to Izzy's place on the sofa. Conversations restarted, but Izzy was conscious of interested looks and whispers behind hands. Her previous refusal of his offer was clearly common knowledge.

"Miss Farrington, how lovely to see you again," Ordsall said. There was a polite smile on his lips but an appraising look in his eyes. "You are looking as beautiful as ever."

Izzy inclined her head.

"I trust you enjoyed your stay in the country," he went on, before she could reply.

"Very much," Izzy replied, picking up her cup of tea. "Wales is a fascinating country—have you ever been there?"

His eyes widened. "Er, no. I thought you had remained at Bedley Park after I... after my visit."

"The family were at Bedley Park, my lord, but I visited a relative in Wales." She'd contemplated mentioning Genie's relationship to her father, and Huw's job, but that could get about and harm Viv's chance of a good match. Lynnie's too, if memories were long in the *ton*.

"Miss Farrington, may I have the honour of a private interview with you?" He looked confident, that smile still curving his lips. Too confident.

"My lord, I gave you an answer last month." She took a sip of tea. She wasn't thirsty, but it helped to give the impression that she was not hanging on his every word.

He ran a finger inside his cravat. "I was given to understand, by your father, you know, that you had changed—"

"I'm afraid Papa may have misunderstood. I said I would be agreeable to getting to know you a little better. For example, will you take your seat in the Lords when you inherit the title? I understand your father votes with Lord Liverpool?"

Lord Ordsall's mouth opened and then closed again.

"Am I mistaken, my lord?"

"No. That is, yes, he agrees with many of Liverpool's policies, but you don't need to bother yourself with politics, Miss Farrington."

It was as if he were reading from a script—one her father also used. Rhys would never say such a thing to her, she was sure.

"A wife's duty is to support her husband's career, is it not?" Izzy asked.

He relaxed a little. "Yes, indeed."

"How are you to take your true part in government without your wife to act as a political hostess? Some knowledge of politics must be essential for that role. It would be my *duty* to learn about such things."

"I… I had not thought. Um, Miss Farrington, when the, hopefully distant, day comes that I inherit my father's estates, I intend to spend much of my time in the country. You would need do nothing more than Lady Bedley does."

Izzy creased her brow in what she hoped was a puzzled frown. "You do not intend to take your seat?"

"Well, I will of course, now and then, naturally. Miss Farrington—"

"But Lord Ordsall, the lives of all your tenants are affected by what the government chooses to do. Lord Liverpool's Corn Law act, for example. After such disastrous harvests last year, is it fair on the poor to keep grain prices so high when people are starving? The government is lucky there have not been more riots."

Ordsall took a deep breath. "Miss Farrington, maintaining prices is necessary for prosperity." He spoke slowly, as if explaining to a child. "How would we go on without revenues from our estates?"

"Does that mean you *approve* of the poor going hungry, Lord Ordsall?" She took another sip of tea while he stared at her. "My lord?"

"Miss Farrington, you really should not be discussing matters you cannot understand!"

Izzy winced at the loudness of his response, suppressing a smile as everyone else stopped talking and looked their way. Across the room Viv was pressing her lips together, as if trying not to laugh.

"But I would *so* like to understand," Izzy said sweetly, hoping she wasn't doing things a little too brown. "Perhaps you could explain something to me?"

Ordsall cast a quick look around. Izzy followed his gaze—most of the conversations had restarted, but she had little doubt that people were still listening. Viv certainly would be.

"What do you wish to know, Miss Farrington?"

Izzy smiled again. "I happened to hear someone discuss the Habeas Corpus Suspension Act. Could you explain what that is?"

The man looked almost like a fish, gaping like that.

"Miss Farrington, really, the debate about how criminals are dealt with should not concern you. It is most unbecoming."

Izzy lowered her lashes. She had probably said enough on that topic. She could, of course, ask him about himself, or his estates, but that would indicate an interest she was far from feeling.

"I'm so sorry, my lord. What would you like to talk about? We must have some conversation, after all."

"I... er..."

Izzy decided that the best plan would be to bore him into submission. "I found I enjoyed embroidery while I was away," she started. "More than I used to, at least. That is a suitable female accomplishment, is it not?"

"Um. Yes, indeed. But—"

"My relative lives in quite a remote part of Wales, you know, and it is difficult to get a good choice of coloured silks. I wanted to make my pattern of roses look as realistic as possible, for I was making little gifts for my hostess' children." Izzy made an effort to conceal a smile as Ordsall's eyes became unfocused. "For the girls, that is, for of course Ioan would not want things embroidering." She giggled, and looked at the floor, as if embarrassed at her mistake. "Silly me, of course not. The two little girls..."

Lord Ordsall was beginning to shuffle in his seat.

"...are learning the piano. I'm afraid to say they are making much better progress than I was at their ages. Do you enjoy listening to music, Lord Ordsall?"

"Why, yes, it has its pl—"

"That's good. I must spend more time practising. The children were so sweet. I do hope they will all be frequent visitors when I am finally settled. It is so refreshing to have energetic young ones around, don't you—?"

"If you will excuse me, Miss Farrington, I have another appointment." Again, his voice was over-loud for a parlour. He stood and made a stiff bow to her, and another to the rest of the room, before taking his leave.

Mama's friends looked at each other, and rose as one.

"I'm afraid I, too, have—"

"So nice to see you back in town, dear Lady Bedley, but I must—"

"Do call on me when you can, Lady Bedley."

They departed in a flutter of shawls and bonnets. Off to spread the gossip that Ordsall had left in a huff, Izzy guessed.

"Izzy, what did you say to him?" her mother asked, when only she and Viv were left in the room.

"I merely made conversation about my stay in Wales."

"He didn't look happy." Mama's eyes narrowed. "Izzy, you didn't tell him who Eugenia's husband is, did you? You must not! My friends would tell—"

"No, Mama, I did not." If Mama's friends were off to spread gossip, Izzy hoped *she* never had friends like them.

"Good—my acquaintance would not like to associate with a family linked to trade, you know. But you must have said *something* to upset him."

Izzy shrugged. The words 'I didn't mean to' were on the tip of her tongue, but she couldn't bring herself to speak such an outright lie. Hopefully she had annoyed Ordsall sufficiently to make him stay away for good.

Rhys admired the luxurious surroundings as Algy—former Captain The Honourable Algernon Pelham—limped to the sideboard and poured two glasses of claret. Rooms in the Albany were well above his touch.

Algy handed him a glass before relaxing back into his armchair and stretching his right leg out in front of him, one hand absently kneading the muscles above his knee. "So, Taffy, cut line. Your note said little, and I doubt you've suddenly developed a taste for seeing the sights. A matter of business?"

"I... no." If he'd come to Town on business he'd have put up at a hotel. "It's a personal matter." Rhys took a large mouthful of wine, strangely reluctant to speak.

"A woman?" Algy asked.

Rhys felt heat rise to his face.

"Ha! More than a passing fancy, eh? Do tell!"

Damn it, Algy was far too perceptive. Rhys took a deep breath and told his tale. Thankfully, his friend didn't laugh at him, but listened carefully.

"So what do you intend to do?" Algy asked, when Rhys finished.

"That's the problem. I don't really know. It would have been easier if she'd still been in Wales—we could have got to know each other better. Or at least I could have found out if I've any chance."

"Did you discuss that at all?"

"No. We only agreed we'd like to see each other again."

"It shouldn't be too difficult to find out where Bedley's London house is," Algy said. "I assume you don't intend to just call on her there?"

"I imagine I'd be out on my ear before I manage two words with her," Rhys said. A mill owner aspiring to a baron's daughter? It wasn't unheard of, but it certainly wasn't common. "Do *you* know her?" he asked.

"Good grief, I don't go to the kinds of places where decent young ladies congregate! My mother's almost given up trying to persuade me to find a wife, and it's not as if I'm the heir, or even the spare." He slapped his leg. "In any case I'm no use at dancing so there's no point in going to balls."

"It's not mending, then?" Rhys asked. Algy had taken a ball in the thigh at Quatre Bras, and was lucky to still have two legs. It was difficult to tell by lamplight, but Rhys thought his friend was looking rather too pale.

"It's better than it was, but not up to hopping around in a ballroom. Enough of that. You and I will haunt Hyde Park—if she's in Town she'll be there at some point. Best place to *accidentally* run into someone. I'll borrow a horse for you."

"Are you sure you'll be—?"

"Exercise'll be good for me," Algy said firmly. "Don't worry about that. Now, are you ready to go out to eat?"

~

Izzy looked around her bedroom as she ran the brush down the length of her hair. This was neither as large nor as familiar as her room at Bedley Park, but it was still bigger and more luxuriously furnished than her room at Plas Coed.

Putting the brush aside, she went to the closet where her gowns hung, fingering the fabrics. They were lovely, and had cost a pretty penny—she never saw the dressmaker's bills, but she'd heard Papa complaining about the expense often enough. There were so many of them, as it just wasn't done to be seen in the same gown too many times in a season. And these were relatively simple gowns, suited to an unmarried woman. Many young matrons of her acquaintance had more lavish wardrobes, with richer fabrics. Would she miss this array of garments if she had to live in reduced circumstances like Genie?

She probably would. But a restricted wardrobe was a small price to pay to *not* marry Lord Ordsall. Or any man who insisted that she obey him, and told her what to think. Rhys would not say—

No. If she was going to thwart her father's plans for her, she should be prepared to end up living with Genie. She wanted to see Rhys again, very much, but although she believed him when he said he wanted that too, it didn't necessarily mean that anything permanent would come of it. His attraction to her might not last once he was back in his normal life. If it did, would he let the difference in their social status put him off?

Izzy did her best to ignore the hollow feeling this thought produced, and picked up the embroidered spoon. Once she had finished working roses around it, she added her date of birth below her initials at the bottom, as if on a sampler. It made an adequate bookmark once sewn onto a scrap of buckram.

The carved wooden spoons were effectively an offer of marriage. She didn't intend this embroidered version to mean quite that much, but she couldn't think of any other way to send a message that her father would not understand. Hopefully Genie would interpret the message and pass it on. Rhys might be thinking similar things about her, so she must let him know she *did* want to see him again. She took a sheet of paper from her drawer and composed another note of thanks to Genie, and then wrapped it around the bookmark. It made a larger than usual letter, but she thought it would do.

She didn't seal it, as Papa would want to see what she'd written. She would ask him to send it first thing after breakfast. Reminding him that she was due to drive in the park with Lord Ordsall in the afternoon might put him in a good enough mood to ignore any suspicions he might have.

Was she doing the right thing?

CHAPTER 15

*M*ama looked up from her novel at the sound of the knocker on the front door. "Now, Izzy, remember what your Papa said."

Izzy sighed. "Yes, Mama."

Unfortunately, Papa had met Lord Ordsall at his club the day before, and had undone most of her good work by assuring him that Izzy did not normally discuss such unwomanly matters. This morning at breakfast, Papa had forbidden her to talk about politics. Izzy wasn't too dismayed. Lord Ordsall hadn't liked her talking about 'men's affairs', but it was her boring talk about embroidery that had finally seen him off. Her ready acceptance of Papa's decree had pleased him, and he had agreed that the bookmark would be a suitable gift of thanks for Genie. It would be on its way today.

"Lord Ordsall will be a good addition to our family, Izzy," her mother went on. "You are lucky your papa persuaded him to try again."

"Yes, Mama." Only lucky in that she'd had a few hours to think up alternative strategies. She smoothed the skirt of her new carriage dress, wondering if the ostrich plumes she'd added to her bonnet were excessive. Mama had made no comment, other than the usual 'you look nice, dear', so she hoped her appearance said expensive rather than vulgar. A vulgar sister would not help Viv's prospects.

Izzy maintained a flow of conversation about the weather and their surroundings as Lord Ordsall drove his curricle to the park. It was amazing how much there was to discuss, if one looked around. "How much money do flower sellers make, do you think?" she asked, as they passed a woman with a basket of colourful blooms. "They must have to work very hard to sell all the flowers before they start to wilt. Where do they get them from?"

Lord Ordsall muttered something unintelligible.

"Selling ribbons and pins must be an easier business," Izzy babbled on, as a dog set off across the road in front of them. She waited until she saw Lord Ordsall's hands pull on the reins. "Those last much longer than—Oh, mind that dog!"

A muscle in his jaw started to twitch.

"I'm glad the little dog managed to avoid you," Izzy went on, watching the oblivious mongrel trot on its way. "I think I'd like a little lapdog when I marry. Two or three, perhaps." She glanced sideways, pleased to see his lips compressed. "They can be a bit yappy, but I shan't mind that. Oh, look at the lovely chest in that shop window! Papa won't let Mama furnish in the Egyptian style, but once I have my own household to run I can follow the latest fashions. I'm sure I'll be able to… Oh, do watch out for that man with the barrow!"

"Miss Farrington, I can—"

"Yes, my lord." Izzy had to admire how well enunciated his words were, given that he appeared to be speaking through clenched teeth. "But what if you *hadn't* seen it? It would be too bad if you collided with someone I'd seen and I had not warned you. Oh, good. Here we are at the park!"

Once Lord Ordsall had tooled the curricle through the park gates and could safely divert some of his attention from the track ahead, she asked him if he liked her gown. "For it is new, you know, although not as fine as I'd like."

"It looks very well on you, Miss Farrington," he said, after a quick appraisal. His expression softened a little as his gaze ran down her body.

"It is rather plain, though." Izzy fingered the silver embroidery down the front, trying to ignore the uncomfortable feeling his inspection had induced. "Seeing my relatives in Wales made me realise how nice it is to have a rich father who can keep me in new gowns." She made a brief pout. "But Mama *will* insist that simplicity is best for unmarried women. I'm so looking forward to being able to decide on my own wardrobe once I am wed."

A surreptitious glance in Ordsall's direction revealed his eyebrows rising.

"There are some lovely new fabrics, you know, with real silver and gold thread in them, or embroidered with pearls." At least, if there were not, there should be. "They are a trifle expensive, to be sure, but my future husband won't mind."

"Miss Farrington, I thought you were aware that I would be spending much of my time on my estate. Such gowns are not required for country living."

"Oh, no, I agree. I will need a completely different wardrobe for that, but even country gowns need to keep up with the fashions, do they not? And I will visit my family in Town often." She smiled at him kindly, noting the crease between his brows deepening. "I need not drag you away from your estates, you know. A married lady has more freedom to go about."

"Miss Farrington, I do not—"

"Oh, look—is that a high perch phaeton?" Izzy pointed at a carriage some distance away. "I do so want to learn to drive. That will be useful in the country."

"Yes, but I have a coachman to—"

"Oh, pooh, that is no fun! A phaeton like that will be just the thing for me, or perhaps a curricle."

His brows were drawing together now, and was that an angry flush on his cheeks?

"Miss Farrington!" His voice was getting louder, too—excellent!

"Ladies do not drive such vehicles."

Fortune really was smiling on her today. As the phaeton approached, Izzy saw that it was driven by a woman of about Genie's age, smartly dressed in a wine-coloured pelisse. A much younger man sat beside her. Izzy recognised the driver as an acquaintance of her mother.

"Do you mean Lady Cleeve is not truly a lady?" Izzy adopted her puzzled expression as the phaeton drew to a halt next to them.

"L-L-Lady Cleeve," Ordsall stuttered, casting a venomous glance at Izzy. "How… how nice to meet you here."

"Lord Ordsall." Lady Cleeve nodded at him and turned to Izzy, her mouth curving in a friendly smile. "Miss Farrington, I was hoping to meet you today. Will you take a turn about the park with me?"

Izzy had no idea why Lady Cleeve wished to speak to her, but this was too good an opportunity to miss. "I'd be delighted, Lady Cleeve."

"But Miss Farring—"

"Miss Farrington, this is my nephew, Mr Somers." Lady Cleeve spoke across Lord Ordsall's protest, turning to the young man beside her. "Charlie, you may wait here for me, or take a turn with Lord Ordsall."

Somers jumped down and held up one hand to assist Izzy down from Lord Ordsall's curricle, then helped her into the phaeton. "I'll wait for you here, Aunt Lucy," he said.

Ordsall's face was thunderous as Lady Cleeve set the horses into motion again. Izzy bit her lips to avoid grinning until he could no longer see her face.

"This is very kind of you, Lady Cleeve," she said.

"Indeed. I would have offered to take you home at the end of our little chat, but I thought it would annoy Ordsall more if he had to wait for you."

Izzy's mouth dropped open. Lady Cleeve was smiling, her eyes dancing. "You seem to have caused him considerable irritation already."

Izzy didn't believe in mind-readers, so there could only be one explanation. "Are you one of Mrs Lloyd's friends, by any chance?"

"Very quick of you, Miss Farrington." Lady Cleeve kept her eyes on the track ahead as she guided the horses around a stationary landau. "Genie wrote to me to explain your situation. I hope you have not changed your mind about Ordsall—I fear my actions will not have endeared you to him."

"Papa wishes me to encourage him to make another offer," Izzy admitted. "I am trying my best to prevent it." She chuckled. "Your timing was perfect, my lady. He had just told me that ladies do not drive phaetons."

"Ah, like that, is he? You will be guided by him at all times?"

"Naturally. Females should not bother their heads with matters beyond their understanding."

"Such as… politics?" Lady Cleeve shook her head. "Genie said you were beginning to take an interest in such things. No, you and Ordsall really would not suit. Now, I will give you my card when I have a free hand. You are to send word if your papa tries to force you into something you do not wish for."

"Thank you, but what…?" It wasn't polite to question the usefulness of an offer of help.

"If it comes to the worst, I can escort you to Capel Bodfan," Lady Cleeve said. "Or I could send Charlie to be a suitor if that might help."

"Mr Somers?"

"He'll help if I ask him, I'm sure. He was about to offer for a young lady near his father's seat—he's the third son of an earl, you know. Sadly, this young woman's father died recently. Charlie is waiting for a month or two before resuming his courtship."

"Oh." That option had possibilities, but also drawbacks. "It wouldn't be very fair on his intended—or him—if word got out he had been courting me."

"True." Lady Cleeve brought the phaeton to a halt, and turned to face Izzy. "Are you intending to put off *all* your suitors?"

"I… yes." It felt more committing to say it out loud. But she wanted to see Rhys again, and to be free when she did so. What happened after that was up to the fates.

"Except for one?" Lady Cleeve asked, one eyebrow raised.

Izzy felt her face heat. What had Genie written to her friend? "Did Genie tell you?"

"No, but it seems an obvious inference to me, along with the idea that your parents would not approve. However, I trust Genie not to be encouraging anyone *totally* unsuitable. Now, was Ordsall's comment about ladies not driving phaetons related to your wish to do so?"

The abrupt change of subject took Izzy by surprise. "I… I had said that, yes, but I don't really want to learn to drive."

"Nevertheless, I think you will take the reins for this last straight stretch."

Izzy looked ahead, to where Lord Ordsall was waiting with his curricle.

"Well?"

Izzy laughed. "Hopefully it will confirm my total unsuitability," she said. "What do I have to do?"

"Lady Bedley wishes to see you in her parlour," Needham said as he took Izzy's bonnet and pelisse.

Mama set her novel aside as Izzy entered and sat down. "Is Lord Ordsall coming in for refreshments?" she asked.

"No, Mama." She hadn't asked him—the tight-lipped silence in which he'd driven her home showed any such invitation would have been declined.

"And how are you progressing?"

Very well. Very well indeed.

"I do not think we will suit, Mama. He did not seem to approve of anything I said."

Her mother sat up straighter in her chair. "What did you talk about, Izzy? You promised not to talk about politics."

"I only talked about the weather and fashion, Mama."

Her mother sighed. "I'm sure that is not the whole story, Izzy. You are too much like your papa."

"Like *Papa*?" Autocratic? Knowing what was best for everyone?

"Stubborn, Izzy."

"I only want to be happy, Mama, is that so bad?"

"No, dear, of course not. But you have had three seasons, and numerous suitors to choose from. It is not unreasonable of your papa to ask you to make a choice."

Izzy bit her lips against the words 'I *have* chosen'.

"Was there no young man you felt you could be happy with?" her mother went on.

"None that you or Papa would have approved of. Mama, why do you both insist on a title?"

"We only want what is best—"

"You don't *know* me." Izzy took a deep breath—losing her temper with her mother would not help. "You are both telling me what I should want."

"Hmm. Young girls do not know enough to know what is good for them."

"Mama, is it so bad to want to have a choice in my future life? I'm twenty years old."

"All the more reason to get you married as soon as possible. You don't want to become an ape leader, do you? If you marry well, you will have a title, your own establishment, and more pin money."

Izzy shook her head, more at the futility of trying to make her mother understand than in answer. In truth, although ending up a spinster was not an attractive prospect, it seemed a better fate than being in the power of a man she neither liked nor respected. Mama would not agree.

"Do you think Lord Ordsall will renew his offer?" Her mother could be annoyingly tenacious on some topics.

"No, Mama."

"Oh, well. You must ride or drive in the park every day the weather is fine, Izzy. Take Vivian with you. If you are escorted by your sister instead of Lord Ordsall, it will be clear that he is no longer courting you."

Advertise my availability, in fact.

"Yes, Mama." Izzy replied, resigned to having to parade herself.

Two days later, Izzy gazed around as Sir Cecil Horton's barouche made its slow way through the park. With Miss Templeton opposite and Viv next to her, Izzy pretended to listen as Sir Cecil described his home in Northamptonshire and his three daughters in need of a new mother. Sir Cecil's greying hair was neatly brushed and pomaded, his clothing immaculate, if a few years out of fashion. Was Mama getting desperate, encouraging a mere baronet as a suitor?

Izzy wondered if Lady Cleeve was in the park. She'd spent the last couple of days considering whether she could write a letter to Rhys and ask Lady Cleeve to send it via Genie. After all, Genie might not guess what Izzy had meant in sending the bookmark. But what could she say? Only that she wanted to see him again, and the embroidered spoon was a more subtle way of saying that. It would be very embarrassing if she was too direct and it turned out that Rhys now saw her as just a passing fancy.

Izzy looked up to the sky. The grey clouds had thickened since they set out, and she smelled rain in the air. With any luck it would start to drizzle soon. All she wanted was enough moisture to make the coachman put the hood up and return them home.

Sir Cecil was still droning on. "...dower house is only a mile away. Mama will remove to that again when I bring my bride home. We are both hoping I will be blessed with a son in my next marriage. A little brother for my daughters, and someone to inherit the title."

Glancing sideways, Izzy was surprised to see Viv looking interested. But then Viv hadn't heard it all already. Twice.

"...Julia loves painting, particularly flowers. Horton House has very fine gardens. Perhaps you will see them some day."

"It does sound lovely," Viv said, when Izzy did not reply immediately.

"I'm sure you would like to see Horton Hall, wouldn't you Miss Farrington?" Miss Templeton prompted.

The governess was only doing as Mama had instructed, but that didn't ease Izzy's resentment. Sir Cecil must be forty if he was a day, and only wanted her as a brood mare. If only his previous wife had been obliging and provided a son.

"Do all your daughters paint, Sir Cecil?" Izzy asked, refusing to respond to the governess.

"Why yes, they have all the talents of proper young ladies," he replied. "They play the pianoforte as well. Julia is looking forward to being presented to society in a couple of years. You... I mean, I hope by then I will have a wife to help me with that. My sister could do so, of course, but is busy with her own..."

Izzy stopped listening. She devoutly hoped that someone else would be assisting dear Julia in her come-out. Luckily Viv responded —thank goodness Mama hadn't sent Izzy out on her own with the man. But a sporty vehicle like a curricle or phaeton would be far too dashing for Sir Cecil, so there was plenty of room for her sister as well as the governess in this lumbering carriage. She looked around at the other people in the park as Sir Cecil rambled on.

"...agree, Miss Farrington?"

Viv's elbow met Izzy's ribs as Sir Cecil stopped talking. About to open her mouth to say 'Yes, indeed', Izzy caught Miss Templeton's encouraging expression and changed her words.

"I'm so sorry, Sir Cecil, I'm afraid my mind was wandering." Sir

Cecil started to speak again, but Izzy's attention was diverted once more. That man in the distance—it looked very like Rhys.

Very like indeed.

"Miss Farrington?"

Izzy took a deep breath. "My apologies, Sir Cecil. I caught sight of Lady Cleeve across the park. I need to speak to her about something."

Sir Cecil twisted round to look in the direction Izzy pointed, his eyes narrowing as he scanned the few people out in this gloomy weather. Izzy took the opportunity to examine the distant rider. He was with another man, both heading for the barouche.

"I'm afraid I don't see her, Miss Farrington. What I was—"

"Perhaps I was mistaken, Sir Cecil. I'm so sorry."

She was not mistaken, though. It *was* Rhys. The two men were close enough now for her to make out their features. She felt suddenly breathless, her heart accelerating. She smiled—she couldn't help it.

"What amuses you so, Miss Farrington?" Sir Cecil was beginning to sound rather testy.

"I… I recalled something Lady Cleeve told me," Izzy said, unable to think of any better excuse. Rhys had seen her now, a fleeting smile crossing his face, but he reined his horse in.

Sir Cecil's barouche would pass within a few feet of them— would Rhys speak to her? Should she introduce him to Sir Cecil? Rhys said something to his companion, who shook his head. Then her heart sank as Rhys touched his hat and the two men turned away.

What was she to make of that? She took a deep breath, her heart still racing, and tried to pay attention to what Miss Templeton was saying.

"Izzy, are you all right?" Viv's hand patted her arm. "Do you have the headache? Should we return?"

Izzy nodded, grateful for this excuse. She put one hand to her forehead, and frowned. "If you please. I'm sorry, Sir Cecil, it cannot be helped."

"Very well, Miss Farrington. I'm sorry our excursion has been cut short." Sir Cecil spoke to the driver, and the carriage headed back towards the gate. Izzy couldn't resist turning her head for one final look at Rhys, but he was lost in the crowds.

Rhys turned the hired hack as the barouche drew away, seeing only the back of Izzy's green pelisse and beribboned bonnet. He'd managed to tear his eyes away from her face long enough to glance at the other people in the barouche. The young woman with her bore enough resemblance to be a sister, and the older woman had the look of a chaperone.

"The one in green?" Algy asked as they rode on. Rhys nodded. "Very decorative, I can see why you took a fancy to her."

"Algy, don't—"

"Sorry, old man. A small payback for the ribbing you gave me about that sergeant's widow in Spain."

"You really don't recognise the man with them?" Surely that hadn't been one of Izzy's suitors—he was old enough to be her father. Perhaps it *was* her father?

"Never set eyes on him before. It's not Bedley, though. Someone pointed him out at the club last night."

Rhys grimaced. A suitor, then. He had declined to accompany Algy the previous evening, not being in the mood for cards after several days of frustration hanging about the different London parks trying to spot Izzy. Algy had found out that the family lived on Wimpole Street, but Rhys still wanted the chance to talk to Izzy before calling on her father. If she didn't want to take things any further, there was no point asking permission to court her.

She'd smiled when she saw him, then the man with them had said something and her expression had become wary. As Algy could not introduce them, approaching to talk to Izzy would have likely involved explanations of where they had met, or hastily improvised lies. Either could have landed Izzy in trouble, so he'd forced himself to ride on. He hoped she would work out why.

He would have to think of something to say if he encountered her again in the park. Could he pretend he'd met her at a ball in London?

Or perhaps he might refer to 'in the country' and hope her chaperone assumed he meant somewhere near her father's seat.

"Rhys?"

Rhys looked up. "What?"

Algy regarded him with an amused smile. "You really are smitten, aren't you? No, don't poker up—come out with me tonight. If you don't fancy cards we can go to the theatre."

Neither activity sounded enticing, but it would be better than sitting in Algy's rooms brooding. And he suspected Algy hadn't been getting out as much as he should. His friend already looked a little healthier from spending a few afternoons in the park.

"Theatre, then. But your leg—"

"I'll borrow a box. Johnnie's mother—you won't know him—his mother keeps a box and is happy to lend it."

"Very well. Thank you."

He *must* speak to her if they met again. If she sent him on his way, at least he'd know how she felt about him.

Izzy maintained her drooping posture all the way home, but managed a civilised farewell to Sir Cecil. After all, it wasn't his fault that Mama was foisting her on any titled man in search of a wife.

"You will be retiring to your room, then, Miss Isolde?" Miss Templeton said, her slightly narrowed eyes giving Izzy the impression that she didn't quite believe in the headache.

"Yes." She wanted some time to work out what had just happened. She'd been so happy to see Rhys, but then he'd turned away without making any attempt to talk to her.

Izzy barely had time to remove her bonnet before her bedroom door opened and Viv slipped through.

"Miss Templeton's gone to make sure Lynnie did her piano exercises," she said. "Who is he?"

Izzy swallowed hard. She'd hoped no-one had noticed her interest in Rhys. "What do you mean?" She turned to the mirror and began to pull pins out of her hair.

"The man you smiled at in the park."

Izzy sighed and put the pins into their dish. "Just someone I met." She looked at her sister. "Viv, please don't say anything to Mama or Papa."

Viv's mouth rounded in surprise. "Izzy, what have you done?"

"Nothing—I recognised someone I met in Wales. A friend of Aunt Genie's. I was surprised to see him in London, that's all."

"Not *pleased* to see him?" Viv wheedled.

Izzy stared at her sister, but did not speak.

Viv's expression gradually became serious. "You really like him!" She took Izzy's arm and walked over to the bed. "Come on, tell me all," she said as they sat down together.

Izzy shook her head.

"He looked very handsome," Viv went on, wriggling backwards and tucking her legs up under her skirt, as they used to when they were younger. "I've always liked men with blond hair. And his blue coat fit him very well."

"He's not blond." Izzy rubbed her forehead. "Viv, please don't tease me—you could have asked me directly which one of them he was."

"I'm sorry."

"Mama and Papa won't approve," Izzy said. "He hasn't got a title." They wouldn't approve of him being in trade, either.

"Do you think he's come to see you?"

She hoped so, but he might be in Town on business. It was only three days since she'd sent the bookmark to Genie—it couldn't possibly have reached Rhys in time to prompt a journey to London.

"Why didn't he stop and talk to you?" Viv went on. "Oh, because Papa would hear about it, I suppose."

Izzy hoped that was the reason, but all her previous doubts had come back. The joy when she saw him confirmed her own feelings, but if he felt the same for her, would he really have turned away like that? If only she might talk to him without Papa finding out. She didn't know where he was staying, but in any case it would be out of the question to call on him. A note would also be improper, but perhaps a little less so. And she didn't have his address; she could probably get it if she wrote to Genie, but that would take days.

"So you do want to see him again?" Viv was nothing if not persistent.

"Yes, but I don't want to talk about it. Not now."

Viv tilted her head to one side. "Very well, sister. I'll keep quiet—for now. You'd best keep it secret from Lynnie, though; you know how much she chatters. She'd be bound to let something slip." She gave Izzy a quick hug and left the room.

If Rhys *had* come to London to see her, what would he do? Might he try to meet her in the park again?

Could she find a way to get a note to Lady Cleeve?

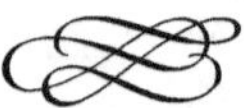

CHAPTER 17

A small packet awaited Rhys at breakfast the next day. Algy was still abed, but Rhys had resolved to get some business done this morning before venturing into the park again. He had to talk to Izzy, even if it turned out to be the end of his hopes.

"It came by messenger half an hour ago, Mr Williams," Algy's man said, pouring Rhys a cup of much-needed coffee.

"Thank you, Saunders." He drained his cup before turning to the letter, trying to dispel the effects of last night's over-indulgence. He should not have allowed Algy to persuade him to go on to his club after the theatre.

He recognised Genie's hand, and broke the seal with sudden interest. A piece of embroidery fell out. From the shape, it was a bookmark, but he'd never seen a bookmark with an embroidered spoon on it before. The letter inside said only that Izzy had sent the enclosed to her with a note of thanks for her visit. However she was fairly certain that she was not the intended recipient of the embroidery.

It wasn't merely a spoon, Rhys realised, looking at it more closely. It was a love spoon. The I.F. at the bottom must be Izzy's initials, and beneath it was a date—8th September, 1796.

Nearly twenty-one years ago. Could it be Izzy's date of birth? If so, it was only a month until she would be of age.

If Genie was right and this had been intended for him, it must surely mean that Izzy did want to see him. He smiled, as a feeling of lightness spread through him. He'd never heard of a woman giving a spoon to a man. Trust Izzy to be unconventional.

He propped the bookmark against the coffee pot, and forced down the coddled eggs Saunders put before him, followed by several slices of toast and jam.

But why hadn't she written? If her correspondence was being monitored, it might have been the only message she could send. He ought not to read too much into it, he thought, his happiness diminishing a little. It might be nothing more than a wish to meet again.

He drank another cup of coffee, his head finally beginning to clear. He would ride in the park again this afternoon. With any luck, Izzy would be there at the same time. He had to find a way to talk to her soon—not only for himself, but because he could not afford to be away from the mill for much longer.

"It's very good of Lady Cleeve to invite you to drive with her," Mama said for the third time, peering out of the parlour window at the street below. "It can only do you good to be seen with such a fashionable countess. I hope it does not come on to rain."

"Indeed, Mama," Izzy agreed. Unlike her drive with Sir Cecil, she did not want this one to be cut short by the weather.

"It's a pity she didn't ask Vivian as well," Mama lamented, also for the third time. She turned to her middle daughter. "You need to find an eligible suitor, too. Perhaps she will invite you when she arrives."

Izzy hoped not. She had to trust that Viv would not tell Mama or Papa about Rhys until she was ready to let them know, and Viv would find that even harder if she'd witnessed a proper meeting between them.

If Rhys was in the park again this afternoon. And if the gathering clouds did not turn to rain.

"Oh, what a shame!" Mama let the curtain drop and returned to her chair. "She's come in a phaeton. I suppose Vivian couldn't fit—?"

"No, Mama," Izzy said firmly. "Lady Cleeve took me up in the park a few days ago. There is no room for a third person." She stood up. "Lady Cleeve won't want to keep her horses standing, Mama. I'll go down now."

Making her escape before her mother could reply, she quickly donned the pelisse and bonnet she'd left ready in the hall. If Lady Cleeve came into the house, she might let drop the fact that Izzy had asked to be taken driving, rather than having been invited.

"So tell me, Miss Farrington, am I assisting in a clandestine rendezvous?" Lady Cleeve asked as she guided the phaeton through the traffic on Oxford Street.

"I hope so, my lady."

Izzy was relieved to see a smile forming on her companion's face. "What are the arrangements?"

"Um. I'm afraid there is no arrangement. Not exactly."

Lady Cleeve glanced towards Izzy, one brow raised.

"I hope to see him in the park, my lady," Izzy went on, casting a nervous glance at the groom on the seat behind them.

"Don't mind Bennett," Lady Cleeve said. "He's rather deaf, poor man, but that is quite useful at times. He is also discreet. Now, you had better start with who this young man is, and why he has not approached your father."

Izzy drew a deep breath. "We had not got so far, my lady." She gave a brief account of her meetings with Rhys, and his business with Huw, nervousness knotting her stomach in case Lady Cleeve disapproved and refused to help. "So, all he said, and I said, was that we hoped to see each other again. Then Papa came to bring me here only a couple of days after Mr Williams left."

"You haven't known him long—you could just forget him," Lady Cleeve said.

Izzy sighed. "I know that I should, but I have not." She clenched her fingers together in her lap. "Lady Cleeve, I find I like him more than any of the young men who have paid court to me over the last few years."

"What does Genie say about this young man?" Lady Cleeve guided the phaeton through the Cumberland Gate into the park and onto the carriage drive.

"She only said I had to be sure I knew what I would be giving up by marrying someone in trade."

Lady Cleeve's eyes narrowed, then she gave a brisk nod. "So we will drive around in the hopes of seeing him."

Izzy let out a breath of relief. "If it is not too much trouble, my lady."

"No trouble at all, my dear. You will pass the time by telling me all about Genie and her family. There is only so much detail that can be conveyed in letters."

~

Algy regarded the grey sky. "Am I to get a soaking to advance your suit?"

"You're turning soft, man," Rhys retorted. "We've only been here ten minutes, and you're complaining already."

"No sign of that barouche yet." Algy looked around the park as their mounts ambled along.

"She might not be in a barouche," Rhys pointed out. She might not be here at all.

"Bang up phaeton, that," Algy said, squinting across to the carriage drive. "Woman at the ribbons, too."

Rhys followed Algy's gaze. The phaeton was proceeding slowly. The driver wore a deep red pelisse and matching bonnet, partly obscuring her companion. The second woman wore white, but even without the green pelisse of yesterday Rhys recognised her as she leaned forward.

"That's her." Rhys urged the horse into a trot, heading for the phaeton, his insides feeling hollow in anticipation.

"Hold on, Taff!" Algy came up beside him. "What are you going to do? Just say hello?"

"Why not? Unless that's her mother with her, but I think she would have said if Lady Bedley drove a dashing vehicle like that."

Algy slowed his mount as they approached the phaeton. "You're in luck, old boy. That's Lady Cleeve, one of Mama's friends. I can introduce you properly."

That would help. But even as they approached, Izzy caught sight of him and her smile left him breathless. She touched her companion's arm and pointed, and the lady in red brought the phaeton to a halt.

"Lady Cleeve." Algy removed his hat. "May I introduce my good friend Captain Williams to you?"

"I am pleased to meet you, Captain Williams," Lady Cleeve said, inclining her head. "I have been hearing much about you." Her smile was not quite an unqualified welcome. Rhys wondered what Izzy had been saying, and *why* Izzy had told Lady Cleeve about him.

"Mr Pelham, this is Miss Isolde Farrington." Lady Cleeve made the introduction.

"I'm happy to meet you, Miss Farrington."

"Bennet, go to their heads." Lady Cleeve turned to face the groom as she spoke, and the man got down and took the horses. "Walk them, if you please. I am not sure how long I will be." She turned her attention to the two men. "Walk with me, Captain Williams. I'm sure Algy will be happy to escort Miss Farrington for a while."

"She should have been a colonel," Algy muttered. "Best do as she says."

Rhys sighed, and fastened his horse to the back of the phaeton. He wanted to help Izzy down, to feel her hand in his if only for a moment, but politeness dictated he offer that service to Lady Cleeve. What did she want with him?

· · ·

Izzy accepted Mr Pelham's hand and jumped lightly down from the phaeton. This encounter had *not* gone as she had expected so far. Her initial rush of happiness had dimmed a little when Lady Cleeve gave her instruction, but she should not have been surprised. Lady Cleeve would want to know something about the man she was helping Izzy to see.

"Miss Farrington?"

Rhys' friend was waiting, one elbow held ready. She'd had eyes only for Rhys yesterday, but now took in his blond hair, more fashionably styled than Rhys'. He was taller than Rhys, but of a slimmer build.

"I'm sorry, Mr Pelham, my wits were wandering."

"I was only saying, Miss Farrington, that unlike Lady Cleeve, I have *not* heard much about you. Taffy's not the talkative kind."

"Taffy? Oh… You know Mr Williams well?"

"Served together in the Peninsula."

She resisted the temptation to look down at his leg. His limp was not pronounced, but their pace was slower than that set by Lady Cleeve, walking ahead of them on Rhys' arm. What was she asking him?

"Is he still a captain, Mr Pelham? I thought he had resigned his commission."

"He did, after Toulouse. But I thought 'captain' sounded more impressive than 'my mill-owning friend Williams'." Mr Pelham glanced at her face. "If your father is anything like my own, Rhys will have a difficult task before him."

Izzy felt her face heat—Rhys had told his friend about her, then. "I… We have not got that far yet," she admitted. "We didn't have much time." She wondered if Rhys had received the embroidered spoon— was that why he'd approached her today? "Is… is he in London on business?" she asked. Yesterday's encounter could have been pure coincidence.

"He's doing some business, yes," Mr Pelham replied. He glanced down at her, a smile quirking his lips. "Do not look cast down, Miss

Farrington. He came to London to see you. I gather the business he is doing is part of the excuse he gave his family."

"Oh." She hadn't given much thought to Rhys' family until now. What would *they* think about her? But she would not worry about that. What her ladyship thought of Rhys was more important at this moment.

Lady Cleeve set a brisk pace along the path. They were soon out of earshot of whatever Algy was saying to Izzy.

"So, tell me about yourself, young man," Lady Cleeve requested. "Have you come to town just to see Izzy?"

"Yes, my lady," Rhys replied, resigning himself to an interrogation—a friendly one, he hoped. "What is it you wish to know?"

"I suppose 'everything' is too much to ask," Lady Cleeve said. She appeared amused rather than critical, to Rhys' relief. "Start by telling me how you come to know Algy Pelham."

"We served in the same regiment of foot. My father died just before Napoleon abdicated, so I sold out after Toulouse and came back home to run the family business."

"And that business is…?"

"Wool, my lady." He wasn't sure how much to tell her, but he started with the basics of the mill and how his father and Uncle John had set the business up together. He kept it concise and was relieved to see that it did not appear to bore Lady Cleeve, or cause her to disapprove.

"And how do you know Mrs Lloyd?" she asked.

Rhys' steps faltered for a moment, surprised at the question.

"I knew Genie Farrington before I married," Lady Cleeve explained. "Genie asked me to help prevent her niece being forced into a marriage she did not want. I met Izzy for the first time only a few days ago. She arranged this drive in the park…" Her voice tailed off and she shook her head.

Rhys' spirits soared. This was no mere coincidence, then. Izzy had not only wanted to see him—the spoon had made that clear—but had taken an active part in making this meeting happen.

But Lady Cleeve had asked him something… Genie? "Mr Lloyd deals with some business for me, and I've been their guest on several visits." Rhys glanced around—Izzy and Algy were some way behind. Was Lady Cleeve going to allow him to speak to her?

"What are your intentions, Mr Williams?"

"My intentions are entirely honourable, I assure you, my lady. For the moment I wish only to have the chance to talk to her. When we said our farewells in Wales it was with the anticipation of seeing each other again within a month or so. If we had known she was about to be taken home things might have been different."

"If she does wish to continue, what then?"

Rhys met her eyes squarely, his chin lifting. "I will discuss that with Izzy, my lady. She knows her own situation and wishes."

Lady Cleeve regarded him closely, her eyes seeming to bore into him. "Very well," she said at last. "However, having helped with this meeting, I feel responsible for Miss Farrington's wellbeing. You may walk with her, but stay in sight of the carriage, if you please."

At last he would have the chance to speak to her in private.

CHAPTER 18

*I*zzy let go of Mr Pelham's arm as Rhys started to walk towards her, hardly aware of her companion stepping aside. She swallowed hard, suddenly nervous. But Rhys' smile looked as uncertain as she felt, and her tension eased into anticipation.

"Are you well, Miss Farrington?" he asked, coming to a halt in front of her.

Izzy looked up into his eyes, her head tilted slightly. "I will not be, *Mr Williams*, if you have forgotten my name!"

This time he gave her a proper smile. He put his hand out and she thought, hoped, he was about to touch her cheek, but he let it drop.

"You look well, Izzy. It is good to see you."

"Have you been in London long?" She closed her eyes for a moment. What a silly way to start this conversation.

"A few days only." He seemed to find nothing odd in what she'd said. "Genie wrote to tell me that your father had taken you away. She said he was pressuring you to marry."

Izzy only half heard him. Watching him speak reminded her how his lips had felt on hers, how his closeness had made her feel.

"Izzy?"

She took a deep breath, glancing around. The park was not busy, but even so it would not do to be seen standing together like this. "Shall we walk?"

Rhys held out his arm, and she rested her hand on it as they set off back towards the carriage.

"Papa does want me to marry, yes, as does Mama. The latest of her prospects is Sir Cecil, the man you saw us with yesterday. He wants a mother for his daughters. He's happy to spend the whole afternoon talking about them; he's not interested in what I think at all. Oh, and he wants someone who can breed an heir for him."

Rhys gave a small choke, and she realised how indelicate her words had sounded.

"I'm sorry if that language shocked—"

"Not at all," he said. "After subjecting you to whole conversations about sheep breeding, how could I object?"

And she had sulked about it, too, the first time. He wore the amused expression she was used to seeing, underlain with something deeper. She looked away again.

"Genie also sent me a most interesting bookmark," Rhys went on. "She assumed it was meant for me, not her. It arrived this morning."

"It was, yes." Only this morning? He had come to London to see her, then, before he got her message. The bubble of happiness inside her expanded.

"Izzy, I spent the ride home from Wales working out how soon I could go back to Capel Bodfan. When I got Genie's letter, I knew I should try to forget you, but I cannot." He put his hand on top of hers where it rested on his arm, and gave a gentle squeeze.

His declaration made her breath catch. "I'm glad," she said, meeting his eyes. "I cannot help comparing the men Papa thinks might suit me with you, Rhys. Some of them I have known for months, years even, but I feel as if I know you better after spending only a few days together." She walked on a few more paces, aware of his body close to hers. Some of Genie's words came back to her: life would be very different. Whatever happened between them now was a decision for the rest of her life. She felt she knew Rhys well—the important things, at least, like his honesty and humour, and the way he dealt with others. But she knew little of what a future life with him might be like.

"Tell me about your home, Rhys. What do you do all day?"

Her question surprised Rhys at first, but he realised she knew little of his life. He hadn't talked of his family when they were together in Wales, but it hadn't seemed of any relevance until that last day under the blue heavens and then in the ruined chapel.

"I live not far outside Shrewsbury," he began. "My father built the house, large enough for all five of his children." Izzy listened as they strolled along the grass, turning occasionally to keep the carriage in sight. He told her about his sisters, and about Alun, his ambitions set on having his own law firm, and Owen, happily running a parish near Monmouth.

"Shrewsbury is an old city," he went on. "There are assemblies and other activities, but nothing like London or even Bath." Her shrug at this information gave him heart. "I spend most of my time at the mill."

Another shrug. "My father spends most of his time at his club," she said, "and some of my suitors seem to do nothing more than gamble in Town, or chase foxes in the country. How big is your mill?"

As he described the business, part of him wondered if it was a mistake to spend what little time he had with Izzy discussing such things. But she *had* taken an interest in what he was doing in Wales, and was asking intelligent questions, so he continued until Lady Cleeve sent Algy to tell them they'd had time enough.

"I should call on your father," Rhys said as they walked back towards the carriage.

"Why?"

"To ask his permission to court you."

There, he'd finally said it. He hoped—he was fairly sure—that she had taken their kiss as an indication that he wanted to, but it was best to be plain. "Izzy, I do not wish to be secretive about this. I should do things properly." Or try to, at least.

Izzy stopped, pulling her hand from his arm.

"Rhys, he will say no. What then? Will you obey him?"

"What do *you* wish me to do, Izzy? I do not like being underhand about—"

Her frown stopped him. Too late, he realised that his words could be taken as criticism of her actions. "Izzy, I didn't mean that you have been underhand."

She shook her head. "No, it's all right. I *have* deceived Papa, but if he wasn't so unreasonable I wouldn't need to." A smile curved her lips, although it did not reach her eyes. "Genie deceived him for more than a decade, although that is no excuse, really." She took a deep breath. "Rhys, can we talk again, *before* you speak to Papa?"

"Of course, if you wish it." He knew what *he* wanted, but he also wanted Izzy to be sure of any decision she made. "Would Lady Cleeve bring you again?"

She shook her head. "We are to go to the British Museum tomorrow afternoon, if that will not interfere with your business."

"*You* are my business, Izzy."

They continued to the phaeton, where Rhys bowed over Izzy's hand and helped her up. "Lady Cleeve, my thanks for the opportunity."

He watched as the carriage pulled away, Lady Cleeve's groom jumping up behind. The last he saw, as it passed between the gate posts, was the pale blur of Izzy's face as she looked back.

"How was your talk, then?" Algy spoke from behind Rhys. "And take a seat, for heaven's sake. You've been staring out of that window for ten minutes."

"Sorry." Rhys sat down, but declined the wine Algy offered. He'd been going over the afternoon's conversation in his head—had he talked too much? She'd commented on yesterday's suitor talking exclusively about himself, but she *had* asked him to tell her about his family.

"Am I due to have another ride in the park tomorrow?" Algy asked.

"No. Would you mind accompanying me to the museum instead? To help me find them, and in case there's a chaperone to avoid."

"You'll owe me some favours, Taffy. I had half an hour of Lady Cleeve interrogating me about why I'm not yet wed."

"Well, why aren't you?" A distraction from his thoughts would be welcome.

"No inclination, old boy. And who wants a beau who cannot dance? I've not got the wealth or title to make up for that."

Rhys looked around—from what he'd heard, apartments at the Albany were not cheap. The furniture, although not new, was high quality. Algy's wine and brandy, too, tasted expensive.

"Father pays for it, and gives me an allowance." Algy shrugged. "He should be glad I've not taken to gaming—there's not a lot else to do. You're lucky; you've got a purpose in life."

The bitter note in Algy's voice surprised Rhys. He was happy with his lot, and it hadn't occurred to him that someone with Algy's connections and status could be discontented.

"Is your leg still paining you?"

Algy shrugged. "A bit, but that's not the cause." He drained the glass of wine in his hand. "Mind you, it'll be exhausting keeping up with your Miss Farrington. Give me someone a bit quieter any day."

"You should marry my cousin," Rhys said. "She's an heiress, and you'd be kept busy managing her half of the business." He tried to imagine Algy sitting in Uncle John's cluttered office, but the image would not come.

"Ha, Father would have a fit."

"Only joking, Algy. I'm not sure Uncle John would approve, either." Rhys rubbed a hand over his face. "Izzy persuaded me to meet her again before asking her father's permission to court her. If I get sent to the rightabout, you may have to be my go-between. Would that be enough occupation for a while?"

"The sister looked pretty," Algy said. "Pretending to court her might keep Mama off my back."

~

The afternoon was sunny, so Rhys and Algy opted to arrive early and loiter in the museum courtyard until Izzy appeared. It was pleasant enough standing in the sunshine reminiscing about times past while they watched carriages arriving and leaving. Rhys finally spotted Izzy as her party alighted from a carriage. She was accompanied by two other women and wore the same white pelisse and broad-brimmed bonnet as yesterday.

"That's not Lady Cleeve with her," Algy said.

Rhys had just worked that out. As they approached he recognised the other two women as the ones he'd seen in the barouche two days ago. Thankfully, Izzy's ageing suitor was not with them. He came to a halt, unsure what to do.

"Go in," Algy urged. "We can meet by accident inside."

Rhys nodded, and they followed the group into the hall where crowds were admiring the Elgin marbles.

"Less of a crush than it was when I came before," Algy muttered, as they tried to keep Izzy in sight beneath a frieze of youths and horses. Suddenly the chaperone turned and pulled the two younger women away, heading in their direction.

Algy sniggered. "Naked men, how unexpected in Grecian statuary." He put a hand on Rhys' arm. "Allow me."

Rhys saw Izzy's smile of recognition turn into a wry twist of the lips as she glanced at her companions. It was unlikely to be a day for private conversation, then. Disappointment stabbed him, although he should not have expected more in such a public setting.

"Miss Farrington, how lovely to see you again." Algy's voice was all well mannered charm. "Won't you introduce me to your companions?"

The older woman's eyes narrowed in suspicion, but she merely inclined her head as Izzy introduced them to Miss Templeton and Miss Vivian Farrington.

"I'm very pleased to meet you, Captain Williams," Vivian said, as her appraising glance turned to a smile. "And you, Mr Pelham."

Algy needed no prompting. "May we walk with you both for a while?" he asked, holding his arm out to Vivian as he spoke. "Perhaps you might like to see the Egyptian exhibits—the crowds are likely to be thinner in there. This way."

"By all means," Izzy said. She took Rhys' arm and set off after Algy and Vivian before Miss Templeton could speak. "I couldn't impose on Lady Cleeve again," she said to Rhys, low-voiced. "I tried to get Papa to allow my maid to accompany us, but he said our governess had to come instead."

"It is a pleasure to see you, Izzy, even if we cannot say much."

Her hand squeezed his arm, and her smile lifted his heart.

"Miss Vivian, slow down if you please." The governess' voice was sharp; Algy and Izzy's sister had drawn ahead, Miss Templeton scurrying to keep up with them.

"Surely no harm can come to us in this public place?" Izzy protested.

"I have strict instructions from your father, Miss Farrington," the governess said over her shoulder. "We will stay together, or we will return home."

That was unfortunate, and the determined thrust of Miss Templeton's jaw indicated that she had every intention of abiding by those instructions. They continued to the Egyptian gallery, and strolled along the exhibits with Miss Templeton between the two couples, close enough to hear everything that was being said. Rhys resigned himself to keeping the conversation away from his deeper feelings and hopes.

"Do you enjoy museums, Miss Farrington?" he asked. "Or do you prefer to be out of doors?" Just being with her was enough for now, he thought, as Izzy described her usual activities when at her father's country seat. His home had no parkland for her to ride in, but he responded by describing the beauty of the countryside around Shrewsbury. He would make time to ride with her.

If she wants you, he told himself sternly.

All too soon the governess brought the conversation to a halt, insisting that she was sure the gentlemen had appointments to keep.

"Pleasant girl, Miss Vivian," Algy said, once they were out of earshot. "It would be no hardship to call on her if it became necessary."

~

"Mr Pelham seems very nice," Viv said, when they were finally free to talk in Izzy's bedroom. "Who is he?"

"One of Rhys' friends," Izzy replied. "That's all I know. Although he did know Lady Cleeve, so he is probably someone Papa would approve of."

"What's going to happen now?"

"I don't know." Izzy sighed. "He said he was going to ask Papa for permission to court me. That's the correct thing to do, but I know Papa will not agree."

What would she say if Miss Templeton reported the meeting in the museum to Papa? To say merely that Mr Pelham was an acquaintance of Lady Cleeve would be lying by omission. She didn't like deceiving her father, but this was her future at stake. She could only hope he would not question her.

CHAPTER 19

*L*uckily for Izzy, her father had been out of the house for most of the day, and if Miss Templeton *had* described the meeting in the museum, Papa had chosen not to ask anything further.

Unluckily—in Izzy's view at least—Papa *was* both at home and at leisure when Rhys called the following afternoon. The weather was warm again; Izzy and Viv were reading by the open window in the front parlour while Mama dozed on the sofa. Miss Templeton was once again drilling Lynnie on her scales.

"It's your Mr Williams," Viv whispered, leaning out of the window in a most unladylike manner. "Needham's let him in."

"Oh, no." Izzy's heart sank. They hadn't had time to plan what they might do if—when—Papa refused his permission. "Viv, can you keep Mama here? Please?" She spoke in little more than a whisper.

"What are you going to do?" Viv looked puzzled and then shrugged. "Very well."

Izzy hurried towards the stairs. As she reached the landing and looked down, she was just in time to see Needham show Rhys into Papa's study.

She paused. What had she hoped to achieve if she'd reached Rhys? Papa would have sent her away.

Needham pulled the study door closed, and then disappeared through the baize door that led to his office and the kitchens. That was all the invitation Izzy needed. She tip-toed down the stairs, her slippers silent on the marble treads, and stood by the study door. All she could hear was the murmur of voices.

Bother.

She would hear better if she pressed her ear against the door, but she had a vision of falling into the room if Papa opened it suddenly. He was likely to be cross enough as it was, after Rhys had spoken to him.

"You are one of the men who met my daughters in the museum yesterday." Bedley dropped Rhys' card on his desk as he leaned back in his chair. "You know Lady Cleeve, I understand."

"I have made her acquaintance, my lord. My friend Mr Pelham is well known to her."

"Pelham? Pelham… Any relation to Lord Dearne?"

"His youngest son. We served in the same regiment."

"Ah, one of our brave soldiers. Damned good job you all did against the Corsican. The country is grateful to you all."

Rhys tried not to grimace.

"And what can I do for you, Mr Williams?" Bedley picked up Rhys' card again. "This says you provide wool yarn and fabric. Are you looking for investors?"

Rhys swallowed. "Er, no, my lord." He may as well get straight to the point. "I came to ask permission to court your eldest daughter."

Bedley's brows drew together. "Court? Isolde? After meeting her yesterday?"

Rhys took a deep breath. "No, my lord. I met her in Wales, when she was staying with Mrs Lloyd."

Bedley's colour rose alarmingly. He stood abruptly, his chair skidding away behind him. "What have you done to her? Damn my sister for allowing this. If you have compromised her reputation, I'll see you in court. I can ruin—"

'You do a disservice to both your sister and your daughter, sir." Rhys' voice had not become louder, but something in it stopped Bedley's rant. "Not to mention insulting my own character."

"Insult? You come to me asking to court my daughter—you, in trade, want my daughter to marry beneath her? She'll get no dowry from me if she agrees to any such thing."

Papa's raised voice carried clearly through the door, and Izzy almost wished she had not come down to listen. Poor Rhys, being berated so for doing what was proper.

Money? He wasn't courting her for her dowry, was he? No, of course he wasn't.

Even as she dismissed the thought, she heard Rhys' denial. He must have moved closer to the door, for he was not shouting.

"I care nothing for a dowry, my lord. Your daughter has value above gold. I have sufficient income to give her a comfortable life."

"Comfort? Pah! What of status? Rank? No, certainly not. I forbid you to see my daughter again. She will marry one of her own kind, someone I approve. Such a decision is too important to be left to females."

Izzy closed her eyes. She'd told Rhys how it would be, and although he'd believed her he'd insisted on doing the right thing. She wasn't sure whether to be cross with him for persisting, or to admire his calm in the face of her father's anger.

"It seems I have far more respect for your daughter than you do. She is a woman capable of making her own decisions about her future."

Izzy stepped back—the voices were louder, as if both men were now close to the door.

"I bid you good day, my lord."

Izzy scuttled to the foot of the stairs as the door opened. Rhys stepped out, her father only a few feet behind him.

"And good riddance. Needham!"

Rhys met Izzy's eyes for a moment as Papa shouted. All Izzy could do was to mouth 'I'm sorry' before her father spotted her.

"Go to your room, Isolde. I will speak to you later. Needham, show this man out, and do not admit him again."

"Miss Farrington." Rhys bowed in her direction, ignoring Papa's spluttering behind him and the ineffectual efforts of Needham to move him towards the door. "I hope to see you again."

"How dare you! When I have expressly forbidden it!"

Rhys walked calmly to the door. Izzy waited at the bottom of the stairs until the door closed behind him.

"Isolde, what were—?"

She ignored her father's question. He had told her to go to her room, so she would do so.

Later that afternoon, Izzy knocked on the door of her father's study and entered without waiting for a response. He had summoned her, after all.

"Well, what have you to say for yourself?" Papa came around his desk and stood directly in front of her, bending slightly to bring his face level with hers. Surprisingly, he no longer looked angry, but puzzled.

"What do you wish me to say, Papa?" Izzy put her chin up. She was nearly of age, and she would act like an adult, not the child her father still considered her.

"Consorting with a merchant? Have you no respect for rank?"

Izzy was about to list Rhys' good qualities, but decided against it. It would make no difference—her father had made up his mind and she doubted anything she could say would change it.

"Why is rank to be respected above personal qualities, Papa?"

"What would this country come to if people did not know their place? Look at what happened to Eugenia, stuck in that tiny house in the middle of nowhere with no society."

Genie was happy, but best not to say that, not now. And Papa had not answered her question.

Her father sighed. "Sit down, Izzy." He took a seat himself beside the empty fireplace. Izzy hesitated, then did as he asked.

"I only want what is best for you, Izzy. You are young; you've seen little of the world. You must accept that, as your father, I know what the consequences would be of a marriage such as that... that young man was hoping for."

Izzy waited. After staying with Genie, she had a very good idea of the consequences, but it was not a picture that would sway her father.

"A sensible match within your own order will be an enduring one," Papa went on.

All marriages were, whether or not the participants wanted them to be. That was no reason to accept someone like Lord Ordsall.

"Tell me you did nothing indiscreet with him, Izzy. Did he lay hands on you?"

Oh yes, and very nice it was, too!

Izzy banished the memory. "He did nothing that would damage my reputation, Papa. But why do you ask this about Mr Williams, when the actions of men like Lord Ordsall did not concern you?"

"Lord Ordsall? Izzy, he is a man of rank and wealth, and would have been a good match for you. He is a man of honour and would not do anything improper."

Izzy's anger rose at the implication that Rhys was not a man of honour, but she said nothing. Rhys had done no more than Ordsall had attempted, and Rhys had asked first.

Better to try to keep her father diverted. She did not regret that kiss in the ruined chapel—how could she? But Papa would manage to make it seem sordid, as if Rhys had taken advantage.

"And Izzy, you did promise you would accept an offer from him."

"Lord Ordsall did not make another offer."

"Why not? What did you do?"

Izzy met his gaze, her eyes widening a little. "Why, Papa, how could I hope to understand the reasons of a man, someone older than me, who has been out in the world more than I have?" She hoped she hadn't overdone the bewildered look.

Her father gaped and then closed his mouth with a snap. Izzy suppressed a smile—showing her satisfaction at winning this minor skirmish would not be wise. And it *was* only a minor victory. Nothing had changed—Rhys was still forbidden to see her.

"May I go?"

Papa waved a hand irritably, and Izzy took her leave before he changed his mind. And before he could ask her to promise not to try to see Rhys again.

She would try, but even if she managed to see him, she might not be able to speak with him privately.

Perhaps Viv could pass on a message for her.

Rhys looked up as Algy came into the room.

"All went well, then?" Algy said, eyeing the glass of wine in Rhys' hand and the half-empty decanter beside him.

Rhys rubbed a hand over his face. "It went as I expected," he admitted. "I've been forbidden to see her again."

Algy poured himself some wine, and sat down. "Why did you do it, you idiot? At least before you were only meeting her without permission, now you'll be doing so against specific orders."

Rhys shrugged. "If we..." He hesitated—he hadn't mentioned marriage specifically to Algy, but his friend must know that it was his aim. He took a deep breath. "If we marry, there will be enough talk about Izzy losing status, or me gaining it, without carrying on a clandestine courtship as well." He sighed and shook his head. "That governess with them yesterday... I meant to arrange what to do if Bedley said no, but that woman was always within earshot. I doubt I'd be allowed to have a private conversation with her again, even if I hadn't seen Bedley today. *You* might be an acceptable suitor—"

"God forbid!"

Rhys refused to be distracted. "I would not, no matter how often you mention my army rank. Bedley was nauseatingly grateful for our efforts in the Peninsula until he realised I wanted to court his daughter. There are limits to his appreciation, clearly."

"Accused you of wanting to marry money, did he?"

"Afraid so." Rhys shook his head. "I wanted to do things properly, on the small chance that he would not disapprove." He drained his glass and stood up. "Come for a ride with me? I need a good gallop— we could go out to Hampstead."

Rhys persuaded Algy take another ride in the park the following day. He wanted to make at least one attempt to talk to Izzy again but then he would have to return home. It would be no use winning her hand if his business failed.

"Is that Lady Cleeve's phaeton?" Algy pointed.

It was, and that was Izzy in a barouche approaching it, the governess sandwiched between her and her sister. Her father sat opposite, with a woman of an age and finely enough dressed to be Lady Bedley.

"Damn." That ruled out any chance of speaking to Izzy at all, let alone having any private conversation. Rhys reined in his horse.

As they watched, the phaeton slowed, and the two vehicles came to a halt next to each other. From the gestures, Rhys guessed that Lady Cleeve was asking if Izzy wanted to drive with her, but Bedley shook his head firmly enough to be visible from this distance, and the barouche pulled away.

"If Lady Cleeve's had the brush-off, you've no chance, old man."

"Why come to the park at all if they're not going to speak to people?" Rhys asked. He was here in the hope of seeing Izzy, but why strolling or riding round this limited and busy area was so popular was beyond him. He enjoyed a fast ride, but galloping was frowned upon here.

"Bedley parading his wares," Algy said. "Some eligible young sprig wouldn't be sent on his way, I'll wager."

Like a damned horse market.

"It's no use scowling, Taffy. It's the way of the world."

"Your world." Even as Rhys snapped out the words, he realised he was being unfair. It was the idea of Izzy, in particular, being subjected to such things that he hated.

Algy shrugged. "Want me to try? I had an enjoyable conversation with Miss Vivian the other day."

"Please."

"What do you want me to say, if I get the chance?"

Rhys shrugged. "Just that I'll take a dismissal only from her, not her father."

Algy set off towards the barouche, but Rhys' pessimism about his chance of success was justified when the barouche paused only long enough for a few words to be exchanged and then moved on again.

"I'd hardly spoken when the damned governess pointed out that I was with you the other day," Algy said when he returned to Rhys' side. "Bedley froze up and ordered the coachman to drive on."

Rhys sat for a few minutes, watching the barouche draw away, and then pulled the embroidered spoon from his pocket. The date on it was a month away. If that *was* her birthday—and he didn't see why else she would have put such a date on it—she would be able to make her own decisions then.

"I'm going back to Shrewsbury," he declared. "Algy, if you can talk to her in the park or at a ball—"

"I don't do balls, old man. The leg, you know?"

"You don't have to dance," Rhys said impatiently. "Just try to talk to her. Let her know I haven't given up."

Algy grimaced, but then nodded. "You did get me out of that mess at Burgos," he admitted. "I'll see what I can do."

CHAPTER 20

*I*zzy sat next to Mama against the wall of Lady Rayston's ballroom, watching Viv dance with a fresh-faced youth apparently too shy to speak to her. She hoped her sister was having more fun than she was. This was not a grand affair, as most of the *ton* were out of Town at their country estates. Unfortunately, the room contained several people she did not want to dance with or speak to, and none of the ones she did.

Papa had been almost rude to Lady Cleeve this afternoon in the park. Lady Cleeve had barely greeted them before Papa said, 'You were a friend of Eugenia, I believe?', and announced that they could not stop as he had an appointment. Really, if he was going to tell lies, they needed to be more believable. Someone must have reported seeing Lady Cleeve allowing her to walk with Rhys.

Then Mr Pelham had been brushed off, too, as soon as Miss Templeton revealed he was a friend of Rhys. And Mr Pelham had only looked at Viv, not herself.

"You should be dancing, Izzy," Mama said, finally turning from the friend she had been gossiping with. "I don't understand—you are usually in demand at events such as this."

Izzy knew why. It was tricky aiming a glare so that only the man approaching her saw it, but it had worked on most of those who had approached her. Only with Sir Cecil had she failed, but she had shown so little interest in his conversation that he had not asked for a second dance. The memory made her rather uncomfortable—Sir Cecil meant well, she was sure, but she could not imagine being married to him even if Rhys did not fill her thoughts and hopes.

"Oh, look, Izzy" Mama pointed across the ballroom. "Lord Ordsall is here. I'm sure if you are pleasant, you could rekindle his interest."

God forbid! But to her relief, Lord Ordsall caught her eye and immediately headed for the card room. Izzy saw him hesitate as her father appeared in the doorway, but he carried on into the room with the briefest of nods.

Viv's partner accompanied her back to where Mama sat, and stammered out his request for a second dance.

Viv blushed prettily, and smiled. "I'd be—"

"I'm afraid Vivian has partners for all the remaining dances, Lord Blaylock." Mama cut across Viv's words. "But I'm sure Isolde would be happy to dance with you."

"Mama!" Izzy protested, as Lord Blaylock looked even more horrified than she felt. Viv frowned, but Izzy caught her eye and gave a shrug.

"Why, thank you, Lord Blaylock. I'd be delighted." She managed a proper smile.

The poor man took it with good grace, and Izzy put herself out to be pleasant as they danced. It wasn't his fault Mama had been so forward. She had to make most of the conversation, but noted his interest when she talked about her sister. He finally managed to work himself up to ask what Miss Vivian's favourite flowers were.

"Roses," Izzy said, having no idea. "Thank you for the dance, my lord." She cast a glance at her mother, looking expectantly in their direction. "If Mama… dragoons you into asking me again, do not worry. I shall read nothing into it."

"That's very good of… I mean…" He swallowed hard, a flush reddening his cheeks as he seemed to realise the implication of his words.

Izzy gave him a sweet smile. "I think my sister might be in need of refreshment," she hinted, and went back to her chair at Mama's side while he headed for the room where tables of drinks and cakes were set out. After a few minutes, Viv muttered something about the ladies' retiring room before setting off after him.

"Sir Cecil was in the card room this evening," Papa began as the carriage started for home. "He tells me he doesn't think you would suit."

Izzy bit her lips against the retort that she didn't think he would suit either. That was good news, though.

"I don't know what you said to him, or didn't say, Isolde, but it's not good enough. A baronet is not as high as I would have liked for you, but he would be a good husband, I'm sure." He sounded sad rather than angry. "And Ordsall almost gave me the cut direct in the card room."

Mama tutted.

"Izzy, I don't know what to do with you," Papa went on. He pinched the bridge of his nose. "Unless you are prepared to be pleasant to potential suitors you will attend no more balls or other events."

"Very well, Papa."

He gave her a pleased smile, misunderstanding as she guessed he would. "Good, good. I'm sure we can find someone suitable, Izzy. You're still very—"

"You mistake me, Papa," Izzy interrupted. "I am quite happy not to attend any further events, as you have directed."

Viv snorted behind her hand as Papa gazed at Izzy open-mouthed and then scowled. Mama patted his hand. "Later, dear," she said, glaring at both her daughters. Izzy sighed, not looking forward to the arguments to come.

～

Rhys pulled his collar tighter about his neck as the coach left the outskirts of Wolverhampton, wondering again what idiocy had prompted him to take an outside seat on the Mail. Thankfully the rain had held off overnight.

He could be warm and dry inside a stage-coach instead. Too warm, no doubt, crammed in with over-inquisitive and under-washed fellow travellers, but he could have feigned sleep. Or he could have waited in London another day and got an inside seat on the Mail that would leave London tonight.

Too bloody impulsive. Like calling on Bedley rather than trying to have another talk with Izzy first.

It was done, and there was no undoing it. He could have stayed in London, but another attempt to see Izzy would have been futile, and likely to result in her being even more closely supervised. Making sure he had a business that would support her was a better use of his time at the moment.

He resisted the temptation to pull out the piece of embroidery again—he didn't want to get it wet. He knew the date by heart, in any case.

Four weeks.

~

"I don't know why you insist on coming here again, Isolde," Miss Templeton complained as they deposited their wet umbrellas in the entrance hall of the British Museum.

"You rushed us away last time," Izzy said. "We haven't finished looking at the marbles, or the Egyptian exhibits."

"Well, if you are hoping to talk to that encroaching merchant, you can think again."

"Poor Izzy would be confined to the house otherwise, Miss Templeton," Viv said as they started up the main staircase. "You wouldn't want her to get fat through lack of exercise, would you? And this *is* educational. There were some very interesting carvings."

Izzy snorted at the memory. The friezes of mounted horsemen

had been interesting, but not nearly as much as a statue of a reclining man they had seen in another room. He appeared to have lost his hands and feet, but it was his lack of clothing that had attracted her attention. Did all men have muscles like that under their shirts? Did Rhys? She found it hard to believe that Sir Cecil did. Sadly, Miss Templeton had seen what she was looking at and dragged her away before she could inspect it more closely.

"Make no excuses for your sister," Miss Templeton said. "Isolde has chosen to remove herself from society. This is not how I have educated the pair of you to behave."

Izzy did her best to ignore the governess' complaints. She'd heard them all yesterday, many times. She didn't know if Rhys might think to find them here again, and what it might achieve if he did, but she couldn't help looking for him. She kept an eye out for Lady Cleeve, too. Miss Templeton would not dare to snub Lady Cleeve to her face.

Her heart accelerated as they turned the corner in the staircase and she spotted Mr Pelham above, leaning on the balustrade. Then her excitement abated as she realised Rhys was not with him—not even waiting somewhere in the background.

Beside her, Miss Templeton came to a momentary halt before walking on stiffly. "You will not speak to that young man either, Isolde."

Mr Pelham caught Izzy's gaze, and Izzy slanted her head sideways to where Viv walked on the other side of the governess. "I think he wants to talk to Vivian," she said, hoping Mr Pelham would play along. When he had approached their carriage two days before, he *had* tried to talk to her sister.

"Miss Vivian, Miss Farrington." Mr Pelham doffed his hat and gave a small bow as they reached the top of the stairs. He gave the governess a cool nod before returning his attention to Viv.

Izzy bit her lips against a smile. He hadn't seemed so supercilious when she talked to him before.

"You are not with your friend today, Mr Pelham?" Viv asked. Izzy, pleased that Viv had remembered what she'd asked her to do, strained to hear the answer.

"No, Miss Vivian. He's returned home."

Izzy had a brief doubt—had Mr Pelham really joined them to talk to Viv? Then he slid a quick glance towards Izzy. "For now."

She let out a breath of relief. Miss Templeton frowned, looking from Izzy to Mr Pelham.

Don't interrupt now, please! Not until Viv has said the next part.

"Oh, dear, that's a shame." Viv looked as if she meant it. "He must enjoy being in Wales, I suppose. Izzy is hoping to visit there again in September. Have you ever been?"

"No, but perhaps I should go some time." Mr Pelham glanced at Izzy again. She gave him a happy smile and a nod. He turned back to Viv and made some inconsequential remarks about the exhibits before taking his leave.

Miss Templeton glared after him, her lips compressed. Izzy wondered what she would report to Papa later—she wouldn't be surprised if Viv, too, was about to be forbidden to talk to Mr Pelham.

Now it was up to Mr Pelham to let Rhys know what had been said —if he even realised that Viv had passed on a message.

"Letter for you, Mr Williams," Griffiths said, laying it on the corner of Rhys' desk. "Have you anything else for me today?"

"No, thank you, Griffiths. I'll see you in the morning." He recognised Algy's scrawl, so he waited until the secretary left before breaking the seal.

A quick scan of the contents brought disappointment—Algy had not managed to speak to Izzy at all. Then he read it again more carefully.

...that dragon of a governess...didn't try to speak to Miss Farrington directly...seemed to be pleased when I said 'for now'...

Izzy had understood his message then.

...no idea of significance...mentioned that she wanted to visit Wales again in September...your Miss F seemed happy when her sister said that... assistance in an elopement might relieve the boredom...

September—she would come of age in September.

Visiting Wales. He leaned back in his chair, his eyes on the grey sky beyond the window. If her father was planning to send her back to Genie, her sister would have said so. Perhaps Izzy was going to attempt to get there herself, and she wanted him to know. Why else would Vivian have told Algy?

He hoped she was not planning on taking the stage on her own. He couldn't help smiling—his Izzy was certainly resourceful, and would probably manage to find help.

He would be in London on her birthday, ready to assist with whatever she planned. If she really did intend to go to Capel Bodfan, that would at least allow him to see her again, to continue their acquaintance. He hoped—he was fairly sure—it was more than that, but all he could do now was to wait.

Reaching for some blank paper, he started writing a letter to Algy. He'd write to Genie, too.

His hand paused as he realised the final thing he had to do. It was time he told Mama and Gwynne about Izzy. He shut his eyes for a moment, imagining the exclamations, demands for details, questions…

Later. He'd faced worse things. He'd finish his letter to Algy first.

CHAPTER 21

"*D*id you enjoy your evening?" Izzy put her book aside as Viv came into her room, clad in her night-rail and robe. That wasn't what she wanted to ask, but it seemed rude to focus on her own concerns when Viv was risking their parents' displeasure by aiding her.

Viv sat at the foot of the bed, resting her back against the bedpost as she smiled happily. "Very much. Lord Blaylock was there. We danced twice."

"And...?"

Viv shrugged. "Not much. He did ask if I would drive in the park with him tomorrow. Papa started to say something about 'My eldest daughter should be wed before...' but Mama stuck her elbow in his side and said I'd be happy to."

Izzy smiled at Viv's imitation of Papa's tone. "Do you really like him, Viv? He didn't look as if he had much to say to you when you danced with him last week. He hardly said a word when Mama made him dance with me."

Viv's blush was visible even in the dim candlelight. "He was a little shy at first, but he's changing." She pointed an accusing finger. "I'm not surprised he didn't say much to you, Izzy, the way you glared at everyone that evening. You can look quite terrifying."

"I know, especially when I do it on purpose." Perhaps one day she would tell Viv about her first encounters with Rhys. She should have learned from that not to judge people by first impressions.

"He's sweet, and he likes me, Izzy. He wouldn't suit you at all." Viv compressed her lips, but a smile escaped. "In fact, I said that to Mama and she had to admit it was true."

"Poor Papa." Izzy shook her head in feigned sympathy. "First me contradicting him, and now Mama!"

Viv giggled. "I looked for Lady Cleeve," she said.

Izzy sat up—this was what she had been waiting for. She'd dropped a few hints to Mary about secretly posting a letter for her, but Mama had told all the servants they would lose their position if they did any such thing. Even if they were prepared to take that risk, she couldn't ask it of them. Viv was too much under Mama's eye, or Miss Templeton's, to take a note, and Lynnie too young to be in a position to help. But Papa could not stop Viv talking to other people at balls.

"I didn't see her, Izzy."

Izzy lay back against her pillows. Bother—Lady Cleeve could have written to Genie for her, or even provided her with an escort to Wales if Rhys did not come.

"I'm sorry," Viv added. "I didn't want to ask anyone if she was there, in case they wanted to know why."

Izzy thought that she might have made up some excuse, but this was her future at stake, not her sister's, and Viv was already being a great help.

"It's all right, Viv. Thank you for looking."

"Mr Pelham was there, though. He asked me to dance, and Mama didn't hear in time to say no."

That was more promising!

"We didn't actually dance. He apologised, and said his bad leg wasn't up to it. He took me for refreshments instead. He's very nice, Izzy. Not as nice as Lord Blaylock, though."

Izzy curbed her impatience with an effort.

"He must have come just to talk to me," Viv went on, "for I saw him leave straight afterwards."

"Viv, what did he *say*?"

"Oh!" Viv covered a giggle with one hand. "Sorry, Izzy. He said he hopes you enjoy your trip to Wales on your birthday. Mama was nearby, and she moved closer then, so he couldn't say anything else."

That was something, though.

"Then on the way home, Mama said he wasn't a suitable person for me to talk to because he's only a third son."

Izzy sighed. Another option gone.

"Izzy, does that mean you want to run away to Wales?" Viv's face creased up, and she bit her lip. "Papa may forbid us from seeing you again if you do."

She'd considered that. "Not forever, Viv. At least, not unless he marries you off to someone like him. I'm sure you could persuade your Lord Blaylock, for example, to allow his wife to see her sister now and then?"

Viv's despondency vanished, but she shook her head. "Izzy, it's far too soon to say things like that. How did you decide about your Mr Williams so quickly?"

"I… He hasn't asked me yet."

Viv's mouth dropped open. "But your plans…? He asked Papa."

"He asked Papa for permission to court me, not to marry me."

"Well, that's almost the same thing."

Izzy hoped so. No, she *knew* so.

"I think he will ask me. But even if he does not, I know that I don't want *any* of the men Mama and Papa deem suitable."

"Is your plan really only to go to Aunt Genie?"

"That's all I *can* plan. I can write to Rhys from Aunt Genie's house." She would find a way to get there somehow, even if she had to wait until Lady Cleeve returned from her travels.

Viv chatted a little longer about her other dance partners and then went to bed, leaving Izzy thinking over what her sister had said. Mr

Pelham's remark about enjoying her trip to Wales could have been a random comment.

What, exactly, had Viv said? September—when Viv had spoken to Mr Pelham in the museum, she'd mentioned visiting Wales in September. But if Viv was reporting Mr Pelham's words correctly, he'd mentioned her birthday. Mr Pelham didn't know her birthday was in September, but Rhys did.

She counted the days in her head—it was five days since Mr Pelham had encountered them in the museum. That was enough time for him to write to Rhys and get a reply.

If Viv had reported what Mr Pelham said correctly. She would just have to hope that was the case. And that it meant Rhys would come for her.

~

"Well!" Mrs Williams regarded Rhys with raised brows. "It's weeks since you came back from Wales, and you only tell me now?"

"Mama—"

His mother flapped a hand at him. "Men never say what's on their mind."

Rhys relaxed a little, leaning back in his chair. He wanted his mother to approve of what he planned; upsetting her would not have been a good start.

"Daughter of a baron, you say?"

"Yes."

"She'll be used to much more than this house. And balls and parties, no doubt."

"She enjoyed staying with Mrs Lloyd," Rhys said. "Their house is not as large as this."

"The attraction of novelty."

Rhys sighed. It was a good point. "I think she knows her own mind, Mama."

"You mean she is used to having her own way?"

Was she? The dissatisfied miss he had first met might have been, but she'd been quite happy with the basic picnic by the cromlech, and she'd settled in well with Genie. She certainly couldn't be said to be having her own way in London at the moment.

"That's not the same thing." Rhys ran a hand through his hair. This was not going as well as he'd hoped.

"Mrs Chambers moved into a smaller house when her son got married," Mama went on. "She couldn't get along with her new daughter-in-law."

Rhys felt a pang of guilt. He hadn't given much thought to what it must feel like to give up the running of a household like this, where Mama had spent her whole married life. "But that is a risk with whoever I marry—unless you don't want me to wed?"

Mrs Williams tilted her head to one side, regarding him with narrowed eyes. "I thought you were going to marry Sophie. Does John know about this?"

"Yes, Mama." Rhys recounted the discussion he'd had with Uncle John before he went to London. "Do you think Sophie *wanted* to marry me?" He hoped not, but it would not change his decision.

To his relief, Mama shook her head. "I don't think she thought about it much at all. From what I've seen of her recently, she takes a fancy to a different man every month. She's only sixteen, after all, too young to know her own mind."

"That's good."

"And you want to elope with this Miss Farrington?"

"No. Not exactly."

"What, then?" Mama shook her head. "No, don't answer that now. Ring for some tea, then you can tell me everything from the beginning."

Rhys told her almost all of what had happened, thankful that he was allowed to stick to events and was not interrogated about his deepest feelings.

"Hmm. So you have an appointment, of sorts, to escort her to Wales in September, but you tell me this is not an elopement?"

Rhys shook his head. "No. If she'll have me, I don't want our life to start in scandal."

"You will need a proper chaperone for Miss Farrington, then. Otherwise that journey is like to compromise her reputation and cause just the scandal you are trying to avoid."

That was something he hoped she could help with. "Can you spare the time? It is a long way, I know, and—"

"No, I don't think that would do. It might show that you *expect* her to become part of our family."

He hoped, yes. He didn't dare expect.

"Let me write some letters, Rhys. Mariah Trent or Caro Walsh might be glad of a change of scenery."

Rhys stood. "Thank you, Mama."

He could call at the jeweller on his way to the mill.

"You wanted to see me, Papa?" Izzy crossed the study and took a seat near her father's desk.

His lips were set in a firm line. "Isolde, it has been a fortnight, and you are still refusing to do your duty as a daughter."

"I have been obeying your instructions, Papa." She quite enjoyed having most evenings to herself to read in the library, finding new interest in some of the books Papa had collected over the years. But the novelty was beginning to wear off.

Papa's face began to turn red. "The instruction I wish you to obey is to be pleasant to your suitors. People are beginning to talk about your absence. Your mother has put it about that you are unwell. You are nearly twenty-one and there will be yet more talk if you are not even being courted by someone at that age."

"Papa, I don't want a life ruled by what the gossips might say."

"Lord Hayworth has expressed an interest in courting you, Isolde," Papa went on. Had he even heard her objection? "He is coming to dinner tomorrow, and you will be polite."

"Very well." She didn't want to embarrass Papa in front of others.

Mama, too, would be mortified if she was rude. But being polite was not the same as encouraging him.

Her father's face relaxed a little. "If he asks you to walk in the park with him, or drive, you will accept."

"Yes, Papa." She might contrive to see Lady Cleeve without Miss Templeton's interference.

"Miss Templeton will accompany you, of course."

Bother!

"And if he asks you to marry him, you will accept."

"No."

"He will be an excellent— What did you say?"

Izzy sat up straight in her chair. "I cannot promise to accept an offer of marriage from someone I've never met." Papa was not usually quite so unreasonable.

Her father took a deep breath. "But you agreed to accept Lord Ordsall if he offered."

That was only because she thought she could put him off before he did so. "That's not the same, Papa."

"Isolde, you will do as you are bid!" The red was creeping into his face again.

Izzy waited for the threat.

"Go to your room. You will stay there until you decide to be sensible."

No need to tell the butler or the footman in the hall—they must have heard his bellow.

Two weeks. It was only two weeks until her birthday, but they could be very long weeks if she antagonised him further.

"Very well, Papa. You had better warn Lord Heyworth I will not be at dinner tomorrow." She stood.

Her father glared at her. After a moment, when it became clear he was not going to speak, she curtseyed, then turned and left.

Things could be far worse, Izzy reflected later that evening. Papa could have fed her on bread and water. Instead she'd had a tray with a selection of the food served to the rest of the family. Viv and Lynnie even crept in after dinner, Lynnie in her night-rail with her hair braided.

"Is Papa still furious?" Izzy asked.

"He didn't say much, but he frowned," Lynnie said. "Izzy, are you really going to stay up here all day tomorrow?"

"Probably. Unless Papa relents."

"Ooh, just like Annunciata, in *The Perils of a Maiden*," Lynnie said, her eyes round.

"Not at all," Viv laughed, and gave one of Lynnie's braids a gentle tug. "Izzy's not actually locked in a dungeon, or being starved into submission. But you won't be able to read any more of those novels; Papa has forbidden it." She put her head back to look down her nose and mimicked their father's voice: "See what reading such rubbish has done to Isolde. Turning down several perfectly respectable matches because of some silly romantic idea."

"Sorry," Izzy said.

"Oh, pooh. This is much better than reading a novel."

"Only if you're not the main character," Izzy muttered. "Time for bed, Lynnie," she added, wanting to talk to Viv alone. "You can come and see me tomorrow."

Lynnie stuck her lip out for a moment, but bade them goodnight.

"I hope he isn't cross with you, Viv," Izzy said, when Lynnie had gone. "He doesn't know you helped me, does he?"

Viv shook her head.

"How is Lord Blaylock?"

Successfully diverted, Viv chattered on for a few minutes. After she left, Izzy went over to the chest where she kept her books. Her hand hovered over the two she'd borrowed from Genie, and she picked up *Conversations in Chemistry*. She would finish reading that—she doubted she'd want to discuss the subject with anyone, but she would at least be a little better informed. It was weeks since she'd read any of it, so she'd need to start again at the beginning.

What other subjects did men learn that Papa deemed unsuitable for women? And how did people know such things were 'unsuitable' when no-one tried to teach them to women in the first place?

She sighed. If everything worked out, she'd soon be able to read whatever she liked, although that would be the least of the advantages.

If Rhys had understood the message.

CHAPTER 22

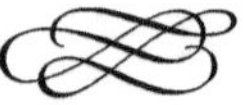

Viv watched as Izzy folded her night-rail into the valise. "This must be the strangest way to spend your birthday, Izzy. What if he doesn't come?"

"Then I will feel a complete idiot, and I'll have to think of some other way of getting to Wales." Viv had found out that Lord and Lady Cleeve were travelling in France, so Rhys was her only means of help. She had to trust that he would come.

No, Izzy *knew* he would come; she just had to trust that it would be today. During the last couple of weeks she'd improved her knowledge enormously with the aid of books Viv had smuggled to her. But even reading palled after a few hours. The rest of the time had been a mixture of boredom and argument, with Mama and Papa taking it in turns to try to persuade her of the error of her ways. But she had still been left with too much time to think, and to wonder what she would do if Rhys didn't arrive.

She strapped the valise closed, and laid her pelisse and bonnet ready. "I've written a letter for Papa. I'll leave it under my pillow—will you make sure someone finds it?"

"Of course I will. I can give it to Papa myself."

Izzy shook her head. "Then he'll realise that you knew my plans and didn't tell him. You'll get into trouble."

"He'll find out anyway. I'm not good enough at hiding guilty secrets." Viv smiled, a combination of mischief and sadness. "And I'm not going to wait until I marry before I see you again. Now I know that Papa *can* be defied, I'll persuade him to let me visit you, even if he won't allow you to come here. I'll make sure Lynnie isn't blamed for any of it, though."

"Will you wait with me?" Izzy asked, a sudden lump in her throat. She could have hours to wait, but more importantly, she might not see Viv again for some time. Lynnie would be under their parents' eyes for even longer, but Viv might be able to smuggle letters to her.

"Of course I will."

They pulled a couple of chairs close to the window, from where Izzy could watch the street.

"Viv, I hope there will be no scandal over this to affect you. I don't want that."

Viv shrugged. "Your life shouldn't be ruled by something that might happen to me. And if Henry—"

"Henry?"

"We are becoming better acquainted," Viv said, with dignity. "*As I was saying*, if Henry lets a little gossip about you put him off, he may not be the man for me." She grinned. "Now, tell me again how you sat in the stream."

That story turned into childhood reminiscences, the familiar memories helping to sooth the fluttering in Izzy's stomach and pass the time. She cast frequent glances out of the window while they talked, not only to look for Rhys, but in the hope of seeing Papa leave for his club. She saw Miss Templeton escort Lynnie down the street, on their way to a dancing lesson. It was a shame not to be able to say a proper goodbye to her youngest sister, but at least Lynnie wouldn't have to witness the unpleasantness that would ensue if Izzy was caught leaving.

"Viv, do explain to Lynnie why we didn't tell her, won't you?"

"Yes, silly! Oh, who is that?" Viv leaned closer to the window.

"Papa is leaving," Izzy said. It was nearly eleven o'clock now, but still rather early for him to depart, so she'd been lucky. Only ten minutes later, she saw a post-chaise draw up outside. A rider following it handed his horse to one of the postilions before mounting the steps to the front door. He did not look up, but Izzy would recognise Rhys from any angle.

"He's here," she said, her breath catching. She grabbed her pelisse with a shaking hand.

"Go!" Viv urged, giving her a quick hug. "I'll bring your bonnet and valise down. Make sure Needham doesn't turn him away!"

Izzy heard the knocker on the front door while she was still on the top landing, and hurried down as fast as she could.

"I have orders not to admit you, Mr Williams," Needham said as she reached the ground floor. Rhys was half-hidden beyond the butler, but he stepped to one side and their eyes met. His expression, his smile, went straight to her heart. This definitely *was* the right thing to do.

"You don't need to let him in, Needham," Izzy said, hearing Viv's footsteps behind her. She took the valise and bonnet, and turned back to the butler. "All you need to do is let me out."

She wondered if Needham was going to allow her to walk into him, but at the last minute he stepped back, his eyes moving to focus on something behind her.

Turning, Izzy saw her mother descending the stairs.

"What is going on here? Izzy, where are you going? Who is this?"

"Mama, may I introduce Mr Williams? He is come to… to escort me to Aunt Genie."

Rhys moved past the frozen butler and took the valise from Izzy.

"Lady Bedley." He made a bow and placed one hand lightly in the small of Izzy's back, hoping his touch would reassure her.

Lady Bedley regarded Rhys with bewilderment before her eyes

narrowed in understanding. "You are the one who wanted to court Izzy?"

"Yes, my lady."

"*Mr* Williams? The one who is in trade?"

"Yes, Mama." Vivian spoke before Rhys could reply. "The one who Izzy *wants* to marry."

Rhys' breath caught at those words, but he ignored the flare of hope. Izzy's sister might be exaggerating.

"You must not go, Izzy!" Lady Bedley's eyes widened as her face reddened.

"I'm leaving, Mama," Izzy said firmly.

Lady Bedley's face screwed up, and she pulled a handkerchief from one sleeve. "Izzy, you can't throw yourself away like this," she wailed, holding the handkerchief to her face. "You could have been Lady Ordsall, or Lady Hayworth. Why are you doing this to us?" She took a deep breath. "The scandal, having my daughter elope! What will Lady Plymouth say when she hears? And Lord Blaylock?" Her voice became louder, shriller. "To think my daughter will disgrace me!"

Izzy stepped forward, but Vivian blocked her way. "Go," she ordered. "I'll see to Mama." Vivian flapped her hands to shoo them away.

"Thank you, Miss Vivian." Rhys was pleased to see a rather wobbly smile from Izzy as he followed her out of the house.

He opened the door of the post-chaise. "Izzy, this is Mrs Trent, who will be your chaperone for the journey."

Mrs Trent smiled in greeting, but Rhys regarded Izzy with concern. Her lips were pressed tightly together and her shoulders drooped. He wanted to hold her close, to show that someone beside her sister cared for her, but now was not the time.

"We will stop just outside London," he added. That would give her a chance to get over her upset, and they could finally have a private talk together.

"Thank you." She managed a watery smile, and he put up the step and closed the door.

"The Swan in Edgeware," he called to the postilions, taking the reins of the hired horse. He mounted as the post-chaise rattled away, and set off after it.

The road was busy, full of hawkers crying their wares, delivery men with carts, and people of all classes pushing their way along the pavements. Rhys, concentrating on not losing sight of the chaise, only noticed a familiar figure walking in the opposite direction when he was almost level with him.

Bedley.

Rhys debated whether to stop and talk to Izzy's father, but the chaise was turning a corner ahead and there was no sign that Izzy had seen him, or wanted to stop if she had.

He shrugged and rode on. If Bedley was going to make a fuss, he'd come after them soon enough.

Izzy settled limply into the seat as the post-chaise lurched into motion, still feeling shaky. Mrs Trent was older than Mama, with greying hair and the beginnings of wrinkles around her eyes and mouth. Izzy attempted to smile but found herself trying to blink back tears instead. It was partly the relief that her plans were finally working, but she was also hurt by Mama's harsh words. She had anticipated some such reaction from her mother, but was more upset by it than she had expected to be.

A hand patted her knee, and Mrs Trent held out a handkerchief. "Have a good cry, my dear; you'll feel better."

"I *never* cry," Izzy muttered as she took it and dabbed her eyes.

"Very wise. It makes your eyes red and your nose run. That's why it's better to get it done now, before we stop, so you look pretty again when you have a proper talk with your young man."

This comment was so unexpected that Izzy giggled, then sniffed. Leaning her head back against the squabs, she took a few deep breaths and decided that perhaps she wasn't going to cry after all. Mama's words had hurt, but they should not have been a surprise. Papa might have expressed things differently if he'd been there, but the overall sentiment would have been similar. At least Viv was happy for her. Lynnie would be too, when Viv had explained.

She gave the handkerchief back. "I'm all right," she said. "Thank you for accompanying me." She hesitated, wondering if she was about to be rude, but decided to ask anyway. "Who *are* you?"

Mrs Trent chuckled. "A very good question. I am a friend of Mrs Williams—Rhys' mama."

"It is very good of you to give up your time to chaperone me," Izzy said.

"It's no trouble, dear. I enjoy travelling, and this is a very comfortable chaise. Now then, I've never been to the part of Wales where your aunt lives. What is the countryside like around there?"

Mrs Trent knew her story then. Izzy wasn't sure if her chaperone was really interested or just making conversation, but describing Capel Bodfan and the surrounding countryside took her mind off her upsetting departure. It was only after they both turned to watch the passing scenery that Izzy wondered if Rhys could have misinterpreted the cryptic message she'd sent via Viv and Mr Pelham. That she really did only want to go and live with Genie. What if he was only helping her as a friend?

Stop finding more difficulties, she told herself firmly. His smile when she first saw him had not been that of a mere friend.

"I reserved a parlour," Rhys said as he opened the chaise door in front of the inn. Riding here, he'd wondered whether to tell Izzy that he'd seen her father not far from their home. No, he decided, not straight away. He wanted to talk to her privately first, without the prospect of an imminent confrontation worrying her.

"Thank you." Izzy took his hand as she stepped down. She smiled, but it wasn't the happy expression he liked to see.

"Are you all right?" he asked.

"I am now. Rhys, it is good to see you." Her smile was more genuine this time, and his worry for her eased.

Inside the coach, Mrs Trent cleared her throat. "If you will assist me to alight, Mr Williams, I will walk around for a little to stretch my legs. I will enjoy a cup of tea in… fifteen minutes?"

Rhys helped Mrs Trent out and offered his arm to Izzy. "This way," he said, grateful for the chaperone's tact. The parlour he had reserved was spacious and clean, with a crackling fire warming it. Izzy entered ahead of him, and he closed the door, pulling off his gloves while she removed her pelisse and bonnet.

Izzy placed her bonnet on a table and turned towards him, her hands clenched together in front of her.

This was the moment of truth. "Izzy, are you intending to live with Genie?"

She shook her head and took a deep breath. "When… when I sent you that spoon, it was the only way I could think of to say I would like to see you again, without Papa understanding."

Rhys took the bookmark from his pocket and laid it on the table, hope growing inside him. "I gathered that." But was that all it meant now?

Izzy picked up the bookmark. "Now, this one has the same meaning as a proper spoon." She bit her lip, and the uncertainty in her eyes went straight to his heart.

"Izzy," he said, taking a step towards her. She dropped the bookmark on the table and walked into his arms, her face buried in the shoulder of his jacket as she clung to him. He pulled her close to him. It felt so right, having her close like this.

"Oh, Rhys." Her words were muffled. "I wasn't sure you'd come. I didn't know if you'd understand the message Viv passed on."

"I got the message, Izzy. I'm here now." The tension in her gradually eased, and he lowered his arms.

"I'm sorry," she sniffed. "I'm not usually a watering pot."

"I think you are allowed to be, under the circumstances." He offered his handkerchief, but she was already wiping her eyes.

He swallowed hard. Her actions had probably told him what he wanted to know, but he should still ask formally. He took the jeweller's box from his pocket. "I had this made for you, Izzy. I'm even worse at wood carving than Huw."

. . .

Izzy took the little box, and opened it with shaking fingers. Inside, a fine silver chain lay coiled, a charm resting on top. A tiny silver spoon, with an ornate handle that looked like intertwined ribbons.

She blinked away a tear. "It's lovely, thank you." She managed to get the words out past a lump in her throat.

He stepped closer, taking the box and placing it on the table. Then he took her hands in his. "Izzy, I love you, and I want to share my life with you. Will you marry me?"

"Oh, Rhys. Yes. Yes, please." She pulled her hands away and reached to pull him close. Then his arms were around her again, one hand tangling in the hair at the back of her head.

"I love you, too," she whispered, hoping he was about to kiss her.

A knock at the door interrupted them as his head bent forwards and he stopped, his arms dropping away. "Damn. Izzy, I'm sorry—"

She shook her head. "There'll be time enough." Although even another minute together would have been good.

Another knock, then the door opened and the landlord carried a laden tray to a table next to the fire.

"Your tea, sir. The other lady is on her way." He set out the pot, cups, and milk, and a platter of sandwiches and cakes.

Mrs Trent entered as the landlord left, one brow rising as she looked at them, still standing close together. "Did I interrupt too soon?"

"No, Mrs Trent," Izzy said, meaning the opposite. "You may congratulate us."

A big smile spread across the chaperone's face. "I hope you will be very happy together. Do we still go to Wales?"

"I will leave that for Izzy to decide," Rhys replied. "It depends on how long an engagement she wants."

A long engagement? Izzy put a hand on his arm. "Rhys?"

"I'll pour the tea," Mrs Trent said, walking over to the table and making a fuss over cups and plates with her back to them.

"Rhys," Izzy said again, keeping her voice low. "Do *you* want to wait?"

He laid his hand on hers, giving it a gentle squeeze. "No. But this is a big change for you, Izzy. You might wish for some time with Genie first."

He put a hand up as she was about to speak. "You can think about it in the chaise, Izzy, and then you can tell me what you have decided later. I hope to stop in Oxford tonight, or somewhere near it. If we are to go to Shrewsbury, you or I can write to Genie this evening."

The plan made sense. And he was allowing her to decide—how could she not like that? "Very well, thank you."

"Izzy." His smile faded.

"What is it?"

"I saw your father on Wimpole Street as we left. He could have been returning home."

"Oh." She took a deep breath, her happiness diminishing. Would he pursue them? Probably. "It will take him some time to catch up, will it not?"

He shook his head. "Not if your butler heard me give directions to the postboys."

"Do you think we should leave now?" She glanced at the tea and sandwiches—she hadn't been able to eat breakfast this morning, and the thought of travelling for several more hours with nothing to eat dismayed her. She moved over to the table. "No," she went on, before Rhys could reply. "I don't want to rush away just because Papa might be on his way. I will have to speak with him at some point. Best to get it over with, if he *is* following."

Rhys looked into her eyes. "Are you sure?"

"Yes," she said. "Besides, I'm in dire need of food." She offered the plate of sandwiches to Mrs Trent, and then took a one herself. The food helped to settle the fluttering in her stomach; the sweetness of the cake helped too.

Rhys smiled, and took his cup of tea over to the window. She had almost eaten her fill when he spoke.

"He's here."

<h1 style="text-align:center">CHAPTER 23</h1>

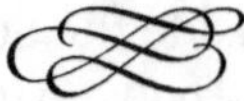

*I*zzy put down her cup and took a deep breath. Papa had no legal right to take her home, and Rhys would not let him do so against her will. But she was fond of her father, in spite of his insistence on controlling her life, and she didn't relish the prospect of acrimonious words.

It was several minutes before the landlord knocked on the door. "Excuse me, sir, ladies. There's a Lord Bedley here asking after a Miss Farrington."

Izzy stood up. "I am Miss Farrington. You may show him in."

"I will leave you to speak in private, Miss Farrington." Mrs Trent stood as she spoke, and slipped out of the room as Papa pushed past the landlord, his face grim. He walked over to Rhys, thrusting his chin out.

"I expressly forbade you from seeing my daughter, and you run off with her! How dare you subject my family to such scandal? I have a good mind to—"

Rhys stood his ground, but Izzy spoke before he could reply.

"Papa, I am not eloping." It was not fair for Papa to blame Rhys for this situation. She glanced behind her—the landlord still stood in the doorway, an interested serving maid behind him. "Can we discuss this

197

without an audience, please?" she went on, more quietly now her father had been shocked into silence. "Unless you want all of Edgeware to know about it?"

Rhys crossed the room to close the door. "Do you wish to speak alone, Izzy?"

She didn't want him to leave, but he would stay within call, she knew. "I think it would be best."

"Very well. I will be just outside the door."

Izzy resumed her seat at the table. "Won't you sit down, Papa?" She was pleased that her voice sounded so calm.

Her father glared at her, but his expression gradually changed from anger to puzzlement. To her relief, he pulled out a chair and sat facing her.

"You went off with a man, Isolde. How is that *not* eloping? Your mama said—"

"Mama said several things, but nothing to the point," Izzy retorted. "She jumped to a conclusion, as you have done."

"What are you doing then?"

"I asked Rhys—Mr Williams—to escort me to Wales, to Aunt Genie. I will choose my own husband. I would like to marry with your blessing, but I will do what I consider is best for me with or without your approval. As of today, I no longer need your permission."

Papa stared at her, and shook his head. "Isolde, you are making a big mistake."

"Why, Papa? Why would marrying Mr Williams be a mistake when you think marriage to Lord Ordsall, or to Sir Cecil, would not?"

"They are of our class. We've been through this before."

"We have, Papa. At that time I asked you why rank mattered more than personal qualities, and you gave me no answer."

"It… that is the way the world works. Rank is influence and power. You cannot change that."

What influence and power did women have? Papa had still not really answered her question, but there was no point in persisting.

"Sir Cecil only sees me as a means to get an heir. I do not want to be a… a brood mare."

"Having children is the purpose of marriage, my dear." He ran his hand through his hair, his brow creased.

"Of course it is, but need it be the *only* purpose? What about taking pleasure in each other's company? Or respect—such as understanding that I am a grown woman and can make my own decisions?"

"I want you to be happy—"

"Papa, if you think marriage to Ordsall or Sir Cecil would have made me happy, then you don't know me at all."

Her father shook his head. "You have not been out in the world, Izzy. Life will be very different if you do this. Lord Ordsall is a gentleman, and—"

"Papa, is it gentlemanlike to force yourself upon a woman?"

"Lord Ordsall—" He broke off, his brows drawing together. "What? What did Ordsall do?"

"He kissed me, Papa. He invited me to stroll in the gardens at a ball. He pushed me against a tree and stuck his tongue in my mouth. It was disgusting. Is that gentlemanly behaviour?"

"Good heavens, no, of course not. But you should have told me, Izzy. I would have insisted he marry you."

Izzy closed her eyes for a moment, despairing of ever making her father understand. "Papa, that is precisely why I did *not* tell you. It was only a kiss." And not even a proper kiss. "I do not want to marry someone who takes no account of my wishes. Is he to be rewarded for that behaviour by gaining my hand? If that is an example of a gentleman I'll be quite happy without one."

"But what do you know of this Williams? Izzy, you were only in Wales a short time. How can you know him well enough to be sure about what you are doing?"

"It does not always take a long time to get to know someone. And he is a friend of Genie and Huw—I trust their judgement that he is a decent and honest man. Papa, what do you really know about Lord Ordsall? Or Lord Hayworth? You insisted I should accept an offer from them, and I know them even less. If this is an example of how men's understanding is better than women's, I want nothing of that, either."

"But to run off? The scandal? Abandoning your whole family, your sisters, and your parents, without even saying goodbye?"

"If I had come to you earlier you would have prevented me from leaving."

Her father did not answer. Izzy kept her gaze on him, and he finally gave a nod. "Yes, I would." His voice was strangely quiet.

"There will only be scandal if you make it so, Papa. Mrs Trent is chaperoning me, and I'm not going to Gretna. Rhys has asked me to marry him and I have accepted."

"Izzy—"

"We haven't yet had a chance to discuss the details, but there will be nothing clandestine or hurried about it. If you choose to forbid me from seeing the rest of my family, then *you* are forcing me to abandon them."

He looked away, his fingers fidgeting with a knife on the table. "He would never be accepted by the *ton*," he said at last, although his tone held defeat.

"Why would he want to be?" At this moment, being banished from the *ton* felt more like a reward than a punishment.

Her father had no answer. Izzy stood, picking up her pelisse and bonnet.

"I bid you farewell, Papa. As I said, I would prefer to marry with your blessing, but I *will* marry the man of my choice."

He did not respond, so she turned and walked to the door. Rhys was outside, as he had promised.

"Rhys, may we leave now, please?"

"Mrs Trent is waiting in the taproom," he said. "I'll get our coats."

Izzy headed for the taproom as Rhys went into the parlour. She hoped her father would not start berating him again, but she could hear no raised voices.

"I left him my address," Rhys said as he rejoined her. The concern in his expression brought a lump to her throat, but thankfully he did not fuss over her.

"Thank you." Papa could not say that she had hidden from him.

. . .

Izzy was silent for the first few miles, pointlessly reliving the interview with her father. Glimpses of Rhys riding beside the post-chaise were comforting, and she finally banished Papa from her mind. She hoped he would relent in time, but she would not let their disagreement spoil her new life. She would see Viv and Lynnie again at some point—she would make sure of that. Her lips curled at the idea of Papa returning home only to find Viv as much a thorn in his side as she had been.

"Are you feeling better now, Miss Farrington?"

"Thank you, yes. And please call me Izzy."

Mrs Trent smiled and patted her hand. "I find conversation helps the miles to pass, but do tell me, dear, if you wish to be without my chatter."

Izzy shook her head. "I have to decide whether we are to go into Wales or to Rhys' home." She didn't want to wait, but there were practicalities to consider.

Mrs Trent was a sensible woman, and happy to talk through Izzy's options. By the time they reached Wheatley, on the turnpike road to Oxford, they had decided between them that she would want some new clothes whether or not her father sent her things on, that these would be far easier to obtain in Shrewsbury than Capel Bodfan, and that calling the banns would only take a few weeks if Rhys could not get a licence. Izzy also discovered that Mrs Trent had been widowed twice, lived in Coventry with her sister, and spent much of her time visiting various friends and relatives.

Rhys waited for Izzy in the private parlour of the inn, looking at the door every time he heard a step in the passageway. She'd seemed happier when they arrived than after the confrontation with her father, but the landlady had insisted on taking the two women upstairs to inspect their room.

"I'm sorry," Izzy said as she finally entered. "The landlady is rather talkative."

"I hope your rooms are adequate."

"Perfectly, thank you. Mrs Trent says she will be down for dinner in about twenty minutes." The suggestion in her smile made his pulse race.

"Good," Rhys said, moving closer. 'We were interrupted earlier."

"So we were." She moved into his arms as if she'd done it a hundred times, and turned her face up to his. The kiss was as wonderful as their first, but he pulled away while still wanting more, conscious of the bustle of waiters and travellers beyond the parlour door.

Izzy put her lip out for a moment in a playful pout. She took a tiny step back, remaining within the circle of his arms. "I have talked things over with Mrs Trent. We will go to Shrewsbury, if you please."

That was what he wanted to hear, but he must be sure he wasn't rushing her into this. "Are you certain, Izzy?"

"Yes."

He listened, nodding as she explained their reasons.

"Rhys, you do know I have no money, don't you? Only what is left of my pin money, and that is—"

"Don't worry about that, Izzy. You will be a guest of my mother. She is looking forward to meeting you." He gave a wry smile. "She will also enjoy helping you to buy new gowns, and whatever else you need."

She shook her head. "I don't need much. But thank you."

"Izzy, you will want some family at the wedding, I think?"

"Genie?"

"Yes. I wrote to her when Algy passed on your message, so she is expecting you to visit her. If I write from here, and if Huw can leave his business for a few days, they could get to Shrewsbury in a week, or just over."

"I would like that, thank you."

"Izzy, are you all right? Your Papa—"

"Rhys, I am fine. I'm sad that Papa forced me to have to choose between him and you, but it is done now."

. . .

Was she all right, really? Izzy felt detached, as if she were watching herself in a play. After being confined to her room for weeks, so much had happened today. The interview with Papa had been upsetting, but she didn't regret it. It was better, really, to have everything out in the open. And now she was engaged to be married and travelling to live with strangers. Rhys had told her a little about his family when they talked in the park in London, but there must be more to know about the people who would soon be her family, too.

That could be remedied. She took a seat at the table, Rhys sitting close beside her. "Tell me more about your brothers and sisters, Rhys."

Mrs Trent arrived while they were talking, and the history of the Williams family lasted them through dinner. When the dishes had been cleared, Mrs Trent asked Rhys to describe Spain. He kept them entertained with amusing stories about places and people, no doubt highly censored for their ears.

"I'm sorry we could not have more private conversation," Rhys said, when Mrs Trent retired, saying she would see Izzy in their room in ten minutes. "Mrs Trent is taking her duties seriously."

"It's for the best, Rhys." She would meet many people who wondered about the reasons for their marriage, and she would be accepted more readily if there were no suggestion of scandal. "Ten minutes isn't long." She stepped towards him. "Let us waste no more of it on apologies."

CHAPTER 24

*I*zzy peered out of the chaise window with interest as it slowed and turned. The house at the end of the short drive was bigger than she'd expected, although the details were difficult to make out in the dusk. Light shone from two large windows on either side of the door, and the height of the shadowy building suggested that there were two more floors above. A flood of light illuminated the steps as the front door opened.

Rhys dismounted, then he was at the chaise door to hand her down. "Welcome to your new home, Izzy." He turned as a servant approached. "Izzy, this is Dobson."

"Welcome, Miss Farrington." Dobson gave a bow. "Your letter arrived earlier, sir. All is arranged."

"Thank you. Send Miss Farrington's valise to her room, would you? And Mrs Trent's luggage."

Rhys offered his arm. Izzy hesitated as she saw two women appear in the doorway.

"They won't bite." Rhys gave her hand a gentle squeeze. "Truly, Izzy, they were happy to know I was finally about to step into parson's mousetrap."

Trap? She caught the curve of his lips and smiled up at him, his teasing putting her at ease.

The older woman bore little resemblance to Rhys, having a thin face and pale hair. But her eyes held a twinkle that Izzy recognised, and her smile was welcoming as she stepped forward. "I am glad to meet you, Miss Farrington. I'm Rhys' mama, and this is Gwynne."

Rhys' sister was a smaller, daintier version of Rhys, with the same grey eyes and softly curling hair. "Welcome, Miss Farrington."

"Thank you. I am pleased to be here. But won't you call me Izzy? All my friends do."

Mrs Williams held a hand out. "Come, Izzy, I will show you to your room. Cook will have some tea ready shortly, and we will dine in an hour." She turned to Mrs Trent, waiting behind them in the doorway. "Mariah, it is good to see you again. I've put you in your usual room. I'll send Sally along to help you settle in."

Mrs Williams led the way to a spacious room on the first floor. The bed hangings were of sprigged muslin, while the wallpaper depicted swags of flowers. Whoever had chosen the décor had taste similar to Izzy's own.

"This was Caris' room before she married," Mrs Williams said, her cheerful expression dimming. "I'm afraid it may not be what you are used to at—"

"It's lovely," Izzy exclaimed. "Mrs Williams, pray do not worry about such things. The value of a home is the people within it, and you have made me most welcome."

"You are, my dear. I was afraid, when Rhys told me who you were, that you would be..." Her voice tailed off. "Do excuse me, Miss Farrington. That was not polite of me."

Izzy laughed; she liked this woman already. "Mrs Williams, I have often been told I am too... forthright. I will be apologising to you soon, I am sure. But speaking plainly has its uses. Please, do tell me if I do or expect something that is out of place here. I'm sure there are some differences, and I mean to fit in as best I can."

Mrs Williams eyed the valise that Dobson had left beside the bed, then Izzy's creased and crumpled gown. "We will take you to a modiste tomorrow," she promised. "Caris left a few things behind when she married. Something may fit you until we can organise better."

"Thank you."

"I'll send Sally in to help you. Do come down when you are ready."

Izzy sank into a chair, feeling limp. She was glad to have finally arrived, but now there would be new challenges.

"When do you plan to hold the ceremony?" Mrs Williams asked, once dinner was served and Dobson had left the room. Izzy looked at Rhys, seated beside her. He would be the one making the arrangements.

"We stayed in Hereford last night," he began. "I managed to see the bishop this morning to get a licence, so we can wed as soon as we wish. But we're hoping that Izzy's aunt, Mrs Lloyd, will come."

Mrs Williams nodded at Izzy. "It will be good for you to have family there, dear."

"We should allow a week, I think," Rhys went on. "I'll talk to the vicar tomorrow."

"Good." Mrs Williams nodded her approval. "That will give us enough time for Izzy to get some new clothes, and to write to Alun and Owen to see if they can be here. Izzy can meet some of our friends, too. Perhaps a dinner?"

That sounded rather daunting.

"Not too many people, Mama," Rhys said. "Izzy's had a trying few days."

"It's all right, Rhys," Izzy said quietly. "I am used to large dinners at home." Long, tedious dinners, with people she didn't know or care about.

"Perhaps two dinners," Mrs Williams went on. Her gaze turned to Izzy. "Small dinners, my dear, with only close friends. Not tomorrow, but perhaps the day after. Will that be acceptable?"

Izzy smiled, and nodded. She could hardly refuse.

"Will you invite Doctor Feltham, Mama?" Gwynne asked. "We could take Izzy to the assembly on Friday as well."

"If you wish, dear." Mrs Williams nodded. "Now, who should I invite first?" She seemed to forget her food as she listed people whose names Izzy quickly forgot, and whose relationships with the family she did not know.

Small dinners? An assembly?

Izzy put her fork down, no longer hungry. It wasn't just the number of new people she would be expected to meet—she did that all the time in the season. But here these new people would matter. Then there was the house. If Rhys' family followed the same customs as the aristocracy, she would be taking over the running of this household from Mrs Williams when she married.

Next week.

The idea had not bothered her before, as Mama had made sure the housekeeper instructed her in all the relevant duties. It felt different when faced with the actual place she would be expected to manage, and the woman who had run it for probably thirty years.

"Don't worry, Izzy," Rhys said, his voice too low for others to hear. "She'll narrow it down to a sensible number."

Izzy shook her head. It wasn't only that.

"Are you going to have a bridal tour?" Gwynne asked. "I'd like to go to Scotland for mine."

"There's time enough to think of that when you're betrothed," Rhys retorted.

Izzy glanced at him, startled by his firm tone.

He put one hand on hers where it rested on the table. "Izzy, would you prefer a tray in your room?" he asked, his voice still quiet. "You are not eating."

"I… No, thank you. That would not be polite." She picked up her fork.

"Polite be hanged. There is something the matter. You should not have to stay here if you are tired or upset."

He had not raised his voice, but sudden silence made her look up from her plate. She flushed as she realised she was now the centre of attention.

"Come, I'll take you to your room," Rhys said, getting to his feet. "Excuse us, Mama, but Izzy is tired."

Izzy stood too, setting her napkin beside her plate, glad for once to be ordered about.

Rhys stopped on the landing outside Izzy's door, and gently turned her to face him. Her set lips had a tiny tremor.

"What is wrong, Izzy? This is more than just tiredness, I think."

"I'm sorry to upset your mama's dinner, Rhys." There was a wobble in her voice, too.

"That doesn't matter." He pulled her towards him, holding her close. She wound her arms around his waist, and settled her head into the hollow of his shoulder. Her body felt tense at first, but gradually relaxed. He wanted to do far more than hold her, but now was not the time.

"I must apologise for telling you what to do," he ventured, recalling what she had said the day she fell in the stream. "I'd hate for you to think of me in the same way as your other suitors."

"In this case, you were right," she admitted, managing a tentative smile.

"What's wrong?" he asked again.

"All those people and plans," she said, her voice muffled by his jacket. "And won't your mama mind me taking over the house? If I am to do that."

"You don't regret your decision, do you, Izzy? It's not too late, if you want to change your mind." Although he'd do his damnedest to persuade her to change it back again.

"No, not at all. It's so… so much at once."

"We need not have dinners if you don't feel like it, or attend the assembly. But do not decide now—wait and see how you feel tomorrow. And don't worry about Mama. I think she may be glad of the chance to hand things over. She was talking about going to stay with Mrs Trent for a while. But that will only be once you have settled in."

He felt her take a deep breath, her body moving against his own.

He would have to avoid holding her like this too often if he was to stay out of her bed until their wedding night.

"Tomorrow, it would be as well to let Mama take you to the dressmaker. But apart from that, you don't need to do anything. If you wish, I could show you around the town, or the mill, or we could just go for a walk or a ride."

"A ride, please. I'd enjoy that, and I'd like to see where you work. Papa confined me to the house for the last few weeks."

"I'm sorry," he said. "That is because I ignored your wishes and spoke to him, is it not?"

She pulled away from him, looking up into his face. "Partly, but I also defied him in other ways, Rhys. And you meant it for the best. It is over now, and I am here, where I want to be."

He so wanted to kiss her, but did not. She was tired, and needed food and rest. "I will get Sally to bring a tray up for you," he said. "And tea, or wine. Eat something, and go to bed. There is nothing we cannot work out, Izzy."

"Thank you, Rhys. I am not normally such a…"

"Watering pot? Wilting flower?"

She giggled. "Either of those!"

"Goodnight, Izzy. Sleep well." He gave her a quick kiss on the forehead, and waited until the door closed behind her. He was tempted to retire himself, weary from his days on the road, but steeled himself and returned to the dining room to discuss dinners and assemblies and Gwynne's Doctor Feltham.

CHAPTER 25

Izzy stood before the mirror, admiring her new gown. In the last week she'd had three new gowns made to supplement the ones she'd brought with her. She would wear this simple one for her wedding. The white muslin was sprigged with tiny blue flowers embroidered onto the fabric, and a blue ribbon marked the high waist. She had some of the same ribbon for her garters, and a blush came to her face as she imagined Rhys unfastening them tomorrow night.

"Very fetching," Genie said, twitching part of the skirt straight. "The blue matches your eyes. It will do well for tomorrow."

"I'm so glad you could come, Genie," Izzy said, turning from her reflection. It wasn't the first time she'd said it, but the fact she had *one* adult relative who did not disapprove helped to alleviate the hurt caused by her parents. And Genie had explained what would happen in the marriage bed. Izzy had guessed at most of it, but she was grateful for the information. Mama, she suspected, would not have emphasised how enjoyable it should be for *both* parties.

"Of course I came," Genie said. "It's a pity Lucy Cleeve is still in France—she'd have liked to come, too."

"You're not just here for the shopping, then?" Izzy added with a grin, determined not to let the absence of the rest of her family cast a shadow over her wedding. The Lloyds had arrived the day before, and were staying at the Prince Rupert Hotel in the town. Huw had escaped from this final day of preparations and was showing the children around the town.

"Shopping is just a bonus," Genie said, eyeing her own new bonnet resting on a chair. "Do you have anything else to do today?"

Izzy shook her head. "Not much. Mrs Williams is organising the wedding breakfast. I want some roses for a posy, and some for Bethan and Alis as well, but I can do that in the morning."

"Where has Rhys escaped to?"

"His brothers have come, and his friend, Mr Pelham. Rhys is showing them all around the mill." He'd given her a tour a couple of days ago, and she'd found it fascinating. And from the way Rhys had talked, she would be able to help with the running of it if she wished to.

Genie chuckled. "Men are best out of the way at times like this."

Both women turned their heads at the crunch of wheels on gravel. Genie walked over to the window as Izzy picked up the enamelled pins Gwynne had lent her, trying to decide how best to fix them in her hair.

"Izzy." Genie's voice had lost its cheerful tone.

Izzy dropped the pins back in the dish. "What is it? Is something wrong?"

Genie peered out of the window, gazing down towards the drive. "That looks very much like Frederick's travelling coach."

Father? Izzy's happiness evaporated. "Oh, no."

"He cannot prevent your marriage, Izzy. Not now."

Izzy reached behind her back to try to unfasten the buttons holding the gown together, her hands shaking. Papa might not be able to stop her, but he could destroy her joy in the day. What if he stood up in church and said there *was* a just cause or impediment? That would cause a horrible scandal, even though it wasn't true.

"Help me out of this gown, Genie. I don't want to wear my wedding dress for an argument with my father."

"Don't rush," Genie admonished, taking her hands. "*He* is not in charge here. Dobson will come to tell you he is here, and ask if you will see him. I'd be inclined to make him wait, although if he's in a bad temper that might make him worse."

Izzy chose one of her other new gowns, a more practical dark blue. She was about to become the lady of this house, and she would act as if she already was.

"This is *your* house," Genie confirmed as she fastened tapes on Izzy's gown. "As near as makes no difference, at least."

Izzy nodded.

"The main thing is not to let him upset you again."

Someone knocked on the door.

"Come in," Izzy called. As expected, Dobson stood in the doorway, but to her surprise one of the footmen from her father's London house stood behind him, next to a large trunk.

"Lord Bedley is here, Miss Farrington," Dobson said. "There are several trunks. Where would you like them?"

"Trunks?" The unexpectedness of the question seemed to have addled her thoughts for the moment.

"I understand they contain your clothing and other possessions, Miss."

Izzy met Genie's gaze. "I'm pleased he sent them, but why would he come with them?"

Her aunt shrugged. "Who knows what men think? Some of them are as illogical as they say we are. Dobson, is there a spare bedchamber they could be left in for now? They will not be needed straight away."

"Yes, Mrs Lloyd." He gave the footman directions and turned back to Izzy. "Lord Bedley also requested an interview with you, Miss Farrington."

"Thank you, Dobson. I will come down shortly."

"What can he want?" Izzy wondered as the manservant left. "Papa cannot think to persuade me to change my mind, not now I've got this far."

"He may not have come to take you home," Genie said. "Why bring your things, if so?"

She hoped Genie was right.

In the parlour, Papa and Mrs Williams sat in facing chairs by the empty fireplace. There had been no sound of voices as Izzy approached the open door. Mrs Williams looked around with relief as Izzy's footsteps sounded on the polished wood floor.

"Ah, Izzy, Lord Bedley wants to talk to you." She stood and hurried past Izzy into the hall. Papa stood up, too.

Izzy sighed; she couldn't blame Mrs Williams for escaping. Papa looked rather grave. "Why have you come, Papa?"

"Won't you sit down, Izzy?" He gestured to the chair Mrs Williams had just vacated.

She ignored his request, not moving from her position near the door. "Why have you come?" she asked again.

"I wanted to talk to you. Please, will you not sit down? We cannot have a conversation across the room like this."

"What more is there to say? You expressed your disapproval; I made up my own mind. It is too bad of you to come all this way to start the argument again." On the day before the wedding, too, when she had just managed to put the upset behind her.

His shoulders slumped. "I did not come to argue, Izzy. Or to give you orders."

Was his expression one of anxiety, not anger? It was difficult to tell. "Why, then?"

"I… I came to apologise."

Izzy had difficulty comprehending what he said. She had never heard Papa apologise for anything before, and wasn't sure she believed him. Crossing the room, she sat down as he had requested.

"The day you left, Vivian asked me if she would see you again soon, or if she would have to wait until she was married to someone more reasonable than me. She was not happy that she could not attend her sister's wedding." He shook his head. "Vivian has never been… argumentative before."

Izzy waited for the accusation that it was her fault, but it did not come.

"She asked if I was going to force her to marry someone she did not know well, just to get rid of her. Izzy, I was not trying to get rid of you, you must know that."

She wasn't sure she did, but said nothing.

"A woman needs…" He cleared his throat. "That is, women are… most women are better off with a husband."

"I am about to get one," Izzy pointed out.

"Yes, and I have not come to dissuade you, Izzy. I am trying to explain why I wanted you to accept an offer from Ordsall or one of the others."

He seemed lost for words, gazing at his hands where they rested on his knees. Izzy waited.

"What you told me about Lord Ordsall," he said at last. "That made me consider your words about gentlemanly behaviour, and about your young man respecting you enough to let you make decisions. I enquired of an acquaintance at Horse Guards about his military record. Exemplary—he was even mentioned in dispatches a couple of times."

A man could be a good soldier and still be a terrible husband, but at least Papa had made some effort to find out more about him.

Her father leaned forward in his chair, looking into her face. "I still cannot see how you will be happy marrying out of our class, Izzy, but I think you were right. I do not really know you."

Izzy felt limp with relief. "I will be happy, Papa. I do not yet know what my life here will be like, but I know that we can make it work between us."

"You *are* certain, Izzy, are you? You are not just going forward with this marriage because you see it as the only way to escape the suitors I arranged for you?"

"I'm certain, Papa. Whatever you may say about foolish romantic notions, I love Rhys and he loves me."

"Very well. You have my blessing, if you want it."

She was surprised to find out how much she did want it. "I do. Thank you, Papa."

"Good, good. Vivian will be pleased, and Lynnette."

"Did they come with you? And Mama?"

"I'm afraid your Mama said she was too unwell to travel this far, but your sisters are here. I left them in the hotel. I wasn't sure if you would even see me."

She hadn't wanted to, but she was glad she had.

"Izzy, who is to give you away tomorrow?"

"Huw. Huw Lloyd, Genie's husband."

"Genie is here?"

"I wanted *some* family at my wedding, Papa."

He had the grace to look guilty. "I should make my peace with her, too," he said, "and with your betrothed."

"Rhys is out at the moment." How would that interview go? Papa had been insulting when Rhys called. "Shall I ask Genie to see you now?"

"If you please, my dear."

Back in the hall, she asked a too-interested Dobson to take some brandy in to her father. He might need it before his interview with Genie.

She felt as if she needed it herself, come to that. An apology from Papa was the last thing she had expected when she came downstairs. Thank goodness for Viv, summoning up the courage to speak to him. And to Papa for actually listening, for once.

Mama? Mama's words still hurt, and Izzy was disappointed that her mother had not come, but she couldn't have everything. Being reconciled with Papa and having him and the rest of her family at the wedding was more than she had dared to hope for.

Rhys rode home with Algy, leaving Owen and Alun to visit Uncle John. "Why this sudden interest in mills, Algy?" he asked, as the house came into sight.

"Tired of the idle life, Taffy. I know it's not the done thing to enter trade, but better than drinking and gambling my life away." He smirked. "You should thank me for rescuing you from a house full of women sorting out wedding gowns and the like."

"Ha, yes."

"Perhaps I'll meet that cousin of yours tomorrow."

Sophie? "Don't get ideas about marrying her for her share of the mill, Algy," Rhys said, not convinced that his friend was joking.

"Would I do a thing like that? You wound me."

"You probably—" Rhys broke off as he spotted the coach drawn up before the house, a groom at the horses' heads with a bucket of water. He urged Seren into a trot for the last few yards.

"Whose carriage is this?" he asked as he dismounted.

"Lord Bedley's, sir. I have orders to wait for him."

Bedley? Damn.

"Take them round, will you Algy?" Rhys handed over Seren's reins and hurried into the house. "Dobson, where's—?"

"I'm here, Rhys." Izzy came down the stairs to meet him, the happy smile on her face reassuring him.

"Your father?"

She drew him into the dining room and closed the door. "He's in the parlour with Genie. Rhys, he came to apologise."

He shook his head. She wasn't making sense.

"He *did* apologise, Rhys, and my sisters have come with him. He wants to speak to you as well."

Rhys felt his lips tightening. After what the man had said to him, and the way Izzy had been treated, he was not feeling very charitable.

Izzy laid a hand on his arm. "For my sake, Rhys? If I have to choose between you and my father, I will always choose you, but I would much rather not *have* to choose."

She had already chosen him, but he didn't want to cause her any more pain. "Very well." He would do his best to be polite if it meant so much to her. "How has your day been, apart from that?"

"I missed you," she said, stepping closer. "There are so many people around all the time."

"There won't be tomorrow night," he said, putting his arms around her. "Are you sure you are happy to go only as far as Llangollen for our wedding trip?"

"Rhys, it sounds lovely. Pretty countryside to walk and ride in."

And a hotel suite to spend as much time in as possible. The last week had been frustrating, having Izzy around with no chance for more than a stolen kiss. Tomorrow night could not come soon enough for his liking, but there was still her father to face.

To Rhys' surprise, Bedley stood as he entered the parlour. Rhys noticed the empty brandy glass on the little table beside his chair and his lips twitched in spite of himself. He'd require fortification, too, if he had to pacify both Izzy and Genie.

"I have apologised to Isolde, and she has accepted my apology. I hope, Williams... *Mr* Williams..." He cleared his throat. "That is, I hope you will also accept my apology."

Rhys sat down. "Izzy said you had given your blessing to our marriage." He kept his voice non-committal; he wasn't yet sure exactly what Bedley was apologising for. "Do take a seat."

"Er, yes. Thank you."

Bedley looked ill at ease, fidgeting in his chair. As well he might, Rhys thought, and there was no need to make it easy for him. He'd put Izzy through a lot, although Rhys did recognise that the man could have done worse. It *was* possible that he thought he had been doing what was best for his daughter. And Izzy had accepted the apology he'd made to her.

"You accused me of being a fortune-hunter," Rhys said, keeping his tone mild. "And of compromising your daughter's reputation."

"I was wrong," Bedley said.

The simple words, with no prevarication, did much to appease Rhys.

"I have put aside dowries for all my daughters," Bedley went on. "I will arrange to—"

"I don't want your money." Rhys' goodwill vanished. Did Bedley think he could not support a wife?

"Should you not let Izzy decide? It could be put into trust for your children, for example."

Bedley was right. After all Rhys' talk of respecting Izzy's ability to make her own decisions, her father had suggested it, not him. The irony was almost amusing.

"Touché, sir. You are quite right. I will leave you to discuss that with her, but perhaps you could delay it until some time after the wedding? You may visit us at any time."

For some reason this seemed to embarrass Bedley. "I… I would reciprocate, Mr Williams, but my wife…" He cleared his throat again. "My wife is not reconciled to Izzy's marriage, I'm afraid." He stood. "I am staying at the Prince Rupert with my other children. I would like to invite you and your family to join us all for dinner this evening. My sister and her family will be present as well."

Rhys wasn't sure Bedley really wanted to dine with the Williams family, but at least he was making an effort.

"Thank you, my lord. I accept." Rhys stood and held out his right hand. A final test.

Bedley shook it. "Until later."

CHAPTER 26

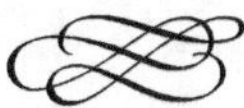

apa had ordered a splendid meal, with two courses and a range of dishes, but much of the food remained untouched as people talked more than they ate. Izzy sat between Viv and Rhys, happy to see Papa in an animated discussion with Huw and Mr Pelham. Papa talking to Rhys would have been even better, but she was happy to have Rhys beside her. Genie was deep in conversation with Mrs Williams.

"Mother knows I stay with the Lloyds when I go to Wales," Rhys told her, "but they've never met."

Gwynne, sandwiched between Izzy's sisters, was discussing gowns and bonnets. While Gwynne answered a question from Lynnie, Izzy took the opportunity to talk to Viv, keeping her voice low.

"Viv, what exactly did you say to Papa? I couldn't believe it when he said he'd come to apologise."

Viv glanced across the table, but their father was concentrating on Huw's conversation. "I asked why I couldn't go to your wedding, and what was wrong with wanting to be happy."

"Did he have an answer?"

Viv shrugged. "Only that marrying into trade was just not done."

219

The same lack of explanation he'd given Izzy. "That can't be all you said to make him change his mind."

"He said that at least I was a dutiful daughter, and encouraging Lord Blaylock. I told him that I was encouraging Henry because I liked him, not because he has a title, and if Henry isn't happy to have Mr Williams as a brother-in-law, I won't be marrying him."

Izzy was touched. Viv had said that before, but she hadn't been sure her sister really meant it.

"But it was Mama who persuaded him, I think," Viv went on.

"Mama?"

"Oh, she didn't mean to. She said some of the same horrid things she said to Mr Williams when he came for you. Then she said there was a price to pay for having a title, but she'd always done her duty even if it was unpleasant." Viv's mouth turned down at the corners. "I think she was talking about… you know."

Izzy could guess.

"Papa stared at her, then he said he wanted his daughters to be happy and locked himself in his study for the rest of the day. With a bottle of brandy."

"Poor Mama."

"Poor Papa, rather," Viv said. "I don't think Mama is really ill—she just used that as an excuse."

Izzy put her hand on her sister's. "Thank you, Viv, for helping to persuade him." She almost choked on the words, and blinked back a tear. She was so lucky to have such a sister.

"That's what sisters are for." Viv grinned. "And I will expect your support when I choose to elope."

Izzy chuckled, and her mood lightened. She was sorry Mama had not come, but at least she had Papa and her sisters here. And tomorrow at this time, she would have Rhys to herself.

On her wedding morning the sky threatened rain, but Izzy didn't care. The carriage was crowded, with Papa squashed between Viv and

Lynnie on one seat, and Alis and Bethan sitting beside Izzy. Four attendants seemed a little excessive, but it was not fair to replace her cousins with her sisters at the last minute. Luckily the rose bushes in the garden had provided enough blooms for all of them to have posies.

The carriage drew to a halt at the entrance to the church. Dobson was on hand to help Izzy and the girls down, and they gathered in the porch. Viv straightened her own gown, then fussed with Izzy's short train.

"Viv!" Izzy protested, irritated at the delay.

"There," Viv said with satisfaction, finally stepping back. "You look lovely, Izzy."

"You do indeed, daughter." Her father held one arm out, and they walked into the church together, Viv shepherding the younger girls behind them.

The church was not full, and Izzy recognised most of the people there: Genie and her husband and son, Rhys' mother and his siblings, and his uncle and cousin, and Mrs Trent. But her gaze fixed on Rhys, waiting by the altar rail with Mr Pelham beside him.

"Thank you, Papa, for being here," she said. Then they were at the altar rail, the love in Rhys' eyes making her breath catch.

"Dearly beloved, we are gathered here…"

While Rhys tipped the porter and arranged for dinner to be served in half an hour, Izzy walked over to the window of the little parlour next to their bedroom. Peering downwards, she made out white streaks of foam on the river below. More of Llangollen lay beyond the water, backed by a wooded hillside. Above that, strange shapes stood out against the darkening sky.

"Castell Dinas Brân," Rhys said, moving over to stand behind her and putting his hands on her shoulders. She rested against his chest. Although they'd spent several hours together in the coach, not until now had she felt truly alone with him.

"Built in the thirteenth century." He put his arms around her and pulled her closer still. "We can walk up to it tomorrow, if you wish." His breath was warm on her ear. "It's very steep."

"If the rain holds off," Izzy said. Warmth spread through her at the feel of his body against her back. She wasn't really interested in the castle, not now.

"I hope it rains for the whole week," he whispered.

"Oh?" She turned in his arms, not stepping away. "What will we do all day?"

She had a very good idea of what they might do. He bent his head and kissed her, gently. She curled a hand around the back of his head to hold him close, feeling his hand tangling in her hair, wanting more of the liquid sensation pooling somewhere below her stomach.

Eventually he pulled away. "Dinner will be here soon," he said, regret in his voice.

"Unfortunately." But they had all evening. All week.

Rhys hardly tasted the food as they sat at the small table, together at last without the need for subterfuge and with nobody around them to demand attention. Their talk ranged from the history of the ruined castle above the town, to how Izzy might get involved in the mill when they returned. More important to Rhys than their conversation were the shared glances, full of promise for later.

Finally, the waiter came to clear the plates, leaving them with a dish of sweetmeats and more wine.

"Another glass?" he asked, his hand hovering near the decanter. Was it too early to go to bed?

"No, thank you." Her eyes slid towards the bedroom, and a delightful rosy tint appeared on her cheeks. "Is it too early—?"

Rhys couldn't help laughing. "I was thinking exactly that," he said. "Shall I ring for the maid to help you?"

Izzy shook her head, the blush deepening. "No. I told her I wouldn't need her again. I can manage." She stood as she spoke, and moved towards the bedroom door, her shawl slipping from her shoulders.

He could wait here while she undressed, or…

"Those buttons look awkward to reach," he said. "Are you sure you don't need help?"

Izzy turned. "Perhaps I do."

"Good," he whispered, and stepped towards her. He turned her around, hearing her gasp as he kissed the nape of her neck. He worked the buttons lose, moving slowly down her back. Her breath hitched as the last one came undone and he moved his hands up to slip the gown off her shoulders.

It pooled at her feet, and she turned around. She was not blushing now, and the look in her eyes took his breath away. He swallowed hard, and tore himself away to lock the door between the parlour and the landing—just in case of interruptions. Then he led her into the bedroom.

Izzy stood near the bed as Rhys closed the bedroom door. It felt strange to be standing before a man wearing just her shift and stays, but it also felt right. The knot in her stomach was something between nervousness and excitement.

Rhys took off his coat and threw it onto a chair. He reached for the buttons on his waistcoat, but Izzy stepped forward and put her hands in his way.

He stilled, and she wondered for a moment if she was being too forward. But the feel of his fingers unfastening her gown had made her pulse race—would he feel the same if she unfastened his waistcoat?

"May I?" she asked, wanting to be sure.

"Please." His voice sounded hoarse, strained even, and she paused uncertainly. "Please do," he said again, more of a whisper this time.

She unfastened each button, feeling the warmth of his body through his shirt. As she worked her way down his chest, he reached up and started to remove the pins from her hair, dropping them one by one onto the rug. She undid the knot in his cravat as she felt the weight of her hair slipping down her back.

"Stays," he whispered, turning her round and loosening the laces. His hands moved faster now, more urgently. The stays dropped to the floor and she stepped out of them, then gasped as he swept her up into his arms and deposited her on the bed.

"I love you." He lay down beside her, stroking her hair away from her face as he looked into her eyes.

"And I you." This was where she belonged.

EPILOGUE

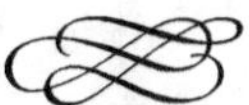

April 1818

"Time to go home, if you've finished?"

Izzy looked up as Rhys entered the office, and put aside the samples of fabric she'd been examining. Even after all these months, she still felt a rush of pleasure at seeing him.

"Yes, for now." Standing, she stretched her back—bending over a desk for too long was not a good idea in her condition.

"Is it time you stopped coming to the mill?" Rhys asked, concern plain on his face.

Izzy put a hand to her swelling belly. "Soon, I think."

She tidied the samples away while Rhys went to get the gig, and donned her pelisse. Outside, the sun had begun to turn the clouds orange and pink, daffodils making bright spots beside the road.

"A letter from Rhodri Evans came today," Rhys said, as he flicked the reins.

"May I read it?" Rhys shared most matters with her. It had seemed strange at first, but now she enjoyed knowing how the business worked.

"You can try, if you like." There was a laugh in his voice.

"Oh, it's in Welsh, I suppose. What does it say?" She'd tried to learn some of the language, but she was finding it hard going—it was so different from English, or the French that she'd been taught in the schoolroom.

"He mainly wrote to thank me for preventing Stannard enclosing some of his grazing land. He's had a few early lambs, and expecting many more soon."

Rhys glanced down at her belly. "How do you feel about going to see them? We could stay with Genie and Huw for a couple of nights. Uncle John's still well enough to take any decisions in the next few weeks."

"I'd like that, thank you." It was six months since she'd seen Genie, although they had corresponded regularly.

"We could go on to Aberystwyth for a few days, if you wish. A bit of sea air might do you good."

She leaned into him as he drove, putting out a hand and squeezing his arm. "That would be lovely." They could have some time to themselves, without the demands of the factory, or the seemingly endless preparations for Gwynne's wedding.

"Good. We can discuss the details after dinner." He pulled up outside the house and helped her down. The gleam in his eye hinted that he was thinking about more than merely discussing their trip.

She smiled at him as they walked up the steps together.

THE END

Thank you for reading *An Embroidered Spoon*; I hope you enjoyed it. If you can spare a few minutes, could you leave a review on Amazon or Goodreads? You only need to write a few words.

~

Find out about my forthcoming books on my website.

www.jaynedavisromance.co.uk

You can sign up to my newsletters via my website. They will tell you about new releases or special offers. I promise not to bombard you with emails. My website also has details about forthcoming books, and links to my Facebook, Twitter, and Pinterest pages.

Read on for notes on Welsh names and pronunciation.

WELSH – PLACES, MEANINGS AND PRONUNCIATION

Capel Bodfan is an imaginary town somewhere between Llanidloes and Aberystwyth (both real places). Llangenydd (mentioned by Rhys and Huw) is also imaginary.

The names of farms and houses are common names in Wales and, like many place names in the country, are very descriptive. Bodfan, Cenydd, Idloes and Collen are all Welsh saints.

Towns:

Aberystwyth – mouth of the River Ystwyth
Capel Bodfan – Bodfan's Chapel
Llangenydd – the parish of St Cenydd
Llanidloes – the parish of St Idloes
Llangollen – the parish of St Collen

Other places:

Y Ddraig Goch – the Red Dragon
Plas Coed – house in the woods
Stryd y Bont – Bridge Street

Hafod Rhos – summer dwelling on the moor
Hafod Uchaf – upper farm
Bryn Moel – bare hill
Castell Dinas Brân – can be translated as Crow's Fortress or Brân's castle (with Brân being the name of a person)
Afon Hafren – River Severn (afon means river)

Animals:

Seren (Rhys' horse) – star
Castan (Genie's horse) - chestnut

Some of my early readers wanted to know exactly what the Welsh words in the story mean, and how to pronounce them. So here they are (in the order they appear in the story):

Diwrnod da - Good day, used in the sense of good bye
Croeso yn ôl – Welcome back
Mae'n ddrwg gen i - I'm sorry
Peidiwch â'i sôn amdano - Don't mention it
Croeso - Welcome!
Diolch - Thank you
Picau ar y maen - Welsh cakes
Da iawn - It's very good

Taffy – Algy sometimes calls Rhys 'Taffy'. This name is often used to insult Welsh people, and is the kind of nickname that an army man might be given if part of an English regiment. Algy means no insult by it. Some say it comes from the River Taff (Afon Taf) in south Wales. Another explanation is that it is a corruption of the Welsh name Dafydd (pronounced Dav-ith).

Pronunciation

The main differences between English and Welsh pronunciations are:

C is pronounced as a K

CH is pronounced as in Loch or Bach

DD is pronounced 'th' as in breathe

LL is roughly 'thl' – there isn't really a direct equivalent

F is pronounced like V, FF like F

W is pronounced as OO

Y can be a U or I, depending on where it occurs in a word.

Some examples from the story

Rhys is said like Reece

Rhodri is Rod-ree

Ioan is Yo-an

Owain Glyndŵr is Oh-wayne Glin-doo-r

Capel Bodfan is Ka-pel Bod-van

Plas Coed is Plas Ko-ed

Llangollen is Thlan-goh-thlen (the o in 'goh' is pronounced like the o in off)

Aberystwyth is Aber-uh-stwith

Thanks to my critique group and beta readers for help with the Welsh. Any errors are my own.

HISTORICAL NOTE - CROMLECHS

The cromlech I describe in the story is based on the one at Pentre Ifan, in Pembrokeshire. I have taken the liberty of moving it to mid-Wales for the purposes of the story.

Cromlechs, also known as dolmens, can be found in many places around the world. The earliest ones date from around 7000 years ago. Although it is commonly accepted that cromlechs were used as part of burial chambers, there is little clear evidence to support this.

England, 1799

Major Matthew Southam returns from India, hoping to put the trauma of war behind him and forget his past. Instead, he finds a derelict estate and a family who wish he'd died abroad.

Charlotte MacKinnon married without love to avoid her father's unpleasant choice of husband. Now a widow with a young son, she lives in a small Cotswold village with only the money she earns by her writing.

Matthew is haunted by his past, and Charlotte is fearful of her father's renewed meddling in her future. After a disastrous first meeting, can they help each other find happiness?

Available on Kindle and in paperback. Read free in Kindle Unlimited.

Book 1 in the Marstone Series

England, 1777

Will, Viscount Wingrave, whiles away his time gambling and bedding married women, thwarted in his wish to serve his country by his controlling father.

News that his errant son has fought a duel with a jealous husband is the last straw for the Earl of Marstone. He decrees that Will must marry. The earl's eye lights upon Connie Charters, unpaid housekeeper and drudge for a poor but socially ambitious father who cares only for the advantage her marriage could bring him.

Will and Connie meet for the first time at the altar. But Connie wants a husband who will love and respect her, not a womaniser and a gambler.

Their new home, on the wild coast of Devonshire, conceals dangerous secrets that threaten them and the nation. Can Will and Connie overcome the forces against them and forge a happy life together?

Available on Kindle and in paperback. Read free in Kindle Unlimited.

A sweet, second-chance novella.

Lieutenant Philip Kempton and Anna Tremayne fall in love during one idyllic summer fortnight. When he's summoned to rejoin his ship, Anna promises to wait for him.

While he's at sea, she marries someone else.

Now she's widowed and he's Captain Kempton. When they meet again, can they put aside betrayal and rekindle their love?

Available from Amazon on Kindle paperback, and Large Print paperback. Read free in Kindle Unlimited.

ABOUT THE AUTHOR

I wanted to be a writer when I was in my teens, hooked on Jane Austen and Georgette Heyer (and lots of other authors). Real life intervened, and I had several careers, including as a non-fiction author under another name. That wasn't *quite* the writing career I had in mind, but finally I am writing historical romance.

www.jaynedavisromance.co.uk

facebook.com/jaynedavisromance
twitter.com/jaynedavis142
instagram.com/jaynedavisromance